GORDON'S GAME: BLUE THUNDER

GORDON'S GAME: BLUE THUNDER

The Biggest Dream! The Toughest Test!

Gordon D'Arcy & Paul Howard

Illustrated by Alan Nolan

PENGUIN BOOKS

PENGUIN BOOKS

UK | USA | Canada | Ireland | Australia
India | New Zealand | South Africa

Penguin Books is part of the Penguin Random House group of companies
whose addresses can be found at global.penguinrandomhouse.com.

Penguin
Random House
UK

First published by Sandycove 2020
Published in Penguin Books 2021
001

Typeset by Jouve (UK), Milton Keynes
Printed and bound in Italy by Grafica Veneta S.p.A.

The authorized representative in the EEA is Penguin Random House Ireland,
Morrison Chambers, 32 Nassau Street, Dublin D02 YH68

A CIP catalogue record for this book is available from the British Library

ISBN: 978–1–844–88462–9

www.greenpenguin.co.uk

MIX
Paper from
responsible sources
FSC® C018179

Penguin Random House is committed to a
sustainable future for our business, our readers
and our planet. This book is made from Forest
Stewardship Council® certified paper.

'Miiissstteeerrr D'Aaarrrcccyyy! Step into my office!'

So many of the adventures I had as a kid ended with me being summoned to the office of the school Principal, Mr Cuffe, and hearing him say those words. But that was how *this* adventure actually started.

A prefect was sent to track me down. Which he did successfully. They were like sniffer dogs, those prefects.

'Mr Cuffe wants to talk to you,' he told me. 'I've been sent to bring you in.'

'Okay,' I said, showing him the inside of my wrists, 'snap the bracelets on me.'

This was my attempt at a joke. They didn't use

handcuffs in Clongowes – although there *were* times when they would have made the job of controlling us a bit easier.

'Do you know what this is about?' I asked, as we walked towards the office.

'You tell me,' said the Prefect. 'What have you done wrong?'

It was quite a long list. I was fortunate enough (or unfortunate enough) to be friends with Conor Kehoe, the biggest practical joker in the school. He'd really ramped up his efforts in the final weeks of term – and, as usual, he'd dragged me into his hilarious schemes. These included:

Sneaking into the staffroom and switching the instant coffee for gravy granules.

Borrowing seventy alarm clocks from the Sixth Year dormitories, then hiding them in the ceiling tiles throughout the school – after setting them all to go off at exactly three o'clock in the afternoon.

Using a bag of flour and a stencil to create little rat footprints in the school foodstore and convince the kitchen staff that we had a rodent infestation.

Conor put a lot of time and effort into his practical jokes. The only downside for me was that I was usually the one who found himself in trouble.

I knocked twice on the door. It was opened.

'Miiissstteeerrr D'Aaarrrcccyyy!' said Mr Cuffe. 'Step into my office!'

'I don't know what I'm being accused of,' I said, 'but I can tell you that it definitely wasn't me.'

He laughed.

'No,' he said, opening the door wider, 'you're not in any kind of trouble – this time anyway. There's someone here to see you.'

'Who is it?' I asked, stepping past him.

And that's when I was forced to do a double-take. Because sitting there, drinking a cup of coffee, was Joe Schmidt – the coach of the Leinster rugby team.

He stood up and extended his hand to me.

'Gordon?' he said. 'I'm Joe Schmidt.'

'Yes,' I gulped. 'I know!'

Joe was from New Zealand – the land of the famous All Blacks.

He sat down and invited me to take the seat next to him.

'So how are you going?' he asked.

'I'm . . . em . . . fine,' I said, momentarily lost for words.

'Mr Schmidt saw you playing for Ireland against Wales,' said Mr Cuffe. 'It seems you impressed him.'

'Did I?' I asked.

'Yeah, you did,' Joe said. 'You did great to come back – especially after the disaster you had against Scotland. It showed real character.'

'Wow,' I said. 'Em, thanks.'

'How would you like to come and play for Leinster?' Joe asked.

He didn't get the reaction from me that he was perhaps expecting. I didn't punch the air, or shout, 'Wa-hoooooo!!!!!!', or jump up on Mr Cuffe's desk and perform a little jig.

I said, 'Leinster.' Then I stopped, trying to think of something to say. 'That's an interesting offer. That's a *very* interesting offer.'

'What's wrong?' he said. 'Here, you're not one of those Lunsters, are you?'

'What's a Lunster?' I asked.

'That's what we call rugby fans who come from Leinster but support Munster.'

I laughed nervously.

'That . . . is . . . HILARIOUS!' I said. 'Lunsters!

Good one, Joe! I see what you've done there! Lunsters! That is absolutely brilliant!'

The reason I was acting so weird all of a sudden was that Dad was a Munster fan. My friend Conor was a Munster fan. My friend Peter was a Munster fan. I was a Leinster fan, like my brother, Ian. But I kind of had a soft spot for Munster too. How could you *not*? They played great rugby. They were the toughest team I'd ever seen. They refused to accept that they were beaten and their second-half comebacks were legendary.

And they actually *won* things!

Like, for instance, two European Cups. Dad had both finals on DVD – the one against Biarritz and the one against Toulouse – and he watched them all the time. Dad would always say: 'Munster play the game the way it *should* be played!'

He even remembered a time, years before I was born, when they beat the All Blacks!

'Look, Gordon,' Joe said, 'I know what you're thinking.'

'Do you?' I asked.

'Yeah, you're thinking Leinster are a bit of a joke. One day, they turn on the style – and they look like the best team in the world. Then, just when you start to get your hopes up, they let you down by losing to a team who aren't even in their class.'

'Yeah,' I said, 'that's, em, kind of what I was thinking alright.'

'Well, all of that is about to change,' he said, taking a sip of his coffee. 'I'm building a new squad. We've got some great players, like Brian O'Driscoll and Shane Horgan. You played with them for Ireland.'

He suddenly pulled a face.

'Eugh!' he said. 'That is the worst cup of coffee I've ever tasted. If I didn't know better, I'd say it was made from gravy granules.'

I had to work really hard to stop myself from smiling.

'Where was I?' Joe said. 'Oh, yeah, I want to bring in some new faces. Have you ever heard of Johnny Sexton?'

'Johnny Sexton?' I said. 'No, I've never heard of him.'

Imagine that! There was a time when I'd never heard of Johnny Sexton!

'He's playing for St Mary's in the All Ireland League,' Joe said. 'I think he's going to be a great number ten. Have you ever heard of Seán O'Brien?'

'Er, no.'

Imagine that! There was a time when I'd never heard of Seán O'Brien!

'He's a really good openside flanker,' he said. 'He's a farmer from Carlow. You see, I want to get rid of this idea that Leinster are a Dublin team. I want us to be a team that represents the entire province. Did you know, according to Seán, that there are people in Carlow who put out red flags when Munster are playing?'

The same thing happened in Wexford.

'That's, em, terrible,' I said.

'I want to change that,' he said, 'by creating a team that everyone in Leinster can get behind. But I want to do more than bring in new faces. For the past year, I've been trying to bring in a new culture, a new way of doing things. Munster have The Munster Way. We're going to have The Leinster Way.'

I had to admit, he made it sound kind of exciting.

'I'm a serious man,' he said, 'especially when it comes to rugby. So what I'm about to say, I don't say it lightly. I think Leinster are capable of winning the European Cup.'

'Really?' I said.

'Don't sound so surprised. We have the potential

to be as good as Munster – maybe even better. So, what do you say?'

Me? Win the European Cup? What else was I going to say?

'Yeah,' I said, 'I'd love to play for Leinster.'

1 *'What's* your *beef?'*

'Welcome to McWonderburger, Wexford! What's *your* beef?'

I can't even begin to tell you how sick and tired I was of saying those words. From seven o'clock in the morning, when the first breakfast customers trudged, bleary-eyed, through the front door, until three o'clock in the afternoon, when my shift ended, I must have uttered the line about three hundred times a day.

'Welcome to McWonderburger, Wexford! What's *your* beef?'

Dad thought it would be a good idea for me to get a summer job.

Unfortunately, while dads are generally a good and useful bunch of people, they do, occasionally, have some crazy notions.

'It'll be the absolute making of you!' he assured me. 'What about working behind the counter in a shop or a restaurant? It'll help you to understand basic monetary concepts, like adding up the prices of things and figuring out how much change to give!'

He tended to get very excited when the conversation turned to maths. He worked as a bank manager. We tried to make allowances for him.

'The price is €7.58,' he said. 'And the customer has handed you a €20 note. How much change do you have to give back?'

'Er, fifty cent?' I speculated. 'Something in that ballpark?'

To be completely honest, I knew that wasn't the right answer. But it was only DAY THREE of the holidays. I had a plan for the summer mapped out in my head and it mostly involved doing absolutely nothing except sleeping late and staying fit, just like Joe Schmidt had asked me to, so that I'd be ready to join Leinster in September.

So I said, 'Er, fifty cent?' because I wanted him to understand how totally and utterly unsuited I was to working in a job that involved handling money.

I hoped he'd drop the subject. But he didn't.

'That's it!' he said. 'You've just proved to me that

a job is EXACTLY what you need! Come on – up you get!'

I forgot to mention that I was still in bed.

'It's €12.42!' I blurted out. 'The change, I mean! I just figured it out in my head! It turns out I don't need a job after all!'

'Come on, get dressed,' he insisted. 'The more I think about this idea, the better it seems. You'll only appreciate the true value of money, Gordon, when you have to earn your own!'

'It's not going to be easy to find a job,' I warned him. 'Especially with the way the economy is at the moment. These are tough times for a kid out of work, Dad.'

But then he remembered something.

'Isn't Peter working in that new burger restaurant in town?' he asked.

'Peter?' I asked. 'Who's Peter?'

'Peter is your best friend, Gordon. He lives three doors down. You share a dormitory together in boarding school. You've been playing rugby with him since you were both tiny. As a matter of fact, doesn't his uncle *own* that new burger restaurant?'

'I'm still trying to picture this Peter guy,' I said.

Mum appeared at the door.

'Conor Kehoe is working there as well,' she added.

'I saw him at lunchtime yesterday. He looked very smart in his uniform.'

She laughed. You'll find out why she laughed soon enough.

'Conor Kehoe?' I said. 'Now why does *that* name sound familiar? Let me sleep on this, will you?'

'Out of bed!' Dad ordered. 'I'll drive you down there now and see if they have any vacancies!'

So that's how I came to spend my summer serving behind the counter of the Sunny South-East's newest, American-style, fast-food restaurant.

'Welcome to McWonderburger, Wexford! What's *your* beef?'

The worst thing about the job was, without doubt, the uniform. It was no wonder my mother laughed. It consisted of a shirt that was – there's no other way of describing it – CANARY YELLOW in colour. The trousers were even more garish. They were BRIGHT GREEN. And, to complete the look, all McWonderburger employees were required to wear a plastic cow snout – which covered your nose and which you strapped to your face using an elastic band – as well as a red baseball cap that had two enormous horns.

The answer to the question 'What's *your* beef?' was usually one of four special menu items.

There was the McWonderburger – a quarter-pound beef patty, with onions, lettuce, tomato and mayonnaise, on a bun.

There was the McWonder Wonderburger – three quarter-pound beef patties and four slices of cheese, with gherkins (eugh!), onions, lettuce, tomato and mayonnaise, on a bun.

There was the McWonder Wonder Wonder-burger – six quarter-pound beef patties, eight slices of cheese, twelve slices of bacon, with gherkins (yuck!), guacamole, salsa, onions, lettuce, tomato and mayonnaise, on a bun.

And there was the McWonder Wonder Wonder

Wonderburger – twelve quarter-pound beef patties, sixteen slices of cheese, twenty-four slices of bacon, black and white pudding, peanut butter, two fried eggs, a deep-fried banana, a slice of pizza, two hot dogs, with gherkins (it's just WRONG!), guacamole, salsa, onions, lettuce, tomato and mayonnaise, not on a bun, but sandwiched between two custard-filled doughnuts.

There was also a hidden menu item: the Mc-Wonder Wonder Wonder Wonder Wonderburger, which was rumoured to be a whole cow on a bun. Although I never saw anyone order one. And we didn't stock whole cows even if they did.

The only thing that made my job at McWonderburger just about bearable was getting to spend the summer with Peter and Conor. We spent our days dreaming up new ways to try to make the job fun.

'We all wish we were playing rugby,' Conor said one day. 'There's nothing to stop us using our imaginations, is there?'

In the late morning, the restaurant was normally quiet. That was when we usually peeled the potatoes to make sure we had enough to make a mountain of chips when the lunchtime rush started.

'Okay, Gordon,' Conor said, 'who's the toughest tackler in world rugby?'

'That's easy,' I told him. 'Ma'a Nonu.'

'Right, let's pretend that this large sack of pota-toes is Ma'a Nonu. Peter, grab the other end of this, will you? We're going to throw it at Gordon.'

'What?' I said, horrified.

'Come on, Gordon, this is going to help toughen you up. You don't want people looking at you and thinking you're soft like all those other Leinster fel-las, do you?'

I sighed.

'Fine,' I said. 'But wait until I'm —'

I was going to say, 'Ready.'

But Peter had already grabbed the other end of the sack and, together, they threw it at me across the kitchen. It hit me full in the stomach, knocking the wind out of me, and I fell backwards against a table, knocking it over and sending a stack of pots and pans clattering to the floor.

'Okay,' Conor said, 'I think you're going to need to practise that before you try it at the RDS!'

There was another game we played whenever we discovered a potato that was rotten. There was a bin in the corner of the kitchen in which we kept all the vegetables that were gone off — to be used, later on, as compost. One of us would hold open the lid while another would try to kick the potato, Garryowen-style, across the kitchen and into the bin.

It took a lot of skill – and one or two broken windows – to get our technique right.

And then we were back serving customers again.

'Welcome to McWonderburger, Wexford! What's *your* beef?'

Occasionally, a customer would look at me in a strange way. And I'd have to repeat myself: 'Welcome to McWonderburger, Wexford! What's *your* beef?'

And they'd sometimes say, 'Do you mind me asking, are you Gordon D'Arcy?'

And I would always reply, 'Er, no, I'm not.'

I was wearing a yellow shirt, green trousers, a plastic snout and a red baseball cap with horns. I didn't want ANYONE to know that it was me.

'It's just, you look really like Gordon D'Arcy,' they would say.

'Who's Gordon D'Arcy?' I'd ask.

'He's a rugby player. He helped Ireland to win the Six Nations this year.'

'No, the name doesn't ring a bell.'

'It's just your name badge there actually says, *Gordon D'Arcy.*'

'I'm, er, a different Gordon D'Arcy.'

And they'd nod and say, 'Actually, that makes sense. I mean, why would Gordon D'Arcy, the rugby player, be working in McWonderburger in Wexford? Especially now that he's just been signed by Leinster.'

And that's when I would get butterflies in my tummy and start wishing that the summer would end, so I could get back to doing what I loved more than anything else in the world.

And that was playing rugby.

2 Stay Fit the Gordon D'Arcy Way!

In a strange way, what I said was true. Sometimes, it *did* feel like I was a different Gordon D'Arcy. It was hard to believe that everything that had happened in the past few months had actually happened to me.

I'd made my debut for Ireland in Paris. I'd helped them to win the Six Nations Championship and the Grand Slam. I'd made lots of new friends. I'd become, well, sort of famous. And, along the way, I'd learned a lot of valuable lessons about the importance of hard work and not letting success go to your head.

But there were times that summer when I wondered had I dreamt the entire thing. When I was hard at work in McWonderburger, serving customers, or sweeping the floor, or peeling chewing gum off the undersides of the table – and what a lot of fun that job was! – it seemed like it had all happened in another lifetime.

But then I'd remember my conversation with Joe Schmidt, especially his warning to me to stay in shape. So, when I wasn't working in McWonderburger, I was devising a fitness programme for myself. Everybody knows that the first thing you need when you're in serious training is music.

More than that, I needed a Gordon D'Arcy Workout Playlist to spur me on.

Unfortunately, I didn't own an iPod. My brother, Ian, had one, but he took it everywhere with him. The nearest thing I could find to an iPod was Mum's old Walkman. Just in case you're unfamiliar with technology from the last century, a Walkman was a portable device with headphones that allowed you to play music anywhere you went – as long as the music was recorded on cassette tapes.

As it happened, Mum owned only one cassette tape. It was the *Greatest Hits of Garth Brooks*. Just in case you're unfamiliar with music from the last century, Garth Brooks was an American country and western singer who dressed like a cowboy and made music that people line-danced to.

But it was the only music I had. So it would have to do. With Garth Brooks plugged into my ears, I applied myself to a nightly regime of sit-ups, press-ups and pull-ups to make myself stronger.

One night my sister Shona shouted out the window, 'GORDON, WHAT ARE YOU DOING OUT THERE?'

I couldn't hear her. I was in the garden. I forgot to mention that I used a branch from our apple tree to perform my pull-ups.

'GORDON!' she shouted. 'GORDON!'

But I was listening to a song called 'Friends in Low Places' and I couldn't hear a word she was saying.

She was forced to come downstairs to talk to me. I opened my eyes and there she was, standing in front of me in her dressing-gown.

'GORDON!' she shouted. 'WHAT DO YOU THINK YOU'RE PLAYING AT?'

'SORRY, SHONA,' I shouted, 'I'M JUST LISTENING TO MY WORKOUT PLAY-LIST WHILE DOING MY EXERCISES!'

'GORDON, WILL YOU TURN THE MUSIC OFF?'

'WHAT'S THAT, SHONA?'

She pulled one side of the earphones off my ear.

'WILL YOU TURN THE MUSIC *OFF*?' she yelled.

'Oh, sorry,' I said, pressing the Stop button. 'I must have had it on a bit loud.'

'Gordon, what in the name of God are you doing? It's eleven o'clock at night!'

'It's called training, Shona. I'm going to be

playing for Leinster in September, in case you haven't heard.'

'Is that Mum's Garth Brooks album you're listening to?'

'Er, yeah.'

'The one she used to practise her line-dancing?'

'Okay, it's not exactly Jay-Z, but it's definitely helping me, Shona.'

It was at that exact moment that Mum and Dad arrived home from the cinema. Mum seemed a bit troubled about something.

It turned out that *something* was me!

'What in the name of all that is Holy are you doing now?' she asked.

She often asked me this question.

'I'm training,' I explained. 'I would have thought that was obvious.'

I was wearing my rugby gear after all.

'It's eleven o'clock at night,' she said.

'Why does everyone keep telling me the time?' I asked.

'The neighbours stopped us on the way in,' Dad explained. 'They said they thought Gordon had gone mad. He was in the back garden singing 'If Tomorrow Never Comes' in a sort of cowboy voice.'

I found it helped to sing along to the music.

'Er, that's how Garth Brooks sings,' I explained.

'Well,' said Dad, 'it's setting all the dogs in the neighbourhood howling.'

'Is that *my* Garth Brooks cassette?' Mum wanted to know. 'The one I used to practise my line-dancing?'

'Yes,' I said. 'I borrowed it because I don't have an iPod. Now, if you don't mind, I'm going to get back to my training.'

'Yes, we do mind,' said Dad. 'And so do the neighbours. They're threatening to call the Gardaí.'

'But I told Joe Schmidt that I'd stay fit this summer.'

'Well, you're not going to get any fitter tonight! Bedtime!'

'You're only saying that because you're a Munster fan.'

'It has nothing to do with being a Munster fan. You've got work tomorrow.'

'Yeah, that is such a Lunster thing to say.'

'Bedtime, Gordon! Now!'

Ian was delighted that I was going to be playing for Leinster. He even offered to help me with my training by coming up with some fun drills to improve my skills. Like, for instance, seeing how

23

fast I could run with my eyes closed. Ian couldn't quite explain which of my skills this was going to improve, but he assured me that the All Blacks had been doing it for years in training. It turned out I was quite good at running fast with my eyes closed – 'A natural!' according to Ian – until the third time I did it, when I ran through six-foot-high nettles and got literally clotheslined by next-door's clothesline, knocking myself out cold for thirty seconds.

Megan was also a great help. I decided that I needed to work on the accuracy of my kicking, so I asked her to open her bedroom window and I'd practise kicking the ball through it. The first three sailed clear through the open window. Each time, Megan threw the ball back down to me, shouting, 'Do it again, Gordon! You're so good at this!'

Confidence was my undoing, unfortunately. The fourth time I tried it, I took my eye off the ball for a split second just before I connected with it. Instead of making contact with the ball with my laces, I kicked it with my toe and it sailed straight through Mum and Dad's bedroom window, which happened to be firmly closed.

There was a loud crash of breaking glass.

'Don't panic,' I told Megan. 'Go and get me the ball and we'll say that a magpie must have hit the window.'

But Megan *did* panic.

'Mooommmmmmmyyyyyy!!!!!!' she screamed. 'Gordon smashed a window!'

Mum and Dad weren't pleased.

'If it's any consolation,' I tried to tell them, 'Ronan O'Gara broke literally hundreds of windows growing up. Probably.'

'You are *not* Ronan O'Gara!' Dad pointed out. 'The glass all over our bedroom floor is proof of that!'

'Yeah,' I told him, 'I'd expect that kind of talk from a Lunster fan. Trust me, when I win the European Cup with Leinster, we'll look back on this day and we'll laugh.'

Mum couldn't help but smile.

'You're never going to change,' she said, 'are you, Gordon? You're still like a big, excitable Labrador, with a red bow around his neck!'

'A big, excitable Labrador,' Dad said, 'who'll be paying for that window with his next wage packet from McWonderburger.'

I didn't mind. I'd been reminded of a valuable lesson – never take your eye off the ball.

'I might as well keep practising,' I said. 'Sure, your window is broken anyway.'

Mum just shook her head.

'Oh, Gordon!' she said. 'Will you ever change?'

3 *Tyrannosaurus Wrecked*

'Oh, no!' I thought. 'Oh, please, God, no!'

It was one Saturday afternoon towards the end of the summer. McWonderburger was hosting a children's party. This happened about three or four times a week. A group of ten or twenty screaming toddlers would arrive like an army of ants on the march.

They would eat Little McWonderburgers and Double Chocolate Sundaes and then they would shout, and scream, and chase each other around, and fall over, and fight with each other, and make up, and laugh, before their exhausted parents took them home again.

While they were there, it was our job to serve them food, but also to entertain them. So we all took turns to dress up as Benji.

Benji was a purple dinosaur, who bore an uncanny

resemblance to another purple dinosaur who was much loved by children everywhere. Due to copyright restrictions, we were not permitted to use the name of the other much loved purple dinosaur – and so we had to call him Benji instead.

On this particular Saturday afternoon, there were twenty very loud and very boisterous children at the party and it was my turn to wear the dinosaur suit. I put it on in the storeroom where we kept the potatoes and the buns and the drinking cups. Then I took a deep breath and walked out to face the madness.

Now, I'd played rugby in the Stade de France in front of 100,000 screaming fans. And yet I'd never felt as nervous as I did stepping out in front of a children's party dressed in that purple dinosaur costume.

Their eyes lit up.

'IT'S BARNEY!' they shouted. 'IT'S BARNEY!'

And I replied, 'No, it's actually Benji' – something I was legally required to say – 'another purple dinosaur with no connection whatsoever to the popular anthropomorphic Tyrannosaurus Rex of the same colour.'

'BARNEY!' they shouted. 'BARNEY!'

They hit me like the South African pack.

BOOOOOOMF!

And suddenly I was caught in the middle of this rolling maul that moved from one side of the restaurant to the other. Conor and Peter jumped over the counter and joined the maul to try to help me.

'BARNEY!' the children shouted. 'IT'S BARNEY!'

And I had to repeat the line that had been drafted by the Legal Department at McWonderburger: 'No, it's actually Benji, another purple dinosaur with no connection whatsoever to the popular anthropomorphic Tyrannosaurus Rex of the same –'

And that – to bring you back to the start of the story – was when I suddenly thought, 'Oh, no! Oh, please, God, no!'

Because through the mouth of the costume, I could see that a group of girls had walked into McWonderburger. And right at the front of the group, expertly spinning a rugby ball in her hands, was none other than Aoife Kehoe.

Aoife was my friend and a cousin of Conor. She was incredibly cool and also one of the best rugby players, boy *or* girl, that I had ever seen. She was the out-half for the Ireland Schoolgirls team and I sometimes helped her practise her kicking by running

and fetching the balls for her every time she put one
between the posts.

I saw her and her friends laughing at the sight of
this purple dinosaur being swept around the floor of
the restaurant by this tidal wave of excited children
while two McWonderburger employees tried to res-
cue him.

And my stupid pride told me that I couldn't
let Aoife see that, inside the dinosaur costume,
was me!

But then there was an unfortunate turn of events.
One of the children had worked himself up to such

a pitch of excitement that he decided to try to rip my head off.

Well, not *my* head, you understand. I'm talking about Benji's head.

I tried to hold onto it, but I couldn't get a firm grip, and it was finally torn from my shoulders just as the maul collapsed in a tangle of arms and legs in front of the counter.

Aoife was staring down at me with a look of surprise on her face.

'Gordon?' she said.

I considered denying it. But there was no point. She knew me too well.

'Hey, Aoife,' I said.

She laughed. So did her friends.

'Are you . . . Barney?' she asked.

'No,' I replied, 'I'm actually Benji, another purple dinosaur with no connection whatsoever to the popular . . . do you know what, it doesn't matter.'

She held out her hand and helped me up. She introduced me to her friends, who were called Sophie, Kate, Emily, Grace and Eva.

'Girls,' she said, 'this is Gordon D'Arcy.'

'Yeah, we *know* who Gordon D'Arcy is,' Grace said. 'Everyone on our road is talking about him at the moment!'

I smiled – I hoped modestly, but probably not.

'So clearly,' I said, 'there *are* a few Leinster fans in this town.'

'I'm not talking about Leinster,' she said. 'I live four doors down from you. You do chin-ups in the back garden in the middle of the night while singing Garth Brooks songs.'

On second thoughts, I recognized Grace now.

'Yeah, it's called training,' I offered weakly.

Suddenly, I heard the sound of Conor clearing his throat.

'Er, can someone help us up here?' he asked.

I forgot that Conor and Peter were still trapped underneath the collapsed maul of hyperactive toddlers. We helped all of the children to their feet and, finally, Conor and Peter, who went behind the counter again to serve Aoife and her friends – or, more accurately, to ask them: 'What's *your* beef?'

Conor and Peter agreed that I could take my break. Let's be honest, I'd earned it. I sat with the girls and I asked Aoife how she was enjoying her summer.

'It's been great,' she said. 'We're playing rugby all the time. But, to be honest, I'm kind of looking forward to going back to school.'

I could understand that. In a few months, she was

going to be captaining the Ireland Schoolgirls team in the Six Nations.

'How was *your* summer?' she asked. 'What have you been doing – when you haven't been dressed up as a dinosaur, or singing Garth Brooks songs in the garden in the middle of the night?'

I laughed. You had to have a sense of humour about yourself if you wanted to spend time around Aoife.

'Mostly, I've been working here,' I said, 'and then doing some training as well. Practising my kicking and my running fast with my eyes closed.'

'Your what?' she asked.

'Doesn't matter,' I said. 'So are you going to come and see me play for Leinster this year?'

'Errr, maybe,' she said.

I was a bit taken aback by her reaction. I thought she'd be pleased for me – just like I was pleased for her.

'What does that mean?' I asked.

'It's just that, well, I'm not really a Leinster fan,' she explained. 'We're all Munster fans in our house.'

'But maybe you shouldn't be,' I said. 'You're *from* Wexford.'

'So?' she said.

'Wexford is in Leinster,' I told her. 'I can show it to you on a map.'

'You don't need to show it to me on a map,' she said.

'I'm just saying, you never hear of Munster fans supporting Leinster, do you? They support their own team.'

'That's because they're worth supporting. They play the kind of rugby that I love to watch – full of passion and hunger and desire. Paul O'Connell roaring at his teammates to give everything they have. Jonny Hayes crying with pride before the match even starts. Donncha O'Callaghan and his red underpants. Leinster don't have anything like that.'

'Joe Schmidt thinks we can win the European Cup this season,' I said.

She laughed.

'I don't want to sound mean,' she said, 'but Leinster are a bit –'

'What?' I said. 'Go on, say it.'

'They're a bit like that dinosaur costume you're wearing.'

'What does that mean?'

'It means they're soft.'

'Maybe that's all about to change,' I suggested.

'Yeah, Gordon,' she said, 'I'll believe it when I see it.'

4 The Holidays are Over

The day had finally arrived. I was going back to boarding school. And I couldn't wait to get back to Clongowes and start playing rugby again.

'I'm still not sure about this,' Dad said.

We were sitting in the bus station in Wexford Town.

'I still think I should drive you there,' he said. 'Come on, let's get back in the car.'

'But, Dad,' I argued, 'they've put this bus on specially. It's going right to the door of the school. All my friends are going to be on it.'

I spotted Conor and Peter across the bus station.

'Look, there they are!' I said.

Conor gave me a wave.

'He'll be fine on the bus,' Mum said. 'Here, I have a little present for you, Gordon.'

She handed me her Walkman.

'I can't take that from you!' I told her.

'You'll need it for your training,' she said. 'And I've left the Garth Brooks album in there for you.'

Dad carried my bags to the bus, then he and Mum hugged me goodbye and said they'd see me next weekend.

I climbed on board, just ahead of my friends.

The bus driver, Hughie, took one look at Conor, then told him, 'I don't want any trouble from you this year.'

'Me?' Conor said, his voice all wounded innocence. 'What have I ever done?'

Conor knew well what he'd done. Hughie had been the victim of more than a few of his practical jokes last year.

'Don't pretend you don't know,' Hughie told him. 'All I'm saying is, I won't be putting up with it this year.'

Soon, we were on the motorway and heading northwards towards Kildare.

Peter spent most of the journey reading his Maths textbook.

'Peter, what are you doing?' I asked. 'We haven't even had a lesson yet.'

'I'm just reading ahead,' he said. 'I'm reading about the 3:4:5 triangle rule.'

Peter got excited about schoolwork the same way I got excited about rugby.

We hadn't been on the road that long when we all became aware of a strange noise coming from the front of the bus — a sort of persistent musical hum. It sounded like this:

HhhooommmmmmWAAAWAAAWAAA!!!!!!

'What's that?' I asked.

Conor winked at me. 'Say nothing,' he said.

HhhooommmmmmWAAAWAAAWAAA!!!!!!

Hughie looked over his shoulder.

'Where's that noise coming from?' he shouted down the bus.

'What noise?' Conor replied.

HhhooommmmmmWAAAWAAAWAAA!!!!!!

That noise!' Hughie said. 'I've been hearing it since we left Wexford.'

'I don't hear anything,' Conor said. 'Gordon, can you hear a noise?'

I shook my head. 'No,' I said, 'I can't hear a thing.'

'I think you've been working too hard,' Conor told Hughie.

HhhooommmmmmWAAAWAAAWAAA!!!!!!

'Conor,' I said out of the side of my mouth, 'what did you do?'

'I stuck a harmonica to the front grille of the bus,' he whispered.

I laughed. Even Peter smiled and shook his head.

'So that's the sound of the wind blowing on it?' I said.

'Exactly,' Conor said. 'But he's going to think there's something wrong with the engine.'

'Conor,' Peter said, 'you have to stop torturing that man.'

I laughed.

'So can I ask you fellas a question?' I said.

'Is it a Maths question?' Peter wondered.

'No, it's a rugby question,' I said. 'Do you know the way you're both massive Munster fans? Is that not weird?'

'Weird?' Conor said. 'Why is it weird?'

'Because you're not actually *from* Munster,' I reminded him.

'Doesn't matter,' Conor said. 'You support a team because you like the way they play – not because of where they come from.'

'Let me put it to you this way,' I said. 'You love the All Blacks, don't you?'

'Yeah,' Conor said. 'Because New Zealand has the best rugby players in the world.'

'But if they were playing against Ireland, who would you cheer for?'

'Ireland.'

'Why?'

'Because I'm Irish.'

'That's my point, Conor. You should be supporting Leinster.'

'It's different, though.'

'How is it different?'

'Because you never hear people saying they're proud to come from Leinster.'

'Maybe we should all be saying that. You always hear people describing themselves as proud Munstermen. But no one ever says they're a proud Leinsterman.'

HhhooommmmmmWAAAWAAAWAAA!!!!!!

Hughie looked over his shoulder again.

'Seriously,' he said, 'what *is* that noise?'

'I think it's your fan belt!' Conor shouted.

Conor knew a little bit about engines.

'Couldn't be my fan belt,' Hughie shouted back. 'I've just had a new one fitted.'

'Definitely sounds like your fan belt to me,' Conor insisted.

HhhooommmmmmWAAAWAAAWAAA!!!!!!

I heard Hughie tut and then sigh, then a second or two later he pulled into the hard shoulder. He got out, walked to the back of the bus and opened the engine cover. We could hear him twisting things and tightening things, then he slammed the engine cover shut again and got back onto the bus.

'I think that's fixed it,' he announced, then he climbed back into his seat and we got on the road again. Thirty seconds later, as soon as the bus built up some speed, the noise started again:

HhhooommmmmmWAAAWAAAWAAA!!!!!!

'Two hundred euros that new fan belt cost me,' Hughie said. 'Bunch of gangsters in that garage.'

'I used to go to all the Leinster matches with my dad,' Peter said. 'But then we just stopped.'

'Why?' I wondered.

'Why do you think? One weekend, they were great. Then the next weekend, they were terrible. He said it was a waste of time and money following a team like that. No offence, Gordon.'

I was a little bit hurt, I had to admit – especially as this was now *my* team they were talking about.

'My brother, Ian, never misses a Leinster match,' I told him. 'He follows them through thick and thin.'

40

'But mostly thin,' Conor said. 'Look, we're delighted that you're going to be playing for them, Gordon. As your mates, we're proud of you – aren't we, Peter?'

'Very proud,' said Peter.

HhhooommmmmmWAAAWAAAWAAA!!!!!!

'But, well, you must have heard the stories about the Leinster dressing-room,' said Conor.

'What stories?'

'Well, firstly, half the players wear fake tan.'

'Fake tan? No way!'

'Have you never wondered why some of them look like they've just come back from their holidays?'

'I just presumed they were abroad – yeah, doing warm-weather training.'

'It's from a bottle. My sister wears the same shade as one or two of them. Medium Mahogany. And that's just *one* of the things I've heard.'

'What else?' I asked.

'I've heard they all bring hair-dryers into the dressing-room.'

'That's okay,' I insisted. 'There's nothing wrong with drying your hair after you've had a shower.'

'No, I've heard they do their hair *before* they play a match,' Conor said.

'No way!'

'That's what I've heard.'

Soon, the bus took a left turn and we found ourselves driving through the famous black gates of Clongowes Wood College, then up the driveway that was so long, it felt like we would never reach the end of it.

Our eyes were automatically drawn to the rugby pitches on our left. I have to admit, I had butterflies in my stomach.

Eventually, the school building came into view. I was so excited to be back at Clongowes.

We joined the queue of boys waiting to get off the bus. As he stepped down onto the gravel in front of me, Conor turned to Hughie.

'There's nothing wrong with your fan belt, by the way,' he said. 'Someone's stuck a harmonica to your front grille!'

'Conor Kehoe,' Hughie shouted, 'that is the last time you are EVER getting on this bus!'

5 *Definitely NOT a Scrum-half*

Vinnie Murray, the school's Director of Rugby, was standing in the middle of the pitch, whistle hanging around his neck, waiting for us to arrive for rugby practice.

'Okay,' he said, 'who wants to run some laps of the field?'

We all froze. Running laps was a punishment. I think most of us would rather have spent our double Free Time period in Mr Rowland's Maths class.

Vinnie smiled.

'I'm only kidding,' he said, much to our relief. 'Will we play some rugby?'

We all cheered.

'Okay,' Vinnie said, doing a quick mental head-count, 'we have enough for two teams,' and then he started to point at each of us in turn, saying, 'Team Red!' or 'Team Yellow!'

The colours referred to the bibs that we pulled on over our rugby gear.

Once he'd assigned us to one team or the other, he told us our positions.

'Gordon D'Arcy,' he said, 'you're playing scrum-half today.'

Now, I was a centre. That's where I played when I won the Six Nations with Ireland. But Vinnie did this occasionally. He knew that players had their own favourite positions. But, sometimes, he liked you to play in a role that was totally alien to you. For instance, he got the smallest boys on the field to play in the second row and contest the lineouts. Or he got the biggest, clumsiest boys to play in a position like out-half, where skilful hands were absolutely essential.

He thought it was important for players to understand how every position on the pitch worked – and there was no better way to understand a position than by playing in it yourself. That way, when you were playing a match and you saw that your full-back was having a nightmare under the high ball, or that your front-row teammates were being out-muscled in the scrum, you would know exactly what they were going through.

As well as that, it taught us not to get a big head.

I was a very good centre. I knew that. But I was a TERRIBLE scrum-half. They might be (usually) the shortest players on the field, but no one covers more ground during a rugby match than a scrum-half. They have to constantly chase the play, to make sure they're there, ready to receive the ball, at every ruck. They have to be able to play the perfect pass from the ground and execute the perfect box-kick under pressure. And that gets harder and harder as your body gets tired.

And if I didn't understand that already, it was something I was about to find out in the most painful and embarrassing way possible. I was on Team Red. Conor and Peter were on Team Yellow. And Conor, as it turned out, was going to be playing opposite me as his team's scrum-half.

The match was about fifteen minutes old when we were awarded a scrum deep in the opposition half. I was already panting hard, exhausted from trying to get to all those rucks. The two packs crouched, then paused, then engaged. I fed the ball into the forest of legs, then ran around the back of the scrum and waited for our forwards to pass it back to me with their feet. I waited and waited. Eventually, it popped out. I picked it up and turned around to find out where my out-half was standing. And suddenly . . .

BANG!

I felt like I'd been hit by the Dublin-to-Wexford train. I fell to the ground, spilling the ball.

Vinnie blew his whistle.

'Knock-on!' he said. 'Scrum to Team Yellow.'

I looked up and saw Conor standing above me with a big smile on his face.

'You have to be quicker than that, D'Arcy!' he said.

I laughed.

He offered me his hand and helped me up. I loved that about rugby. No matter how hurt or humiliated you felt after being dumped on your back by a tackler, you had to accept the hand of help if it was offered.

Ten minutes later, it happened a second time. I fed the ball into the scrum. I raced around the back again, this time even quicker. The ball emerged from between the number eight's feet. I gathered it up. This time, I didn't even get the chance to turn around.

BANG!

Conor hit me again. Down I went – again, spilling the ball, although this time it went backwards and it was Conor who gathered it up, then offloaded it to Peter, playing in the centre, who ran the length of the pitch to score a try.

'It's a good job you can play centre,' he pointed out helpfully as he pulled me to my feet for the second time, 'because you are no number nine!'

'Thanks, Conor!' I told him. 'I'll never complain about slow rucks again!'

As the match went on, I kept arriving later and later to rucks. My teammates were looking around, asking, 'Where is he? Where's Gordon?' and then I'd finally arrive on the scene, puffing and panting. And because I was tired, my passes always missed their target.

When Vinnie blew the final whistle, he announced that Team Yellow had beaten Team Red by 41–12.

And I knew that I had been the worst player on the pitch.

As we walked off, Vinnie called me over.

'Are you okay?' he asked. 'You're not hurt, are you?'

'Just my pride,' I replied. 'I'll never, EVER criticize a scrum-half again!'

'When are you training with Leinster?' he asked. 'Isn't that happening this week?'

'Yes, Mr Murray,' I said. 'It's tomorrow after school.'

'Well, best of luck with it. And give Joe Schmidt a message from me, will you?'

'Yeah, what is it?'

'Tell him you're definitely NOT a number nine!'

I had to laugh.

Vinnie looked around him then.

'Where's Conor Kehoe?' he asked. 'Conor, can I have word with you, please, in private?'

I watched a look of worry spread across Conor's face. We'd only been back at school for one day. He couldn't be in trouble already, I thought.

I went back to the dormitory with Peter. We changed out of our rugby gear and into our uniforms, then we headed for A3, where our next class of the day was Geography, which I absolutely HATED.

It wasn't helped by the fact that Mr Trent, the teacher, had the most BORING voice in the entire world.

'And these lakes are called what?' he asked. 'Anyone? They're called Pater Something Lakes. Anyone know the word? Pater? Pater?'

A few minutes into the class, Conor arrived. He apologized to Mr Trent for being late, then sat next to me in the free seat to my left.

'What happened?' I whispered. 'What did you do?'

'I didn't do anything,' he said, 'for once in my life. Well, nothing bad anyway.'

'So why did Mr Murray want to talk to you?'

'He asked me if I'd ever considered making scrum-half my permanent position.'

Mr Trent was still going on about lakes.

'Anyone?' he asked. 'I'll give you another hint. Pater Nos-Something Lakes. Anyone? No? It's Pater Noster Lakes!'

'I'm not surprised,' I told Conor. 'You were amazing today.'

'I told him I was a hooker,' Conor said. 'But he said lots of players start out in one position and then discover that they're better suited to playing somewhere else.'

It was true. I'd started out playing in the front row as well. As a matter of fact, Conor and I first met when we played opposite each other in the front row – me for Wexford Wanderers and Conor for the Gorey Gladiators.

And we were sworn enemies in those days.

'I never thought of myself as a scrum-half before,' Conor said. 'But he said he was really impressed with me today. He's going to have a word with Frank Kelly.'

'What?' I said. 'Really?'

Frank Kelly was the coach of the Clongowes junior team.

'They need a scrum-half,' he said. 'He wants me to go for a trial.'

I was delighted for him.

'That's great!' I said.

'I told him I might go,' he said, 'provided nothing else came up in the meantime.'

Conor was the funniest person I knew. But he also had the potential to be a great rugby player – if only he took himself seriously enough.

'Why do you always do that?' I asked.

'Why do I always do what?' he said.

'Make jokes.'

'I thought you liked my jokes. You're always laughing anyway.'

'But there's a time for jokes and there's a time for being serious,' I reminded him. 'The great Vinnie Murray picked you out today and told you he thought you might be good enough to play for the Clongowes junior team! Aren't you excited about that?'

'If you never get your hopes up,' he said, 'then you'll never be disappointed.'

'But if you never get your hopes up,' I told him, 'then you'll never achieve anything. You'll just be the class clown forever.'

I didn't mean to hurt his feelings, but I think I may have accidentally done it.

'That didn't come out the way I intended it to,' I said.

'Hey, there's worse things you can do than put a smile on people's faces,' he said.

'I know that,' I explained. 'I just think you could be a great rugby player one day – if you put your mind to it. Will you go for the trial?'

'Yes, I will.'

'Do you absolutely promise, Conor?'

'Yes, Gordon, I absolutely promise.'

6 *The Leinster Way*

It was the smell that hit me first. It wasn't a bad smell. It was actually quite a nice smell. It reminded me of one Christmas when Mum took me to Brown Thomas in Dublin and we walked through the cosmetics hall at the front of the shop. It smelled of lemon, and hazelnuts, and freshly cut grass, and blueberries, and fir trees, and burning wood, and sea air – all at the same time.

Yes, it was a very nice smell.

It's just, I knew that it wasn't how a rugby dressing-room was supposed to smell – especially BEFORE training!

I'd had to take two buses to training – one from Kildare to Dublin City Centre, and another from Dublin City Centre to the stadium in Donnybrook, where we were due to train at 7 p.m. I'd made it with five minutes to spare. I tried to slip in without anyone noticing me, but Joe saw me in his peripheral vision.

Joe saw everything, I would soon discover.

'You're late,' he said, without even looking at me.

As if I wasn't nervous enough meeting my new teammates, every set of eyes in the dressing-room was now fixed on me.

'Er, I'm actually five minutes early,' I said, looking at my watch. 'You did say seven o'clock, didn't you?'

Joe pointed at Brian O'Driscoll, who, I noticed, was already dressed in his training gear – just like every other player.

'Tell him the rule,' Joe said. 'The one I brought in at the end of last season.'

'To be five minutes early is to be late,' BOD said. 'To be twenty minutes early is to be on time.'

'Er, okay,' I said, pretending that this made perfect sense to me.

'The players who take their job seriously,' Joe said, 'arrive half an hour before I tell them to be here. That's The Leinster Way.'

This was seriously embarrassing.

'But you're new to the set-up,' Joe said, 'so I'm going to let it go this time. Everyone, I want to introduce you to Gordon D'Arcy. Some of you will already know him, having played with him for Ireland. And the rest of you, I'm sure, will have seen him in action against France and Wales, so you'll know he can be a pretty decent player on his day.'

Pretty decent? On his day? He wasn't filling me with confidence.

There were one or two hellos and a few nods. But they didn't exactly roll out the red carpet for me.

I sat down and I looked around me. Some of the players I already knew from the Ireland set-up, like Brian O'Driscoll, and Shane Horgan, who everyone called Shaggy, and Leo Cullen. Others I recognized from TV. There was Shane Byrne, the hooker known as Munch, who was built like a photo booth and had long, wavy hair like a rock star. There was Felipe Contepomi, the out-half, who was as bald as a billiard ball and who stared intensely into the distance, like he was already visualizing the training session. There was also a tall, skinny guy with dark hair and a sulky face, whom I'd never set eyes on before, but whose name, I would soon discover, was Johnny Sexton. And sitting next to him was a stocky lad with a smiley face, who turned out to be Seán O'Brien.

It was their first training session as well and they seemed even more nervous than me. But at least they'd been on time!

'Well, are you going to sit there looking around you,' Joe asked me, 'or are you going to put that gear on?'

On the bench beside me, freshly pressed and folded into a neat pile, was a Leinster training jersey, a pair of shorts and a pair of socks.

'Hurry up and get changed,' Joe said, 'and we'll see you outside.'

I put my gear on as quickly as I could, then I joined everyone else out on the pitch for the warm-up. I was performing a few lunges, to stretch out my hamstrings, when another player, who was warming up beside me, introduced himself.

'I'm Damn Handsome!' he said, offering me his hand. 'But then that's obvious to anyone with eyes in their head!' and he laughed like it was the funniest thing anyone had ever said.

'Damn Handsome?' I said. 'What, that's your actual name?'

'No,' he said, 'my *actual* name is Dan Hansen. But everyone calls me Handsome for short.'

'Wouldn't it be shorter to just call you Dan?' I wondered.

Again, he laughed, but then he turned serious again.

'It's Handsome,' he said. 'Or Damn Handsome – okay? I'm trying to get the name to stick. It's part of my online brand.'

'Er, okay,' I said, then I continued with my lunges.

Handsome was a winger and he was part of a little group of players who seemed incredibly cool. They were so tanned and their hair so neatly styled that I began to wonder if Conor was right about some of the Leinster players.

Oh, and that smell of lemon, and hazelnuts, and freshly cut grass, and blueberries, and fir trees, and burning wood, and sea air? It was coming from them.

When we'd finished our warm-up, Joe separated the backs from the forwards. He said he wanted to work with us on some basic handling drills. He'd watched twenty or thirty hours of video footage of Leinster matches from last season and he'd decided that the team had a habit of drifting sideways on the pass. He wanted us to practise running in straight lines. The pitch was marked out into a series of fifteen narrow lanes. Each player had to pick one. Then we all had to sprint the length of the pitch, passing the ball backwards to each other at high pace, while making sure not to step outside of our lanes. It was really difficult to do, but Joe said that the secret to perfection was perfect practise – and lots of it.

After we'd tried it twenty times, Joe told us to take a break. Felipe caught my eye and gave me a thumbs-up, which I hoped meant that he thought I was doing well.

As I was catching my breath, another Leinster player introduced himself to me. He had tight hair, a hard face and eyebrows that met in the middle. His name was Graham Bull, but he was known to one and all as Bully.

'I just wanted to make sure there was no awkwardness,' he told me.

'Awkwardness?' I said. 'What do you mean?'

'Well, you play inside-centre, don't you?'

'Er, I did for Ireland, yeah.'

'It's just that I play inside-centre as well.'

'Oh,' I said. 'Right.'

'So we're both looking for the number twelve jersey,' he pointed out. 'Some people would say that makes you the enemy. But I actually think competition is a good thing.'

'Do you?' I asked.

'Absolutely,' he said. 'Competition is what spurs

us on to become better players. Look, just because we're rivals for the same position doesn't mean we can't be mates. And if Joe happens to pick you ahead of me, I'll be as happy for you as you would be for me if the roles were reversed.'

'Wow,' I said. 'That's, em, great to hear.'

'Hey, a few of us are going for a coffee after training,' he said.

'Er, yeah,' I said, 'I'd love to go.'

He looked at me with a quizzical expression.

'What?' he said.

'I'm saying I'd love to go for a coffee,' I told him.

'I wasn't inviting you,' he said. 'I was just telling you that a few of us are going for a coffee.'

Behind him, a group of slightly older players, with hard, heavily scarred faces and misshapen ears, laughed.

'Nice one, Bully!' one of them said.

Bully stuck out his hand to me. I went to shake it, but he pulled away at the last second, making me look stupid again.

'You can forget everything I just said about us being mates,' he said. 'Because if you think I'm going to let you waltz in here and take my place on the team, you're dreaming, D'Arcy.'

He turned around and walked off, high-fiving his mates as he did.

When training was over, Joe didn't say, 'Well done!' or 'You worked well tonight!' or 'Thanks for really putting in the effort!'

He said, 'We are what we repeatedly do every day. Remember, perfection is a habit.' And then he walked off in the direction of the dressing-room.

I felt a tap on my shoulder. I turned around. It was BOD.

'What did he mean by that?' I asked.

'That was a Joe-ism,' he said. 'You'll get used to them. I see you didn't wear your golden boots tonight?'

He was talking about the ones with the words TOTAL and LEGEND written on them, which I'd worn against Scotland – and had a disaster of a match.

'No,' I said, 'I only wear those when I want to make a fool of myself in front of millions and millions of people.'

BOD laughed.

'You did well tonight,' he told me.

'It's, er, very different, isn't it,' I said, 'to the Ireland set-up?'

With Ireland, there was a sense of togetherness,

that we were all on the same team. It didn't feel like that with Leinster.

'There's a lot of cliques within the squad,' he said.

'What are cliques?' I asked.

'They're smaller groups within the bigger group. Like, for instance, Dan Hansen has his little gang. Graham Bull has his little gang. They've all got their own way of talking and their in-jokes. Joe is trying to break them up and get us to act more like a squad. Like Munster, I suppose.'

'Right.'

'Take my advice, Gordon – just arrive early, work as hard as you can while you're here and don't get sucked into any of that stuff. Playing for Ireland is an honour. But playing for Leinster is a job.'

Yes, it felt like a job alright. And there was one thing I was already certain about.

I absolutely hated it.

7 The Gollymochy

'Well?' Conor said.

'Well, what?' I asked.

'How was it? Training with Leinster?'

It was after eleven o'clock when I got back to the dormitory that night. Again, it took two buses to make the reverse journey from Donnybrook to Clongowes and I was exhausted by the time I climbed into the top bunk. I definitely wasn't in the mood to talk.

'It was, em, different,' I told him.

'Different to what?' he asked from the bunk below me.

'Different to training with Ireland,' I said.

'Different, better?'

'Different, different.'

Peter was fast asleep. He was snoring the way he usually did. Which sounded like this:

HOOOCCCKKK . . . ZZZUUUUUU!!!!!!
HOOOCCCKKK . . . ZZZUUUUUU!!!!!!
HOOOCCCKKK . . . ZZZUUUUUU!!!!!!

I suddenly remembered the trials for the junior team.

'Hey, how did *you* get on?' I asked.

'I did alright,' Conor replied. 'I think.'

'What do you mean, you *think*?'

'It's not always easy to tell with Mr Kelly, is it? I mean, I think I played quite well. But afterwards he didn't really say anything. He just asked me some questions. Why did I do this and why didn't I do that instead?'

'Mr Murray does that as well. That's a good sign.'

'Is it, though?'

'Yeah, if you do something that they like, they want to make sure you know exactly why you did it.'

'That's one way of looking at it.'

'Conor, seriously, that means he thought you did well.'

Peter's snoring was growing louder:

HOOOCCCKKK . . . ZZZUUUUUU!!!!!!
HOOOCCCKKK . . . ZZZUUUUUU!!!!!!
HOOOCCCKKK . . . ZZZUUUUUU!!!!!!

'I'm going to have to wake him,' I said – because I wasn't going to be able to sleep with that going on.

'PETER!' I shouted. 'PETER, YOU'RE SNORING AGAIN!'

Suddenly, he sat bolt upright in the bed and said: 'Welcome to McWonderburger, Wexford! What's *your* beef?'

Conor and I laughed. It took a few seconds for Peter to realize where he was.

'Sorry,' he said, 'I was having that dream again.'

We had *all* had that dream!

'Hey,' he said when he'd properly woken up, 'how did you get on with Leinster?'

'It was, em, fine,' I lied.

'Just fine?' he asked.

'*Different* was the word he used to me,' said Conor.

'The Leinster squad is just full of, em . . . I can't remember what the word is – groups within a group.'

'Cliques?' said Peter.

'Cliques,' I said. 'Exactly.'

'So which clique do *you* belong to?' Conor asked.

'None,' I said. 'That's the problem. I didn't feel like I belonged there at all.'

'It's bound to feel strange at the start,' Peter said. 'It's like when you played for Ireland. It took you a while to get your bearings, didn't it?'

'I suppose.'

'It'll be the same with Leinster. I'm sure of it.'

'Anyway,' I said, 'I'm going to try and get some sleep.'

But Conor had other ideas.

'You're not going to sleep,' he said. 'We're sneaking out tonight!'

'Sneaking out where?' I asked. 'It's not to bring another cow into the staffroom, is it?'

'No.'

'We got caught for doing that last year. Mr Cuffe will definitely know it was us.'

'Relax, Gordon. We're not bringing a cow into the staffroom. Some of the older lads are going to try to jump the Gollymochy tonight.'

The Gollymochy was a river that cut through the grounds of Clongowes Wood College – and still does to this day. For over a hundred years, there was a tradition where the older boys would attempt to jump it at its widest point. It was famously difficult. It was said that for every one boy who succeeded in making the jump, there were fifty more who ended up in the water. And if you failed to make it to the bank on the other side, you weren't allowed to attempt the jump again for another year.

So when someone announced that they were going to try to jump the Gollymochy, it was a massive deal – and the news spread through the school very, very quickly.

'Come on,' Conor said, 'let's get dressed.'

I agreed to go. I thought it would be a good way to forget the events of the evening. So I jumped down from the top bunk and I pulled on my clothes again. Conor and Peter got out of bed and got dressed too. Then, as quietly as we could, we crept out of our dormitory, down the corridor, through the fire door and outside.

It was a quiet, moonlit night. We crossed the rugby pitches and walked down the steep bank of a hill to the River Gollymochy. Then we followed its course until we reached the point where it was at its widest. There must have been a hundred boys there, all waiting around excitedly to watch two of the senior boys, Michael Purcell and Brian McGuinness, attempt to clear the river.

There was an air of nervousness.

Michael Purcell was the first to attempt the jump. His nickname was The Rabbit, so we all presumed he was a good jumper. He walked back a good distance, to give himself a long run-up, while the crowd started to perform a slow clap, to pace him. He closed his eyes for a moment to try to focus on what he was about to do.

Then he set off on his run, the clapping of the boys becoming faster as he gathered pace and neared the river.

He reached the bank and leapt high into the air.

The crowd *whoaaa-ed* as he took off.

But I knew from the moment he left the ground that he wasn't going to make it to the other side.

The crowd *aaah-ed* as he came down again. And then . . .

SPLAAASSSHHH!!!!!!

The crowd *oooh-ed* as he disappeared beneath the surface of the Gollymochy.

GLUUUUUUGGGGGG!!!!!!

A few seconds later, he stood up again, looking disappointed and soaked to the bone, but acknowledging the help of the crowd as he stood in the freezing river with the water lapping around his waist.

Next, it was Brian McGuinness's turn.

Brian took a longer run-up. Again, the crowd started clapping rhythmically as his face filled with resolve, then he took off like a sprinter from the traps.

He took off from the bank like it was a springboard and he was suddenly flying through the air,

arms and legs flailing to try to give him added distance.

He was going to make it. You could hear the excitement rising in the crowd as he descended towards the ground.

THOOOMMMPPP!

Brian landed with two feet on the far side of the bank! The crowd went wild! He'd done it! Whatever else happened in his life, he would *always* be able to say that he'd jumped the Gollymochy!

He lifted his hands above his head in triumph.

About thirty or forty boys waded through the water to the other side. They lifted him onto their shoulders and carried him back across the river, chanting, 'Le-gend! Le-gend! Le-gend!'

'That'll be us one day,' Conor said.

It was a nice thought.

Then, out of nowhere, we heard a roar:

'WHAT ARE YOU BOYS DOING?'

It was Mr Cuffe. He lived in a house next to the river.

We scattered like pigeons.

'BACK TO YOUR DORMITORIES!' he shouted. 'THIS INSTANT!'

And we laughed and laughed as we sprinted all the way back to the school.

8 *Bully Boy Tactics*

I'd learned my lesson. The next time I trained with Leinster, I made sure to arrive early. As a matter of fact, I was sitting in the dressing-room for a whole hour before anyone else showed up.

Joe walked in and saw me sitting there in my training gear.

'You got here before *me*!' he pointed out.

'Er, yeah,' I said.

He winked at me.

'The Leinster Way!' he said.

While we were warming up, Shaggy decided he was going to have a crack at the Leinster chin-ups record. It was held by Bully and it stood at fifty-eight in one minute.

At 6'4", Shaggy was an absolute giant. He didn't

need to jump up to reach the crossbar. He just raised his two arms and gripped it in his hands.

'Okay,' he said, 'someone time me.'

Malcolm O'Kelly, one of our second-rows, went inside and got a stopwatch.

'Right,' he said, 'sixty seconds. Starting from . . . NOW!'

We all stood around and counted off Shaggy's pull-ups:

'Forty-one . . . Forty-two . . . Forty-three . . .'

'STOP!' Malcolm shouted. 'TIME'S UP!'

Bully burst out laughing.

'Forty-three?' he said. 'Not even close, Shaggy! Not! Even! Close!'

Then BOD said, 'What about you, Darce?'

'Me?' I said.

'Yeah, you're pretty good at pull-ups, if I remember correctly?'

He didn't remember correctly. I'd been the third worst in the Ireland squad, which was why I'd spent the entire summer practising them while listening to Mum's Garth Brooks cassette.

'I don't know if I'm ready,' I said.

But then they all started chanting my name . . .

'D'AR-CY! D'AR-CY! D'AR-CY! D'AR-CY!'

. . . until I said, 'Fine, I'll give it a go.'

There was one problem. When I jumped up to grab onto the bar, I discovered that I couldn't reach it.

Bully laughed.

'Someone give him a lift!' he said.

Big Leo Cullen stepped forward and picked me up like he was lifting a trophy. I grabbed hold of the bar.

'Sixty seconds,' Malcolm declared, 'starting from . . . NOW!'

I blazed through the first thirty seconds and a big cheer went up when I hit the forty mark. I knew I must have been close to the record because I heard Bully say, 'He's not pulling his chin above the bar!'

But Leo said, 'Yes, he is.'

BOD shouted, 'Go on, Darce!' while everyone else counted them off.

'Fifty-four . . . Fifty-five . . . Fifty-six . . . Fifty-seven . . . Fifty-eight . . .'

'STOP!' Malcolm shouted. 'TIME'S UP!'

There was a huge cheer as I let go of the bar and dropped to the ground again.

'He's equalled the record!' Shaggy said. 'Well done, Darce!'

But Bully wasn't pleased.

'Are we training today or not?' he asked, then he

started performing his stretches, refusing to even look at me.

It was a tough training session. It was our last before we played Toulouse in the European Cup the following night and Joe worked us really hard. At the end, he thought it might be fun to finish with a game of Sevens.

I loved Sevens rugby. It was fast and exciting because the ball was in play all the time. And, with only seven players on each team, you had so much more room to run with the ball and beat players. Plus, there were always loads of tries.

Handsome volunteered to captain one team while Bully offered to lead the other. We all lined up while they took it in turns to pick the players they wanted. There was no way in this world that Bully wanted me on his side, so I ended up on Handsome's Team, as a sub. I watched the first half unfold from the sideline and I finally started to relax. Everyone was laughing and letting off steam. Then, at half-time, Handsome told me that I was going on.

I took up my position in the centre – directly opposite Bully. The half kicked off. Inside thirty seconds, I got the ball in my hands for the first time. I ran towards Bully, made a move to go one way, but then went the other, totally wrong-footing him, before throwing a really wide pass for Felipe Contepomi to score a try.

Felipe clapped his hands together twice while giving me a look of approval.

A minute later, I managed to burn Bully for pace, before playing a switch pass with Felipe to allow him to score again.

This time, I got a thumbs-up and a look of approval. And I suddenly realized that, in four hours of training together, Felipe still hadn't said a single word to me. But then, weirdly, he was one of those people who didn't need words to communicate with you – the man could say everything he needed to say with just a look.

The game was almost over when I got the ball in my hands again. Seán O'Brien played it to me through his legs. I went outside Munch, his long hair blowing in the wind as he chased after me. He tried to tackle me, but missed.

There was just one player between me and a certain try under the posts – and it was Bully. I was running straight for him, but it was too late for me to change direction. He positioned himself for the tackle. I braced myself for the contact. But, at the very last second, he stepped out of the way – and I ran straight into the post.

I hit the padding hard and bounced off it, managing to jar my shoulder and spill the ball. Bully laughed as he scooped it up and said, 'The great Gordon D'Arcy – tackled by the post!'

I climbed to my feet, rubbing my shoulder. I was in severe pain, so Handsome had no choice but to sub me off.

Once again, when training was finished, Joe didn't praise our efforts. He just said:

'Remember, hard work beats talent when talent doesn't work hard!'

Another Joe-ism.

I decided I would have to start writing them down to remember them.

'See you at the RDS on Friday night,' he said.

I noticed that Felipe and Johnny Sexton were staying behind to practise their kicking. Rather than seeing him as a rival for his position, Felipe saw Johnny as a sort of apprentice – someone he had to help along. I looked over my shoulder and I saw that Felipe was talking to him really intensely, like a teacher would, moving his arm in an arc, like he was discussing the flight of the ball. I wondered why it couldn't be like that between me and Bully.

'That looked sore,' a voice behind me said.

I turned around. It was Handsome.

'It's just a bruise,' I told him. 'I'll survive.'

I'd been tackled by Mathieu Bastareaud in my time.

'You don't want to pay attention to Bully,' he said. 'His nose is out of joint.'

'Is it?' I asked. 'I didn't notice.'

'It's an expression, Darce! It means he's jealous of you!'

'Of me?'

'Of course! He's getting on in years. You're a young player who's coming in and you're threatening to take his place in the team.'

'But I could say the same about Felipe and Johnny Sexton. But Felipe is helping him.'

'Felipe is Felipe,' he said. 'Bully is Bully.'

'What am I going to do?'

'Look, you've only been with the squad for two training sessions. You'll find your feet. You've just got to try harder to fit in.'

'But how do I fit in?'

He laughed.

'Well, you could definitely do with smartening yourself up a bit,' he said.

'Smartening myself up?' I said. 'In what way?'

'Your hair, for starters. It's a bit 1990s, isn't it?'

'This is considered a fashionable haircut in Wexford.'

'I'm tempted to comment on that, but I won't. And look at the colour of you.'

'What's wrong with my colour?'

'Er, you don't *have* any colour. You're as white as Casper the Ghost.'

'But what's wrong with that?'

He just shook his head like I was being hopelessly naïve.

'Dude,' he said, 'you're playing with Leinster, not Munster! Our fans expect you not only to play well, but to look well too!'

9 *Practice Makes Perfect*

It was the following day and I was sitting in Mr Rowland's Maths class. It was particularly boring this afternoon.

'The 3:4:5 triangle rule says that if one side of a triangle measures 3 and the adjacent side measures 4, then the diagonal between those two points must measure 5 in order for it to be a right-angled triangle.'

I wasn't really listening to him. I was staring out the window, thinking about what happened in Donnybrook the day before. My shoulder hurt. I didn't mind the pain so much. Injuries were part of the game. That wasn't what had upset me. It was the fact that Bully had set out to humiliate me in front of all my teammates.

But then I started to think about what Handsome

Dan Hansen had said. Maybe things *would* settle down. Playing for Ireland had seemed strange at the beginning. It had taken me a while to find my feet. Perhaps he was right. Maybe I should try harder to fit in. I know BOD told me not to, but maybe I just had to join one of the cliques.

'Miiissstteeerrr D'Aaarrrccccyyy, I asked you a question.'

I looked around from the window to find Mr Rowland glowering at me.

'Er, sorry, Mr Rowland – what was the question?' I asked.

'The question,' he said, 'was how would one go about calculating the hypoteneuse of a right-angled triangle?'

'The hippopotamus?' I asked.

There was a burst of loud laughter from the other boys.

Out of the corner of his mouth, Peter attempted to give me the answer: 'Square the length of the two sides –'

'DON'T TELL HIM!' Mr Rowland roared.

He walked down to my desk and stood over me.

'Have you been listening to anything I've been saying about the Pythagoras's Theorem, Mr D'Arcy?'

'Er, no, Sir,' I told him.

I could feel my face redden with embarrassment.

'And what was so fascinating,' he wondered, 'that it drew your attention away from a subject that's almost certainly going to come up in your end-of-year exams?'

End-of-year exams? It was only September!

'I was thinking about rugby,' I told him.

'You were thinking about . . . rugby?' he asked, scarcely able to believe it.

'Yes, Sir.'

'Go and see the Principal. I want you to tell Mr Cuffe that you were thinking about rugby when you should have been thinking about Pythagoras and his exciting Theorem.'

I left the class to a chorus of titters from the other boys.

I walked to Mr Cuffe's office, but his secretary said he had gone out for the afternoon and he wouldn't be back until tomorrow morning.

I breathed a sigh of relief. I was off the hook for now. And, having been thrown out of Mr Rowland's class, I had the next half an hour to myself.

I went outside to get some air. And that was when I spotted Aoife walking through the grounds of Clongowes with a kicking tee in one hand and a bag of rugby balls slung over her shoulder.

Aoife attended St Bridget's, a boarding school for girls, across the road. But her school had no rugby pitch of its own, so Aoife used our pitch to practise her kicking.

I called her name and she turned around.

'Hey, Gordon,' she said. 'How are things going?'

'Er, with what?' I asked.

'You know what! With Leinster?'

'Oh, em, fine. Hey, can I carry that bag for you?'

'I'm well capable of carrying a bag of rugby balls, Gordon.'

'Sorry.'

'Why aren't you in class anyway?'

'I got thrown out of Mr Rowland's class because I didn't know how to calculate the hippopotamus of a triangle.'

'I think the word might be hypotenuse. Gordon, you can't neglect your schoolwork just because you're on the Leinster team now.'

'I just find Maths really boring.'

'Lots of things are boring, but they still have to be done. I find practising my kicking boring.'

'What? Really?'

'Of course! Standing on a rugby pitch for two hours every single day after school? Taking kick after kick after kick? In the cold and the wind and the rain? There's loads of fun things I'd much rather be doing. But the more I practise, the better I get.'

Aoife had made it onto the Ireland Schoolgirls team and would be captaining them in the Six Nations against France in the New Year.

'Can I watch you practise?' I asked.

'You wouldn't find *that* boring?' she wondered.

'No, I could run around and retrieve the balls for you – like I used to last year?'

She shrugged.

'Okay,' she said, 'please yourself.'

We walked to the pitch. Aoife threw down her kicking tee at the corner of the pitch, where the touchline and the tryline met. She was going to see how many times she could hit the post with the ball.

'Would you, er, not start with something a little easier?' I wondered.

'Why would I want to practise the easy kicks?' she asked. 'I know how to kick the easy ones.'

'Just to warm up, I mean.'

'No, I have to push myself even harder now. The thing is, I have a rival.'

'A rival? How could you have a rival? You're the best out-half they have. And you're the captain of the team.'

'Do you know Emma Ormsby?'

'Emma Ormsby? I don't think so.'

'She's the full-back on the Ireland team. She's a really good full-back – but she's also an amazing kicker.'

Just because you play in the out-half position, it doesn't necessarily mean that you get to kick the penalties and conversions for the team. In fact, there are lots of number tens who don't take their team's kicks because someone else on the team – often a full-back – is better with the boot.

'I don't want to give up my kicking duties,' Aoife said. 'So I have to keep improving – to make sure that I'm better than Emma Ormsby.'

She put a ball in the tee, then she nodded in the direction of the goal.

'Are you going to go over there and kick the balls back to me or not?' she asked.

'I will,' I said. 'But can I ask you a quick question first?'

'What is it?'

'What do you know about fake tan?'

She laughed.

'Absolutely nothing,' she said.

'Nothing?' I said, unable to hide my surprise. 'But you're, like, a girl.'

'Gordon, not every girl in the world is obsessed with stuff like that.'

'Fine. I was just, em, making conversation.'

A look of realization crossed her face. She'd figured out why I was asking about fake tan.

'Oh my God,' she said, unable to keep the smile off her face, 'it's for you, isn't it?'

'What?' I said, trying to buy myself some time.

'Gordon,' she said, 'are you *seriously* thinking of wearing fake tan?'

'It's just that a few of the guys on the Leinster team wear it.'

'A few of the *guys*?'

'A guy called Dan Hansen – and one or two of the others.'

'Do you remember what happened when you wore green hair dye playing for Ireland?'

'This is a totally different situation, Aoife.'

'How is it different?'

'Because I did that to try to stand out. I'd be doing this to try to fit in.'

I watched her take four steps backwards and three to the left. She stared down at the ball, then up at the posts, then down at the ball again. Then she ran at it, kicked it and sent it wobbling through the air and narrowly wide of the post.

She didn't get annoyed. She just picked up another ball and put it in the tee.

'Gordon,' she said, 'fitting in doesn't mean being the same as everyone else. There's nothing wrong with just being yourself.'

Deep down, I knew that Aoife was right. But, as was so often the case, I had to learn the hard way.

10 'It's for My Mother – I Swear!'

The woman in the chemist shop gave me the strangest look.

'Fake tan?' she asked.

'Er, yeah,' I replied.

I was trying to act all casual, but I could feel myself blushing.

'Well,' she said, 'there are lots of different *types* of fake tan. Can I ask – is it for yourself?'

'Absolutely not!' I told her. 'What, me? Wear fake tan? I don't think so!'

'It's not only women who wear fake tan these days, you know? Increasingly, a lot of men are looking for healthier alternatives to a natural tan.'

'It's not for me. I want to make that clear. It's definitely, DEFINITELY not for me.'

'That's okay. So who *is* it for?'

'Who is it for?'

'Yes.'

'You're asking me who is it for?'

'Yes, that's what I'm asking you.'

'It's for, em . . .'

'Yes?'

'My mum.'

'Your mum?'

'That's right. She wears it all the time.'

'But she didn't give you any indication of what kind of fake tan she wears?'

'Unfortunately not, no.'

'Do you think she'd want something long-lasting with an even colour fade? Something that's water-proof? Something with no odour? Something that's made with only natural ingredients?'

'Er, I don't know.'

'Okay, when are you planning to wear it? Sorry, what I meant was, when is your mum planning to wear it? Is it for, say, a wedding?'

'A wedding,' I said. 'That's exactly it. She's going to a wedding.'

The woman picked a bottle from the shelf and handed it to me.

'This one,' she said, 'comes highly recommended.'

I read the label. It said:

'Self-Tanning Lotion. No Streaks!'

'This looks fine,' I said. 'And, just for the sake of argument, if she wanted to play rugby at some point, would this be okay to wear?'

'Does your mum play rugby?' she asked.

'No – but say if the mood took her and she decided she might fancy playing a match in, say, the RDS, against Toulouse, tonight? With rain forecast.'

'Well, this one *is* waterproof,' she said. 'You won't have to worry about it running.'

'*She* won't have to worry about it running, you mean.'

'I'm sorry, I thought that's what I said. It's very confusing, isn't it? So you're going to take this one?'

'Yes, I am. Yes, *she* will.'

'That'll be thirty euros.'

'Excuse me?'

Thirty euros? Fake tan was a *lot* more expensive than I expected it to be.

I pulled a handful of coins from my pocket and I spilled them onto the counter.

'I've only got one, two, three, four . . . eight euros and twenty cents,' I said.

She snatched the bottle from me.

'I'm sorry,' she said, 'you don't have enough.'

'Do you have anything for eight euros and twenty cents?' I asked.

She turned around and looked at the rows and rows of bottles behind her. Then she took one from the bottom shelf.

'This,' she said, 'costs exactly eight euros and twenty cents.'

She handed it to me. It didn't even have a label.

'And is this a good one?' I asked.

'I seriously doubt it,' she replied, 'but it's exactly what you get for eight euros and twenty cents.'

I paid for the bottle and I left the chemist shop. I checked the time. It was four o'clock in the afternoon. I had just enough time to get back to school to apply the tan to my arms, legs and face, before Dad and Ian arrived to drive me to Donnybrook for the match.

Peter was alone in the dormitory when I got back to Clongowes. He looked up from his study desk. He had a worried expression on his face.

'Gordon,' he said, 'where you have been?'

'I've been doing some preparation for tonight,' I told him. 'We're playing Toulouse in the European Cup, remember?'

'It's just that Mr Cuffe was looking for you.'

'Oh? Do you know what it's about?'

'It might have something to do with the fact that you were missing from all of your classes this afternoon.'

'Like I said, I was getting ready for tonight.'

'What were you doing?' he asked. 'Were you training?'

'Er, sort of,' I said, 'yeah.'

I put the bottle with no label on my study desk.

'What's that?' he asked.

'It's fake tan,' I told him.

'Fake tan? You're actually going to wear fake tan for the match?'

'It's not only women who wear fake tan these days, you know? Increasingly, a lot of men are looking for healthier alternatives to a natural tan.'

'Where did you read that?'

'It's just something the woman in the shop told me. Plus, a lot of rugby players wear fake tan.'

'Paul O'Connell doesn't wear fake tan,' he said.

'He could do with wearing it,' I told him. 'I've always thought he looked a bit pasty.'

I took the bottle over to the sink and I looked in the mirror. I tipped the bottle upside-down and squeezed some of the liquid into the palm of my hand.

It was orange in colour.

I rubbed it into my face, covering my forehead, my cheeks, my nose and my chin, then I moved down to my neck.

Conor walked into the dormitory.

'Where were you this afternoon?' he asked.

'I was getting ready for tonight. Er, we're playing Toulouse at eight o'clock. My dad's going to be collecting me any minute now.'

He noticed what I was doing then.

'Oh my God,' he said, 'are you putting on fake tan?'

'Yes, I'm putting on fake tan,' I told him.

'So it's true?' he said. 'It *is* a Leinster thing.'

'It's not *just* a Leinster thing,' I pointed out. 'A lot of men wear fake tan.'

'Ronan O'Gara doesn't wear fake tan.'

'Okay, can everyone stop naming Munster players who don't wear fake tan? ROG is another one who could do with some. He's very pale.'

I squeezed out some more of the orange liquid and rubbed it onto my arms and onto the back of my hands.

'It's not *very* dark,' I said, 'is it?'

I could barely see any difference.

'It takes a while for the colour to show,' Conor assured me. 'My sister always looks like she's just come back from holidays. She uses a really expensive brand, though.'

'Right,' I said.

'What brand are you using?'

'I don't know. It doesn't have a name.'

'What does it say on the label?'

'It doesn't have a label.'

I started to rub some of the liquid onto my legs.

'Hey, big news,' Conor said. 'Mr Kelly is announcing the junior squad tonight!'

'Whoa!' I said. 'That *is* big news! Has he given

you any hints yet about whether you're going to be in it?'

'No, nothing – but he's announcing it in the sports hall at seven o'clock!'

'I wish I could be there. I really hope you make it.'

'If I do, it'll be all thanks to you, Gordon.'

'Me?'

'Yeah, you were the one who told me to take myself more seriously. You were the one who told me to aim high – otherwise, I'd never achieve anything. Thanks.'

'Hey, no problem, Conor. I'd better get going. My dad is picking me up outside.'

'We'll be watching on TV,' Peter said. 'Even though it clashes with Munster versus Clermont Auvergne.'

I laughed.

'You're missing a Munster match to watch Leinster play?' I said. 'You'll be converted yet!'

'Good luck,' Conor told me. 'Hopefully, we'll both have something to celebrate later on.'

11 *My Big Chance*

Ian was more nervous about the match than even I was.

'Joe Schmidt was on the radio earlier,' he said. 'He reckons this Leinster team has the potential to win the European Cup. Did he mention that to you, Gordon?'

'He did,' I said. 'He really believes it.'

I was sitting in the back of the car, while Dad and Ian were in the front.

'Munster have won the European Cup twice,' Dad pointed out.

'Why are you telling us how many times Munster have won the European Cup?' Ian asked. 'We're not talking about Munster. We're talking about Leinster.'

'I'm just trying to put it in context,' Dad explained.

They were hilarious when they argued about rugby.

'Well, Munster lost two finals before they won one,' Ian said. 'Joe was making the point last season that you learn more from your defeats than you do from your victories.'

'In that case,' Dad said, 'Leinster should have learned an awful lot over the years!'

'Funny man!' Ian said. 'Why have you got that thing anyway?'

He pointed to the air freshener hanging from Dad's rear-view mirror. It was a scented cardboard Munster jersey that he'd bought in the souvenir shop in Thomond Park.

'It makes the car smell nice,' Dad said.

Ian tugged on it and the elastic snapped.

'What are you doing?' Dad asked.

'You're driving your son to Ballsbridge to make his debut for Leinster,' Ian said, 'and you've got a Munster air freshener in the car.'

Ian opened the window and threw it out onto the road.

'Well, you don't any more!' he said. 'Sorry you had to look at that, Gordon.'

'Ian,' Dad said, 'I liked the smell of that. It was sandalwood and . . . something else.'

'We'll go to the shop in the RDS,' Ian said, 'and we'll get you a Leinster one.'

I had to admire my brother. As usual, he was decked out, from head to foot, in blue. Ian always bought the new Leinster jersey when it went on sale each summer, even though most of his friends waited until Christmas, to see was it going to be a season like every other season. He was totally dedicated to his team. And, despite all the disappointments he'd endured while following them, he never stopped believing that this year would be their year.

'So, Gordon, you never told us,' he said, 'what are they like?'

'Who?' I said.

'The Leinster fellas. They seem like a sound bunch, are they?'

'Er, yeah, they are.'

And they *were* – well, mostly.

'What's that Graham Bull like?' he asked.

I couldn't bring myself to tell him the truth. These players were his heroes.

'He's, em, great,' I told him. 'He's been very welcoming to me.'

'That's very big of him,' Ian said, 'especially considering that you're his main rival for the number twelve jersey. A lot of fellas would feel threatened by you.'

'So how are you feeling about the match?' Dad asked.

'Don't keep asking him that,' Ian said. 'You'll make him even more nervous.'

'I'm fine,' I told them. 'I don't even know if I'm playing yet.'

'Joe was talking about bringing in new faces,' Ian said.

'I think he meant that over the course of the season,' I told him. 'Not all at once.'

'I'd be shocked if you didn't get on the pitch at some stage,' he said.

I hoped he was right.

We eventually arrived in Ballsbridge. The was a real buzz in the air. Ian always said there was something special about Friday night matches in the RDS, and this was my first taste of it. The roads leading to the ground were thronged with fans, excited about the start of a new season.

Dad pulled up at the players' gate. There were two security guards standing there. They were built like props and dressed all in black. One of them approached the driver's side of the car.

'I'm sorry, Sir,' he said, 'this entrance is for players only.'

'My son is a player,' Dad said proudly.

'Really?' the man said. 'Who is he?'

'Gordon D'Arcy,' Dad said. 'That's him in the back there.'

The man squinted his eyes and looked through the window at me.

'He's very young,' he said, 'isn't he?'

'The youngest player ever to play for Ireland,' Ian pointed out, 'and now the youngest ever to play for Leinster.'

'We don't know that I'm playing yet,' I reminded them.

'We can let him in through this gate,' the first security guard told Dad, 'but not you, or your car. You'll have to find a parking spot on the road somewhere.'

Dad turned around in his seat.

'Okay,' he said, 'you jump out there, Gordon. And we'll see you back here after the match.'

'Okay,' I said.

I picked up my gear bag, containing my boots and my gumshield, and I got out of the car.

'Good luck, Gordon,' Dad said.

'Yeah, do us all proud,' Ian added.

Then, as I walked through the players' gate, they shouted:

'D'AR-CY! D'AR-CY! D'AR-CY! D'AR-CY!'

12 *Dropped*

Everyone was tense.

The jerseys – numbers one to twenty-three – were hanging from hooks, right the way around the four walls of the dressing-room. But no one dared to sit down, because Joe hadn't announced the team yet. Even players like BOD, Felipe and Leo, whose names were usually the first down on the team sheet, didn't take it for granted that they would be picked.

With Joe, you couldn't take anything for granted.

So, instead of sitting down, we all gathered around the snack table.

'Try this,' Shaggy said, handing me a tiny cup.

'What is it?' I wondered.

'It's a beetroot shot,' he said. 'It's supposed to help get the oxygen to your muscles.'

I knocked it back in one mouthful. It was the

most disgusting thing I'd ever tasted. And I ate snails in Paris. I didn't want to admit that I hated it, so I said, 'Mmmmmm!' and then, when Shaggy wasn't looking, I ate three Jaffa Cakes to try to take the taste out of my mouth.

A moment or two later, Joe Schmidt walked into the dressing-room. In his hands was a sheet of paper. And on his face was a serious expression.

He was about to name the team to face Toulouse.

A knot formed in my stomach. I wanted to play so much. Joe had promised to make big changes this season. And, as he prepared to read out the team, all of the players braced themselves, not knowing whether they'd made the cut.

He started to read out the names of the starters. All around the dressing-room, you could hear players exhaling with relief when their names were called, then each one went and sat on the bench next to his jersey.

When he got to number twelve, I was surprised to discover that I was holding my breath. But the news wasn't good.

'Number twelve,' Joe said. 'Graham Bull. Inside-centre.'

I felt a horrible, sinking feeling of disappointment. He was starting the match with the same group of players who'd finished last season. There was no place in the starting XV for Johnny Sexton, Seán O'Brien, or me.

My name was the last to be called.

'Twenty-three,' he said. 'Gordon D'Arcy.'

I went and sat down next to my jersey and tried my best to hide my disappointment.

'Substitutes,' Joe said, 'remember, you could be called upon at any minute – so make sure you're ready.'

I have to admit, I daydreamed my way through Joe's team talk. He might as well have been Mr Rowland talking about the 3:4:5 triangle rule for all the interest I had in what he had to say. I'd never started a match on the bench before and I presumed that his words had no relevance to me now.

I sat there, looking around me. I noticed that someone had stuck little signs on the wall with words on them, like 'Humility' and 'Discipline' and 'Respect'.

And then I noticed Bully, grinning at me across the floor of the dressing-room.

Joe finished his team talk and everyone stood up and clapped their hands together and shouted, 'Come on, Leinster!' and 'Let's beat these guys!'

Some players went off to have Deep Heat rubbed

into their sore muscles, others to have various parts of their arms and legs strapped. Malcolm O'Kelly wore so much bandaging that Leo Cullen called him The Mummy!

Dan Hansen and one or two others made one final check of their hair. That was when Handsome caught sight of me in the mirror.

'Hey, Darce,' he said, pulling me to one side. 'What are you wearing, Dude?'

He was looking at my face like there was something interesting written on it.

'Just a little bit of, em, fake tan,' I told him.

'Fake tan? What brand did you use?'

'Er, I don't know. It didn't have a name.'

'What did it say on the label?'

'It didn't have a label.'

He nodded.

'Did I put enough on?' I asked.

'Oh, you put plenty on,' he said. 'The colour is just starting to show.'

I looked in the mirror. To my horror, my face was starting to turn orange.

'Alright,' said Joe, 'let's go out there and show this crowd what The Leinster Way is all about.'

Oh, no, I thought to myself. My face looks like an Easy Peeler!

13 *Typical Leinster*

'YYYYYYEEEEEESSSSSS!!!!!!'

The crowd was going absolutely wild.

There wasn't even a minute gone and Handsome had scored our first try of the game. It was an absolute beauty as well – one of those tries that you knew people would be watching on YouTube for years to come.

Felipe did all the hard work. He was gliding along with the ball in his hands, when he performed a double step, dragging two defenders onto him. With a flick of his wrist, Felipe played a reverse pass straight into the hands of Handsome, who blazed through a tiny gap in the Toulouse defence to put the ball down underneath the posts.

The Leinster supporters went crazy. They were chanting:

He's Handsome!

He's Handsome!

He's Handsome Dan Hansen!

The credit really belonged to Felipe, but Handsome was more than happy to accept the praise, performing what I soon discovered was his trademark celebration – standing in front of the crowd with his chin in his hand, as if to say, 'Yes, you're right – just look at this beautiful, suntanned face!'

Felipe kicked the conversion and we were well on our way.

I watched most of the first half from the deadball area. Joe didn't believe that substitutes should sit around, waiting for their time to come. He wanted us running as if we were involved in the match. So I made sure to keep moving. I thought, at least the crowd might think the reason my face was orange was because of all the effort I was putting into staying warmed up.

Usually, Toulouse played beautiful, running rugby, but the early try had rocked them, and they failed to get their passing game going. Only once in the first half did they get beyond our twenty-two-metre line.

Near the end of the first half, we doubled our lead when Frédéric Michalak, the French out-half, threw a terrible pass under pressure from Keith Gleeson,

one of our flankers. We were lucky he did, as we were badly exposed and Toulouse had four players out wide just waiting to receive the ball. Fortunately for Bully, the ball bounced up into his arms and he ran half the length of the pitch to score our second try.

Then Bully did his trademark celebration, kissing his two biceps, then striking a pose like a body-builder in front of the Leinster supporters.

Felipe converted it to make it 14–0 and it was shaping up to be a good night for us.

But watching the match unfold from behind the goal was a new experience for me. And it was even harder, I was finding out, when things were going well. Bully was the best player on the pitch in the first half. And if he kept playing the way he was playing, I knew I was never going to break into the team.

At half-time, Joe warned us not to be complacent in the second half. Toulouse would come back at us, he said, and we had to be aware of their attacking threat.

I caught a glimpse of myself in the dressing-room mirror and I looked like an Oompa Loompa. What was I thinking?

Malcolm said to me, 'I think you may have slightly overdone it with the tan, Darce.'

I felt so stupid.

But with everything going to plan on the pitch, at least no one was focusing on me.

The second half was only five minutes old when Bully scored our third try. It came from a move that

Joe had dreamt up with Toulouse in mind and he'd made us practise it over and over and over again. The move started from a scrum – a simple, loop play between Felipe and Bully. Shaggy came on a hard line from the openside wing, BOD slipped in behind him, with Handsome and Girvan Dempsey for support. Bully was supposed to offload the ball to Girvan, but he dummied the pass and went on to score the try himself.

Our fans went wild. They started singing: '*Olé, olé, olé, olé . . .*'

Felipe kicked the points with no fuss. We were 21–0 in the lead and coasting – or so it seemed. Behind me, I could hear people in the crowd telling each other that this was definitely going to be Leinster's year.

And then it all started to go wrong.

Horribly wrong.

Toulouse did what Joe said they would do. They came back at us. They started to put together phase after phase, making slow but steady progress towards our tryline. We were lazy defending around the ruck. Isitolo Maka, the giant Toulouse number eight, picked up the ball, one-handed, from the middle of the ruck and ran, untouched, to score a try.

I was still running and stretching in the deadball

area when Johnny O'Hagan, our kitman, ran down to get me.

'Joe's sending you on for Bully,' he said.

I thought I might have misheard him. Bully was still having a great game out there.

'What are you waiting for?' he asked.

So I ran back to the bench, stripped down to my rugby gear and did a few final stretches. As I did, I could see Bully staring over in my direction. He'd clearly figured out that he was about to be taken off.

'Just keep it simple,' Joe said to me. 'Don't take any risks. It's still a two-score game – we have to just see it out now.'

'Okay,' I said.

An official held up the board with Bully's number on it.

The stadium announcer said: 'Substitute for Leinster in the seventieth minute, number twelve, Graham Bull, is being replaced by a player making his Leinster debut tonight – Gordon D'Arcy!'

The crowd cheered. But Bully wasn't happy about having to make way for me. He walked off the pitch with a furious expression on his face.

He shouted in Joe's direction: 'Why are you taking *me* off? I'm on a hat-trick!'

He didn't shake my hand to wish me luck. He

didn't even look at me as he walked past me. He just grunted at me and told me not to mess it up, although the exact phrase he used wasn't quite so polite.

I ran onto the pitch. I could suddenly hear Dad and Ian in the crowd shouting:

'Go on, Gordon!'

We were about to take a lineout deep inside our own half. I got into position, ready to receive the ball if it came my way.

But Fabien Pelous, the Toulouse second-row, who looked like Buzz Lightyear, stole the ball when it was in the air. With just two long, raking passes, they managed to move the ball to the opposite flank, leaving our defence badly exposed. Yannick Jauzion, one of the Toulouse centres, had the ball. BOD tackled him hard and low, almost stopping him dead in his tracks. But Jauzion managed to flick the ball to Clément Poitrenaud, the other centre, who seemed to appear out of nowhere, too late for me to do anything about it. I made an attempt at a tackle, but he pushed me away with a palm in my face, before running on to score.

Suddenly, our lead was cut to 21–14. There was now just one score in it with nine minutes of the match remaining. Our fans were silent.

BOD clapped his hands together and said, 'Come

on, guys, let's not focus on the result, or even winning the match. Let's focus on winning this next moment.'

You could see that some of our players understood it immediately – just do your job and only your job. But you could see others shrinking. Handsome was looking across at Joe and muttering: 'Please take me off. Please take me off. Please take me off.'

Maybe Joe read Handsome's lips. Or maybe he just sensed in his body language that he wasn't up for the fight. But a moment later, an official on the sideline was holding up his number and I heard Handsome say, 'Thank God for that!' He was being replaced by Luke Fitzgerald and he ran from the pitch as fast as his feet could carry him.

Girvan Dempsey, our full-back, kicked the ball deep into the Toulouse half. We defended for our lives. But their offloading game was like nothing I had ever seen before. You couldn't see where the danger was coming from because they attacked from so deep.

The time was almost up when I got the chop on Isitolo Maka, tackling him low, around the bootlaces, and bringing him to ground. BOD knocked the ball out of his hands. I scrambled to my feet and gathered it up. Suddenly, I heard the horn sound, announcing that time was up and the match would be over the next time the ball went dead.

And in that moment – I don't know why – I made eye contact with Bully, sitting in the stand with a sneering look on his face.

I could hear Joe shouting, 'Kick it out!'

I could hear my teammates shouting, 'Kick it out!'

I could hear fifteen thousand supporters shouting, 'Kick it out!'

But I delayed too long. As I prepared to put my foot through the ball, I was tackled hard by Pelous and I went to ground, spilling it out of my hands.

I heard the crowd groan as one.

By the time I picked myself up, Michalak had taken the ball and sprinted the length of the field to score a try. I could barely watch as the try was converted to level the game.

The Toulouse players danced around in celebration. I fell to the ground with my face buried in my hands. There was silence in the crowd. We had thrown it away – and it was all my fault.

Malcolm held out his hand to me, to help me up.

'Come on,' he said. 'It was a bad night. But no one died.'

He dragged me to my feet.

Most of our players told me to forget about it, to put it behind me, but I knew that I had let them down.

The ground was emptying out fast. People couldn't get out of there quickly enough. They were streaming towards the exits and I could only imagine what they were saying.

'Typical Leinster,' one old man shouted in my general direction. 'You turn it on for an hour, then as soon as you're asked a few questions, you fall to pieces. Thirty years I've been following this team – but I won't be coming back again.'

Back in the dressing-room, the players were conducting their own post-mortem into what went wrong. Most of them couldn't bring themselves to look at me.

'Why didn't you just kick it out?' Bully asked me. 'What were you waiting for? Christmas?'

'I don't know,' I said. 'I think I just . . . froze.'

'You can't afford to freeze at this level,' he said. 'You cost us the points today. Which I knew you would. You and your orange face – you're an embarrassment.'

Joe Schmidt walked into the dressing-room. To say he didn't look happy would be the understatement of the century. I braced myself for the worst. But he didn't say anything to me.

'You're all going to get changed,' he said, 'then you're going to walk outside and sign autographs for the fans – that's provided anyone still wants one. You're going to listen to what they have to say to you. If they're disappointed in you, then they're entitled to tell you. You're going to own this result. You will own it and you will learn from it. I'll see you all at training tomorrow night – seven o'clock, Joe Schmidt time.'

Joe walked out of the dressing-room.

'He should never have taken me off,' Bully said, then he turned to me. 'Congratulations, D'Arcy. You just played your first and your last game for Leinster.'

14 *A Bad Break*

I wasn't in the mood to talk during the drive back to Clongowes that night. I could tell that Ian was disappointed, but he tried to cheer me up by reminding me that at least Leinster didn't lose.

'The first hour,' he said, 'was the best rugby I've seen Leinster play in about three years.'

'Until Joe took Bully off,' I said, 'and put me on.'

'That's not what I meant, Gordon. I actually thought you played well, apart from –'

'Apart from not kicking the ball out of play,' I said, 'and gifting them the chance to equalize.'

'Maybe you were just out of sorts tonight,' Dad said. 'You don't look well, Gordon. I said it to Ian when I saw you coming out of the tunnel before the match. I said I thought you looked a bit, well, orangey.'

'It's fake tan,' I told him.

'Fake tan?' he said. 'You mean like that River-dance crowd wear?'

'Yes, exactly like the Riverdance crowd wear.'

'Why did you put that on you?'

'Because I was trying to fit in. Look, I don't want to talk about it, okay? Can we just *not* talk?'

There was silence in the car until we arrived back in Kildare and Dad took the turn up the driveway to the school. They both made one last effort to persuade me that it would all look different the following morning. Or maybe several mornings later.

'You've come back from bigger disasters than this,' Dad reminded me.

'Do you remember the Scotland match?' Ian asked.

'That was definitely worse,' Dad said. 'Not only did you have a nightmare that day, you did it wearing golden boots.'

'And the green hair dye,' Ian added. 'Do you remember it was pouring down his face? A few weeks later, you won a Grand Slam, Gordon.'

'Exactly,' Dad said, pulling up in front of the school. 'Everyone makes mistakes. Even the great Ronan O'Gara has missed vital kicks in his time.'

I was suddenly reminded of something.

'How did Munster get on against Clermont Auvergne?' I asked.

'They, em, won,' Dad said.

He seemed embarrassed to tell me.

'What score?' I asked.

'It was 42–9. We listened to the end of it on the radio while we were waiting for you at the players' gate. The great Donal Lenihan thinks there's no one will stop them from winning the European Cup this year. Their fans will be on the Internet tonight,' he said, 'booking their tickets for the final.'

I'd heard enough. I said goodbye to Dad and Ian and I got out of the car.

It was almost midnight. The entire building was in darkness. I made my way to the dormitory as quietly as I could, not wishing to face anyone.

I decided to take a shower.

I stood under the warm water and tried my best to forget what had happened. Then I rubbed shower gel into my face and scrubbed it with a facecloth to try to get rid of the tan. I did the same with my arms and legs, rubbing harder and harder until the water running off me looked like orange juice. I got out of the shower and looked in the mirror. But somehow, I'd made it worse. My colour had gone from ripe Easy Peeler to wrinkly old Easy Peeler.

I gave up and decided to go to bed. I stuck my head around the dormitory door. There wasn't a sound out of Conor or Peter, so I presumed they were both asleep. I tiptoed into the room, put on my pyjamas, then clambered up the ladder into my bunk.

I was lying there, staring at the ceiling, waiting for sleep to come, when I heard Conor's voice from the bunk below me.

'We saw what happened,' he said. 'Are you okay?'

'Not really,' I told him. 'But I don't want to talk about it.'

'You'll bounce back from this, Gordon. It wasn't as bad as what happened against Scotland.'

Then I remembered that Mr Kelly was announcing the Clongowes junior squad that evening.

'Hey, how did *you* get on?' I asked. 'Did you make the cut?'

He didn't reply. There was silence for about ten seconds, then I heard the sound of sobbing.

'Conor?' I said. 'Why are you crying?'

'Mr Kelly says I'm not ready,' he said. 'He thinks I probably need one more year.'

'You're still young,' I reminded him.

'You've already played for the *senior* team.'

'I know.'

119

'You've played for Ireland. You played for Leinster tonight.'

'Yeah. And look how *that* worked out!'

'He told me I was still a bit on the small side,' he said. 'Peter Stringer is small. But he's the best passer of the ball. What does size matter?'

'Don't lose heart,' I told him. 'You never know what's going to happen. The boy he picked ahead of you might get injured and he'll have to bring you in.'

'Are you listening to me, Gordon? He thinks I'm too small – even to play scrum-half. This is all your fault, by the way.'

'*My* fault?'

'Yes,' he said, 'you were the one who told me to take myself more seriously. You were the one who told me to aim high – otherwise, I'd never achieve anything. Thanks a lot, Gordon.'

'I'm sorry,' I told him. 'I really wish you'd made the team.'

Suddenly, he threw back his bed sheets and got out of bed.

'Where are you going?' I asked.

'Too small,' he muttered. 'I'll show him.'

'Conor, what are you doing?'

And that's when he said it:

'I'm going to jump the Gollymochy.'

I couldn't believe what I was hearing.

'Are you mad?' I said. 'Conor, get back into bed.'

'No,' he insisted. 'I'm going to jump the Golly-mochy. And you're coming with me.'

'No, I'm not.'

'Yes, you are – the rules say I need two witnesses. Peter, let's go!'

I watched him cross the room and shake Peter awake.

'What's going on?' Peter asked, opening his eyes a crack. 'I haven't overslept, have I?'

'No,' I said. 'Conor wants to jump the Gollymochy. You need to help me talk some sense into him.'

But, by then, Conor was already pulling on his clothes. So we got dressed and we followed him outside into the pitch-black night, across the rugby pitches and down the steep bank to the river, begging him not to do it all the way.

'I'm doing it,' Conor insisted.

'But you won't make it to the other side,' I said. 'You're too –'

'Do NOT say I'm too small!'

'I was going to say you're too young. No one our age has ever jumped the Gollymochy.'

'I have to aim at being something other than the Class Clown – right, Gordon?'

'Look, I didn't mean it to come out like that. I love that you're funny. I just don't know what you think *this* is going to prove.'

'Stand aside there, lads.'

Conor was taking a very lengthy run-up. But me and Peter were standing in his way.

'No,' I said, 'I'm not going to let you do it.'

'I'll just run through you,' Conor said.

Peter and I looked at each other. He probably would. We'd get injured in the process and he'd end up in the water anyway.

'What's the worst thing that can happen?' I asked Peter. 'If he falls in the river, he'll just get wet. Then it'll be over and we can all go back to bed.'

Peter nodded. Then we stepped aside.

Conor had a look of hard resolve on his face.

'I'll show you who's too small!' he said.

Then he ran towards the river. He covered the ground in no time at all. He let out a determined roar as he reached the riverbank and launched himself high into the air.

Oh no, I thought. He wasn't going to make it. I knew. Peter knew. And I suspect Conor knew it, because his roar of determination turned into one of terror as he plunged towards the icy water of the Gollymochy.

SPLAAASSSHHH!!!

In he went.

Peter and I moved towards the edge of the water to pull him out. But suddenly the air was pierced by a scream:

'AAAAARRRRRGGGGGHHHHH!!!!!!'

It sounded like a wild animal caught in a trap. It was Conor. And it was clear that he'd hurt himself very badly.

We jumped into the water.

'Conor!' I shouted. 'Conor!'

Peter and I managed to grab hold of him. We pulled him out of the water while he continued to howl in agony:

'AAAAARRRRRGGGGGGHHHHH!!!!!!'

We laid him down on the riverbank on the far side of the Gollymochy.

'What's wrong?' I asked. 'What happened?'

Conor nodded his head to indicate his right leg. I looked at it and I was forced to turn my head away when I saw what had happened.

His leg was broken.

'AAAAARRRRRGGGGGGHHHHH!!!!!!'

'He must have hit a rock,' Peter said.

'What are we going to do?' I wondered, staring off into the black night.

'I'll go for help,' Peter said. 'Mr Cuffe's house is just over there.'

While Peter ran off to get the Principal, I tried to comfort Conor by telling him that an ambulance would be here soon.

'Why did you let me do it?' he asked. 'AAARRR GGGHHH!!!'

'What?' I said. 'We begged you not to!'

'You should have stopped me. AAARRRGGG HHH!!!'

'There was no stopping you.'

'AAAAAARRRRRRGGGGGGGHHH-HHH!!!!!!'

15 *A Stern Warning*

Mr Cuffe was absolutely furious with us.

'I'm absolutely furious with you,' he said.

But then, he didn't need to tell us. We could see it. His face was an angry shade of red and you could almost see steam billowing out of his ears.

Peter and I were standing in his office, with our heads bowed.

'I'm surprised at *you*, Peter,' he said.

Which I took to mean that he expected it of me.

'A boy is in hospital this morning,' he said, 'with one of the worst broken legs the ambulance crew said they'd ever seen. What on Earth were you thinking, allowing him to jump that river?'

'I don't know, Sir,' I said.

'And in the middle of the night!' he added. 'In the dark! Honestly, Peter, I thought *you* had more sense.'

'I'm sorry,' said Peter. 'Is Conor going to be okay, Mr Cuffe?'

'I've just spoken to his mother,' he replied. 'He's likely to be on crutches for months. And who knows after that. And all for what – mmm?'

The question was directed at me.

'I don't know,' I told him.

'Just so he could say that he'd jumped over a river,' he said. 'How utterly ridiculous. I'm putting you two boys on litter-picking duty every lunchtime until Christmas – do you understand?'

'Yes, Sir,' we both said.

'Peter, go back to class. Gordon, I wish to speak to you further.'

Peter left the office. Mr Cuffe stood up from his desk.

'I've been hearing reports about you,' he said, 'and I'm concerned.'

'Is this about what happened at the RDS last night?' I asked. 'Because if you're going to ask me why I didn't kick the ball out –'

'I'm not talking about rugby,' he said. 'I gather Mr Rowland asked you to leave his Maths class the other day and told you to come and see me.'

'I did go to see you, but you weren't in, Mr Cuffe.'

'Well, since then I've had conversations with

several other teachers, who all have similar complaints about you. Not concentrating in class. Not handing in homework.'

He picked up his phone and dialled the number for his secretary.

'Joyce,' he said, 'can you ask the Director of Rugby to come in here, please.'

A few seconds later, Vinnie Murray walked into the room.

'Gordon,' he said, 'how are you?'

'I'm fine,' I said.

'I was at the match last night. I thought you did well when you came on – apart from, well, you know. That could happen to anyone, though.'

'Yes, Mr Murray.'

'The important thing is that you learn from it.'

'Ahem,' said Mr Cuffe, clearing his throat theatrically. He hadn't called us into his office to listen to us shoot the breeze about rugby. 'The reason I asked you to come in here on a Saturday morning was to tell you that a boy was seriously injured last night, attempting to jump the so-called Gollymochy.'

'Who was it?' he asked.

'Conor Kehoe,' Mr Cuffe said.

I could see the look of concern on Mr Murray's face.

'And in the process of attempting to jump that confounded river,' Mr Cuffe added, 'he managed to break his leg – very badly, as it happens. Miiissstt-teeerrr D'Arcy here was present when it happened.'

'Gordon, what happened?' Mr Murray asked.

'He was upset because Mr Kelly didn't pick him for the junior team. He said he was too small. I think he was trying to prove that he wasn't.'

'However,' Mr Cuffe cut in, 'we are not here to discuss Miiisssttteeerrrr Kehoe's behaviour. We are here to discuss the behaviour of Miiisssttteeerrr D'Arcy. I've been talking to a number of his teachers and they are unhappy with the – shall we say – *less* than enthusiastic way he's been approaching his schoolwork this year.'

I hated to disappoint Mr Murray. But I knew that I had.

'Is this true, Gordon?' he asked.

'Er, yes, Mr Murray,' I told him.

'While we are justifiably proud of your achievements,' said Mr Cuffe, 'I would like to remind you of something I told you last year – Clongowes Wood is a school, not a rugby academy.'

'Yes, Sir.'

'Whether you like it or not, Miiisssttteeerrr D'Arcy, you have to hold yourself to a higher standard of behaviour. Because a lot of students in this school look up to you. They follow your example. I wanted Mr Murray to be present when I informed you of this. Unless I see a marked improvement in your attitude towards your schoolwork over the coming weeks, then there will be no more rugby for you.'

'We did tell you this last year,' Mr Murray said. 'Rugby is a privilege. And, like all privileges, it can be taken away from you' – and then he snapped his fingers – 'like *that*.'

As usual, I wasn't listening. All I could hear was: 'Blah, blah, blah, blah, blah . . .'

16 *Different for Girls*

Conor was lying in bed with his leg raised. The entire thing was encased in plaster from ankle to hip. He looked miserable – and seeing me and Peter arrive didn't seem to cheer him up at all.

'I'm an idiot,' he kept saying. 'I'm a complete and utter IDIOT!'

'Conor,' I tried to tell him, 'it's not the end of the world. Loads of players have come back after breaking a leg.'

'But it's a really bad break,' he said. 'The doctor said I'll have to wear this cast for six months.'

'Six months?' Peter said.

'Then, after that, he said it'll be months and months of rehabilitation before my leg is strong enough to play any kind of sport. He told me to

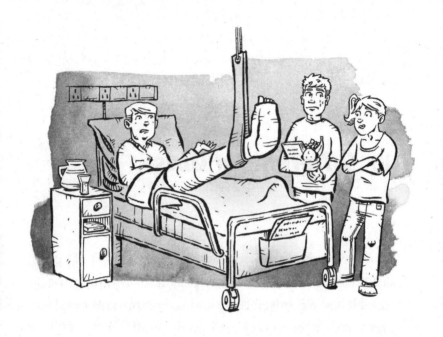

forget about playing rugby for at least a year. And maybe even . . .'

His voice trailed off. Whatever the doctor had told him, he didn't want to say it out loud.

'What?' Aoife asked. 'What did he say?'

'He said I might end up with a permanent limp,' he said.

'A limp?' I said. 'Wait a minute, does that mean –?'

'That's right,' he said. 'There's a very good chance that I'll never play rugby again.'

Two nurses arrived then to change Conor's sheets. They asked us to step outside for a few minutes. We headed for the waiting area. Peter went to get drinks from the vending machine, leaving me and Aoife alone.

She asked me how I was doing.

'I'm fantastic,' I said, 'considering I made a complete fool of myself at the RDS on Friday night.'

'On the upside,' she said, 'at least your fake tan is fading.'

I had to laugh.

'So what happened?' she asked.

'I don't know,' I said. 'I went to kick the ball out – but I just . . . froze.'

'What did Joe Schmidt say?' she asked. 'He must have been mad at you.'

'I suppose I'll find out at training tonight,' I said. 'That's if I go.'

'*If* you go?' she said. 'You're not thinking of giving up, are you? What, just because of one mistake?'

'I don't like it,' I told her. 'I don't like the Leinster set-up.'

'Can *I* tell *you* something?' she said. 'I don't like the Ireland set-up.'

'What? Why?'

'We're treated like second-class citizens, Gordon.'

'Really?'

'We train in Herbert Park, which is fine. But we

don't even have a dressing-room. I have to get changed into my gear in the back of my mum's car. Then I have to go back to school to have a shower.'

'That's terrible.'

'Plus, we have to pay for our own kit. We have to buy our own Ireland jerseys.'

'What, even though you're representing your country? That doesn't sound right.'

'You haven't even heard the worst bit yet. Do you know what I found out yesterday? When we go to Paris in February to play France, we all have to pay our own expenses.'

'But it's a Six Nations match!'

'We all got a letter yesterday. It said we have to pay for our own flights, our hotel accommodation, all of our meals.'

'When I played for the Ireland men's team,' I said, 'I didn't have to put my hand in my pocket once.'

'Unfortunately, it's different for girls.'

'That's a disgrace.'

'I know it is. My mum and dad don't have the money to send me to Paris for a weekend.'

'So what are you going to do?'

'There's nothing I *can* do. I won't be able to go.'

'You *have* to go – you're the captain of the team!'

'That doesn't mean very much when you're a girl.'

Aoife was miserable. I was miserable. Conor was miserable. Rugby could do that to you. It could make you feel the highest of highs and the lowest of lows.

17 *Showing My Face*

I was more nervous going to training that night than I had been travelling to the match. Once or twice, I thought I'd have to ask the bus driver to let me off, because I was convinced I was going to be sick.

I tried to listen to Garth Brooks on Mum's Walkman, but my mind kept wandering back to what I was about to face.

Joe Schmidt would have watched the video of the match over the weekend and he'd be furious with me. Bully was probably right. He'd give me a serious dressing-down in front of the rest of the players, then he'd tell me, sorry, it was all a mistake, that I wasn't ready to wear the Leinster number twelve jersey yet.

And would that be such a bad thing? At that precise moment, I didn't think so. It would actually come as a relief. I could play for Clongowes in the Leinster Schools Senior Cup. I could play for Vinnie Murray – and rugby would be enjoyable again, not a job that I hated.

I got off the bus in Donnybrook and I headed for the ground. More than once, I thought about turning around and getting back on the bus. But I remembered the lesson I learned when I messed up playing for Ireland – taking responsibility for your mistakes is a sign of character. And, as my dad told me at the time, sometimes the bravest thing you can do is to just show your face. And I was determined to do that, even if it was the last time I ever set foot in the Leinster dressing-room.

I walked in – and every conversation in the room stopped.

I could see Dan Hansen and his friends trying to avoid making eye contact with me. They were talking to each other out of the corner of their mouths. I guessed they were saying, 'He's here! Oh my God, I can't believe he actually came back!'

Some friend Handsome turned out to be, I thought.

I put my gear bag down on the bench.

'Not there!' a voice said. 'Sit somewhere else.'

It was Bully. He was sitting a few places down.

'This bench is for winners,' he said. 'And you're certainly not one of those.'

It was awful. For a second or two, I thought I was going to burst into tears.

'Sit over here,' a voice said.

I turned around. It was Liam Toland, our number eight.

'Are you sure?' I asked.

'Yeah, of course,' he said. 'How are you?'

'Er, not great,' I said, sitting down next to him. 'Especially after, you know, what happened last night.'

'Just remember,' he said, 'every mistake we make is an opportunity to learn. And if you learn something, then it's not a mistake at all.'

I wondered whether Joe would feel the same way.

He was waiting for us on the pitch when we walked out. It was a cold and dark September night and he cast four shadows on the pitch in the glare of the floodlights.

He didn't say anything. He just told us to train.

We warmed up and then we practised different passing moves. Some of them were a little bit difficult to get the hang of at first. But it always happens that the longer you practise something, the easier it becomes.

I started to enjoy myself and had nearly forgotten about what had happened last night. But then I told Handsome we should maybe practise the switch pass for a little bit longer and he said, 'Er, Gordon, would you mind *not* talking to me when Joe is looking?'

'What?' I asked.

'I just don't want him to think we're, you know, friends or anything.'

I couldn't believe what he was saying to me.

A few minutes after that, Joe clapped his hands and told us to gather round because he had something to say to us.

I noticed that Bully was giving me a sideways look.

'Nice knowing you,' he said, then he smiled and faced the front again.

'Okay,' Joe said, 'I want to talk to you about what happened last night. There's one reason why we didn't win that match.'

'Er, just to point out,' Bully said, 'that he *is* actually here tonight, Joe – so, you know, you might want to go easy on him. In case he starts crying in front of the group.'

'Who are you talking about?' Joe asked.

'I'm talking about Gordon whatever-he's-called?'

Bully said. 'That's hilarious. I've already forgotten his name.'

'Gordon didn't cost us the win,' Joe told him sternly.

'I beg to differ,' Bully shot back. 'He should have kicked the ball out of play and he didn't.'

'That was a mistake. It could happen to anyone. It's not the reason we didn't win. We should never have been in that position in the first place. Remember, when you point a finger, Bully, you've always got three fingers pointing back at you.'

'I don't have any questions to answer. I scored two tries. I was man of the match.'

'According to who?'

'All the papers.'

'All the papers aren't the coach of this team. You want to know why I took you off? Because you were playing for yourself and not for the team. The reason you were in a position to score the first try was because you weren't helping Keith Gleeson to defend. The reason you scored the second try was because you threw a dummy pass to Girvan Dempsey because you wanted the glory for yourself. That's the kind of selfishness I'm trying to coach out of this team. The reason we didn't win was down to you. And to you . . .'

He pointed at Handsome.

'And to you,' he said, pointing at Malcolm.

And suddenly he was pointing his finger at every one of us in turn and saying, 'And you ... And you ... And you ...'

Finally, he pointed his finger at himself.

'And me,' he said. 'We're all to blame. Because you're not a team – not like Munster are a team. You're a group of talented players – some of you are even world-class – but you don't play together the way those boys do. You don't even *think* together as a team. Look at the way you're trying to distance yourselves from the player who failed to kick the ball out of play. Look at the way you're trying to get him into trouble. That's not what a team does. A team takes collective responsibility.'

'If he'd kicked the ball out of play,' Handsome said, 'we would have won the match. That's all there is to it.'

'What about last season?'

'What about it?'

'How many matches did you guys lose from a winning position in the last quarter?'

'I, em, don't know.'

'The answer is seven. There were seven matches in which you were leading going into the final twenty minutes and you still managed to lose. And those weren't Gordon's fault because he wasn't on the team at the time. So whose fault were those ones?'

'Two of them were your fault,' Bully said to Handsome. 'Remember you gave the penalty away against the Dragons? And then you should have scored a try against Edinburgh, but you dropped the ball.'

'What about you?' Handsome said to Bully. 'You got yourself sin-binned against Connacht. We lost that day because we had to play the last ten minutes with fourteen men.'

Joe just smiled. They had proven his point for him.

'*My* fault,' he said. '*Your* fault. *His* fault. *Their* fault. That's all I'm hearing from you guys. And never *our* fault. Where do you think the phrase "Typical Leinster!" came from? I heard people saying it leaving the ground on Friday night. There is a weakness in this team. And Toulouse picked up on it, just like a lot of other teams have picked up on it. When the pressure comes on, we crack. We make selfish decisions. That's what makes us soft. Real teams do their best work when the pressure comes on. They do the simple things well and they work for each other.'

I could see Felipe and BOD nodding in agreement.

'Joe's right,' Leo said. 'We don't play together as a team.'

'Until you want your mate to win as much as you want to win yourself, you'll never be a team,' Joe told us. 'Munster will go on winning European Cups and you'll win nothing.'

When he'd finished talking to us, I went back to the dressing-room with the others. Bully was sitting opposite me with three or four of his friends from the team. He started talking about me as if I wasn't there at all.

'Can you imagine if he did that under the last coach?' he said. 'He would have been bawled out of it in front of everyone, then told that he'd never wear the Leinster jersey again.'

I packed up my things with the intention of getting back to school as quickly as I could. I looked inside my bag and that's when I realized that my Walkman was missing. I checked the pockets of my coat and then I checked my bag a second time. It wasn't there.

For a moment, I wondered if I'd left it on the bus. But then I looked at Bully and I noticed that he was wearing my headphones around his neck.

'Hey, that's my Walkman,' I said.

'What was that?' he asked.

'I said that's my Walkman!' I repeated. 'Well, actually, it's my mum's.'

'Your mum's?' he said, laughing.

'Yes,' I said, 'it was in my bag. And now you have it.'

'This is *my* Walkman,' he said. 'Isn't that right, guys?'

He turned to his friends, who sniggered, then nodded their heads.

'It's mine!' I said. 'Give it back!'

But, instead, he put the headphones over his ears, stood up and pressed the Play button. Then he walked out of the dressing-room, singing along to Garth Brooks's 'If Tomorrow Never Comes'.

18 *Tummy Ache*

'This is SO unfair!' I said.

It was lunchtime. Peter and I were outside on litter-picking duty. A high wind was sweeping across the Clongowes rugby pitch and Peter was chasing after a crisp packet that clearly didn't wish to be caught.

He finally jumped on it like he was pouncing on a loose ball in the in-goal area.

'Got you!' he said.

I opened the rubbish bag and he dropped it in.

'We tried to STOP Conor from jumping the Gollymochy,' I reminded him. 'And this is SUCH a waste of our time.'

'I know,' Peter agreed. 'I could be in the library now, reading about the Spanish Civil War, or quadratic equations, or the life cycle of the earthworm.'

'I meant that we could be having fun!'

'That *is* fun for me, Gordon.'

I bent down and picked up a Coca-Cola can that had been flattened.

'Well, *I* was talking about rugby,' I said, putting it into the bag. 'We could be playing rugby right now. Me and you just throwing the ball back and forth to each other. Instead of this.'

'Hey, at least you'll be playing rugby tonight,' he said. 'You've got training with Leinster, don't you?'

'Er, yeah,' I said – because I'd been trying to forget. 'I, em, do have training with Leinster, yeah.'

In two days we would be flying to Wales to take on the Dragons. And, while I liked Joe Schmidt as a coach, I felt no excitement at all. Only dread at seeing Bully again.

We'd been friends for so long now that Peter knew instinctively when something was bothering me.

'What's wrong?' he asked.

'I don't think I'm going to go,' I told him.

'Really?' he said. 'Why?'

'I'm, er, not feeling well,' I said. 'Yeah, I'm feeling a bit dizzy.'

'When did this come on? Because you never mentioned it.'

'It just came on a few minutes ago.'

'Maybe you should go and see the school nurse.'

That was a good idea, I thought. It would also get me out of litter duty.

'I'll go and see her now,' I said, handing the bag to Peter.

'You're not going to leave me to do this by myself,' he said, 'are you?'

'Peter,' I told him, 'I'm a very sick boy!'

Nurse Mavis had been the school nurse for as long as anyone could remember. She was a rather large lady, who was built like a wardrobe – a double wardrobe – and she never seemed to smile. As a matter of fact, the last time anyone in the school remembered her smiling was fourteen years ago. Although it later emerged that she wasn't smiling at all, but was in fact attempting to remove a poppy seed from the back of her front teeth using her tongue.

Nurse Mavis had an uncanny ability to look at a boy and tell instantly whether or not he was faking illness. It was like she could smell a lie before it was even told.

She also had a wide range of absolutely DIS-GUSTING homemade cures that she would prescribe to those she suspected of what she called 'malingering' – which means pretending to be sick to avoid work.

Her speciality was a cocktail of her own creation called The Truth Teller. It was made from mushroom juice, cold tea and liquidized turnip and it got its name because anyone who was faking sickness to get out of school immediately confessed when they smelt it.

She was tough.

But if I was going to get out of playing for Leinster, I was going to need a sick note from the school.

When I arrived at her office, she was already examining another boy – well, cross-examining would be a more accurate description.

I could hear her through the door.

'And when did this *dizziness* come on?' she asked.

I could tell by the way she pronounced the word *dizziness* that she didn't believe him.

'Er, just a few minutes ago,' I heard the boy tell her.

'Did you know,' she said, 'that a new cure for dizziness has just been developed? And you're in luck because I happen to have some of it here.'

'Er, what is?'

'It's mushroom juice, liquidized turnip and cold tea.'

'Eugh.'

'Have a little sip there.'

'You know something? I'm already feeling better.'

'Are you?'

'Definitely.'

'Well enough to take the Maths test that Mr Rowland has set for you this afternoon?'

'Yes, Nurse Mavis.'

The door flew open and a terrified-looking boy shot past me.

'Are you sure you won't take some of this medicine to go?' she shouted after him.

'No,' he yelled over his shoulder, 'I feel great again.'

'Well,' said Nurse Mavis, almost to herself, 'it's certainly cured your dizziness.'

She turned her head and noticed me sitting there then.

'Step into my consulting room,' she said.

I followed her into her office, which contained a desk and chair, an examination table and a shelf filled with bottles of her revolting potions. She sat behind her desk and I sat in a chair opposite her.

'So what about you?' she asked. 'You're not feeling dizzy as well, are you?'

'Er, no,' I told her, at the same time trying to come up with something – and quickly.

'So what is it that you *claim* is wrong with you?' she asked. 'And before you say anything, I want you to know how much I can't stand malingerers. You're not a malingerer, are you?'

'No, Nurse Mavis. I'm not a malingerer. I've never, er – malingered?'

'So what's wrong with you, then?'

'I have, em –'

'Yes? Come on, spit it out!'

'A tummy ache.'

'A tummy ache?'

'Yeah, a tummy ache.'

She laughed like this was the funniest thing she'd ever heard. And I cursed myself for not coming up with something better.

'A tummy ache, eh?' she said, looking deep into my eyes. The trick was to stare back and not break eye contact with her – although that was easier said than done. 'A tummy ache, is it?'

'Yes, Nurse Mavis.'

'And what exam do you have this afternoon?'

'I don't have any exam this afternoon.'

'You're not in Mr Rowland's Maths class?'

'I had Maths with Mr Rowland this morning, Nurse Mavis. I did my exam then.'

She was still staring into my eyes.

'Very good,' she said, then she broke eye contact, apparently satisfied that I was telling the truth. 'Hot milk and bed rest.'

'Excuse me?' I said.

'I want you to drink lots of hot milk and get plenty of bed rest. That should fix you.'

'Thank you, Nurse Mavis,' I said, standing up.

'Please tell my next victim – I mean, *patient* – to come in.'

I walked out of the consulting room. I was surprised to meet Mr Murray outside. He was standing with a boy who was holding his arm like it might have been sprained. A rugby injury, no doubt.

'Gordon?' he said. 'Is everything okay?'

'Er, not really,' I told him. 'As a matter of fact, I was going to come to see you.'

'Really?'

'Yes, Mr Murray. I was wondering could you phone Joe Schmidt and tell him I won't be able to make it to training tonight?'

'You're not injured, are you?'

'No, Mr Murray, I have a tummy ache.'

'A *tummy* ache?'

It was like he'd never heard of such a thing.

'Yes, Mr Murray,' I said.

'And did Nurse Mavis give you anything for it?'

'She suggested hot milk and plenty of bed rest.'

'She didn't offer you her mushroom juice, cold tea and liquidized turnip concoction, did she?'

'No, Mr Murray.'

'Good God, it must be serious, then. Okay, I'll phone Joe Schmidt and tell him the news. Will you be well enough to travel to Wales for the match this weekend?'

'Unfortunately not.'

'When do you think you'll be feeling better?'

'Em, maybe a few weeks.'

'Weeks?'

'Might even be a month or two.'

'A month or two? Gordon, if there's a reason you don't want to play for Leinster, it's okay to say it, you know.'

'I really do want to play. But it's this stupid tummy of mine. Maybe it would be better all round if you told him that I would be unavailable for selection until further notice?'

'Okay,' he said, then he nodded and smiled.

Mr Murray was even better than Nurse Mavis at recognizing when a boy was faking it. But I was certain of one thing:

I had played my last match for Leinster.

19 'Joe Schmidt is in our kitchen!'

The weeks went by and things returned to normal.

Conor arrived back to school, picking his way around the place on crutches. His attempt to jump the Gollymochy might have failed in the most spectacular way, but his courage earned him a lot of respect.

On his first day back, there was a queue of people in the cafeteria, waiting patiently to sign his cast. They wrote things like:

'MASSIVE respect, Conor!'

And:

'TOTAL legend, Conor!'

And:

'You ROCK, Conor!'

And Conor grew to enjoy his new-found fame.

But it was no substitute for playing rugby with us. He didn't enjoy standing on the sidelines, leaning on his crutches, watching me and Peter play rugby during Free Time. Especially because he still didn't know whether he'd ever play the game again. I really felt for him.

Mr Murray never mentioned Leinster, except occasionally . . .

When he'd see me score a brilliant, solo try, finished off with a swan dive . . .

Or when he'd see me put in a chop-tackle on the ankles of a bigger boy . . .

Then he'd say, 'That pain in your tummy seems to be definitely improving, Gordon – is it?'

And I would reply, 'Er, it comes and goes, Mr Murray. It comes and goes.'

Leinster were doing just fine without me. They went to Wales and beat the Dragons 30–14. Then they went to England and beat Bath 24–6. Then they played the Dragons at the RDS and they won 18–0. Then they played Bath at home and won 32–9.

Graham Bull had scored seven tries in the five games so far, while Dan Hansen had scored four.

And all the doom and gloom surrounding Leinster had suddenly gone. They were top of the group and they just needed to beat Toulouse in their final group game to be sure of reaching the quarter-finals. No one was rolling their eyes and saying, 'Typical Leinster!' any more.

The newspapers stopped mentioning my name when they wrote about Leinster's injured players. Everyone forgot about me. And that suited me just fine.

Hallowe'en Week arrived. I was back in Wexford, along with Conor and Peter. We were hanging out in the forest near where we lived. I had climbed up a tree and hung a rope from a high branch and me and Peter were having fun, swinging out over the sixty-foot drop below us.

Conor was making us laugh, reminding us about some of the tricks he'd played on us to try to put us off our game when we played for Wexford Wanderers and he played for the Gorey Gladiators. Then he was reminding us of the time in school when we got up in the middle of the night and drew moustaches on the faces of all the other boarders while they slept. Then he did funny impressions of some of the customers we knew from the time we worked in McWonderburger.

He was so funny. We laughed and laughed until my tummy really *did* hurt.

Peter got off the swing. I saw him and Conor exchange a look, like they had something they wanted to talk to me about.

'Gordon, this, em, tummy ache of yours,' Conor said. 'It's a bit weird the way it only seems to come on in the week of a Leinster match.'

'Er, yeah,' I told him, 'it is a bit of a coincidence. Here, Peter, give me the swing, will you?'

'Yeah, before I do,' he said, holding it away from me, 'me and Conor were just wondering – is there a reason you don't want to play for Leinster?'

'Have you just decided that Munster are the best team after all?' Conor asked.

'Or is it because of what happened against Toulouse?' Peter wondered. 'Because if it is, I have to say, it's very unlike you to give up because of one mistake.'

I thought about it for a moment. I took a breath. Then I decided to tell them everything. They *were* my best friends after all.

'Look, please don't tell anyone this,' I said, 'but you're right, there's nothing wrong with my tummy. I've been faking it for weeks now.'

'So it *is* because of what happened against Toulouse?' Conor said.

'Kind of,' I told him. 'I know it sounds stupid,

but the reason I didn't kick the ball out of play was because I noticed that Bully was staring at me.'

'Staring at you?' Conor said. 'What are you talking about?'

'He doesn't like me,' I said. 'And he's been really mean to me from day one. He offered to shake my hand, then he pulled *his* hand away. He made me run into a post and pretended it was an accident. And he stole my mum's Walkman.'

It felt good to share all of these secrets that I'd been carrying around inside my head for weeks. It felt better than good. It felt great.

'It sounds to me like Bully has really earned that nickname!' Peter said. 'Bully by name! Bully by nature!'

Conor shook his head angrily.

'But it's not right,' he said. 'You shouldn't have to give up playing for Leinster just because he has a problem with you. There's only one way to deal with bullies and that's to stand up to them!'

'GORDON! GORDON!'

I suddenly heard my sister Megan calling me. She ran up to us, out of breath.

'Mum said you have to come home,' she said. 'She wants to talk to you.'

'Er, did she say what it's about?' I wondered.

Mum had asked me a couple of times if she could have her Walkman back because she was thinking of going back to line-dancing. Both times, I'd just made an excuse.

'I don't know,' Megan said, 'but a man called to the door. I think he said his name was Joe Smith.'

'Joe Smith?' I said. 'Do you mean Joe Schmidt?'

'I can't remember,' she replied. 'But he's in the kitchen now.'

Conor laughed. 'Oh my God!' he said. 'Joe Schmidt is in your house!'

'I wonder what he wants,' I said.

'Whatever he wants,' Conor replied, 'I hope your mum and dad remembered to de-Munsterfy the place before they invited him in.'

'What do you mean by de-Munsterfy it?'

'All the Munster rugby stuff in your house. I don't think Joe would be happy looking at that.'

Oh, no, I thought. He was right.

I told Conor and Peter that I'd see them later and I ran all the way back to the house with Megan.

I pushed open the kitchen door.

Joe Schmidt was sitting at the kitchen table, having a cup of tea with my parents. I noticed that Mum had taken out the good china, which was only

ever used if the parish priest or the President called to the house.

The President rarely called to the house.

Okay, that's a lie. The President NEVER called to the house.

Dad was pouring Joe a cup of tea from a teapot, instead of pouring boiling water into a mug with a tea bag in it, like we did for ordinary visitors.

'Hey, Gordon,' Joe said, 'how are you going, mate?'

'Er, hello,' I said.

'It's Joe Schmidt!' Dad said. 'Joe Schmidt is in our kitchen, Gordon!'

160

Munster fan or not, this had clearly impressed him.

I looked around the room. I was relieved to see that the framed photo of Dad in his Munster jersey with his arm around Ronan O'Gara had been turned face-down on the sideboard. And also the one of him with Peter Stringer, holding the European Cup. And also the one of him with Paul O'Connell and Donncha O'Callaghan, where Donncha is giving him rabbit ears.

'How are you feeling?' Joe asked me.

'Em, a little bit better,' I told him.

'He *must* be feeling better,' Mum said, 'because he's been out playing on that swing since seven o'clock this morning.'

'That's good for me to know,' Joe said. 'Because I still get asked from time to time for an update on your, em – what was it, Gordon? – your tummy?'

'Yeah,' I said. 'It, er, comes and goes.'

Oh, no. Dad had made sure to turn down all of his Munster photographs, but he'd forgotten about the picture on the wall that said:

There's No Place Like ~~Home~~ Thomond!

I walked over to it and I turned it around to face the wall.

'Anyway,' Joe said, 'the reason I called was to

find out when you think you might be ready to come back to us. Or whether you want to come back to us. You might not want to come back at all.'

It was becoming clear to me that he hadn't bought the upset tummy story.

'Look,' he said, 'I understand that it's a tough dressing-room. There's a lot of big characters in there. Some of them are worried about younger players like you coming in and taking their places. Some of them are still a bit too fond of the way things were done in the old days. There's one or two of them are a bit too interested in how their hair and their tan looks.'

Ouch, I thought.

'Why do you even want me back?' I asked. 'You're doing great without me. You've won your last four matches.'

'Because you're a great player and I see you as part of this team's future,' he said. 'I'm not building a team to win the European Cup once. I want to build a team to win it over and over and over again. I want to build a team that thinks it has a right to win things, a bit like –'

A worried look suddenly crossed Joe's face. He was staring past me.

'Is that a Munster Rugby mug on the draining board?' he asked.

Dad jumped up from the table like there was a chip pan on fire.

'Where did *that* come from?' Dad said, pretending he'd never seen it before in his life.

'You're not Munster fans in this house, are you?' Joe asked.

'God, no!' said Dad. 'I'd rather stick pins in my eyes than watch that rubbish.'

'It's just there seem to be a lot of Munster fans in this part of the world,' Joe said, 'who *should* be Leinster fans.'

'Oh, don't worry, I've heard about the famous Lunsters!' Dad said, dropping the mug into the bin. 'I've no idea who brought that into the house. But it's gone now, Joe, and you won't have to look at it again.'

Joe turned his attention back to me.

'Gordon,' he said, 'do you want to know why you didn't the kick the ball out against Toulouse?'

'Er, why?' I asked.

'Because you weren't concentrating.'

'I thought I *was* concentrating.'

'I'm not talking about when you came on the pitch. I'm talking about before that. I saw you warming up in the deadball area – you were looking around you.'

That's true. I was trying to find Dad and Ian in the crowd.

'You weren't watching the match. You see, a lot of substitutes make the mistake of thinking that the game doesn't start for them until they step onto the pitch. Do you know why I never let the subs sit down during matches?'

'Because you want us to be warmed up when we're called upon.'

'No, it's because I want you to be mentally up to speed with the game. When I pick a player as a substitute, I want him to imagine he's on the field of play. I want him studying every move, playing every pass, feeling every tackle, looking to see where the opposition are weak, where we can improve – so that when he steps onto the pitch, he's already involved in the match in his head.'

'Okay.'

'That's why you didn't kick the ball out of play. It was because you weren't up to the pace of the game mentally when you came on.'

I nodded. He was right.

'I know you had a hard time in the few weeks you were with us,' he said. 'I told you at the start that I was going to change the culture around the team – and that's slowly happening.'

'I didn't really know what you meant by culture,' I said.

'By culture, I mean the way people behave as a group. Right now, you're right, we're winning matches. But the culture is still poor. The reason I say that is because I'm still having to lay down the law. If the culture was good, I wouldn't have to do that. I want a dressing-room where the players enforce the standards, not the coach, where everyone takes responsibility when something goes wrong. I talked to Warren Gatland about you. He told me you're one of the most resilient players he's ever worked with.'

'Resilient?' I said.

It was a new word to me.

'Resilience is toughness of character,' he said. 'The ability to bounce back when things go wrong. *That's* why I want you in my team, Gordon. I need not only great players but players who are prepared to work hard when things aren't going well. I know you're one of those players. That's why I drove down to Wexford today. I'm going to be making a lot of big changes – starting from next week. I'm moving our training base to UCD. We're going to have the best of facilities. I'd love to see you come back to us, Gordon. In time for the second match against Toulouse. Provided your, em, tummy sorts itself out. What do you say?'

20 *Serious Sports People*

'So what *did* you say?' Peter asked.

'I told him I'd think about it,' I said.

Conor couldn't believe what he was hearing.

'Joe Schmidt came to your house,' he said, 'and practically BEGGED you to play for Leinster –'

'He didn't beg me,' I said.

'– and you told him you'd have to THINK about it? Oh my God, Gordon, do you know what I would give to be in your position? To have two fully functioning legs and to have the coach of the Leinster rugby team in my kitchen – BEGGING me to play for him?'

'He didn't beg me. And anyway I thought you were a Munster supporter?'

'I am a Munster supporter. But I'd be happy to

play for anyone – if I could just take this cast off my leg.'

We were standing on the sideline of the rugby pitch in Herbert Park, watching Aoife train with the Ireland Schoolgirls team. They were playing a Sevens match at the end of the session and Aoife was having the match of her life. She had scored two tries. The first came after she launched a Garry-owen deep into the opposition half; then, when the ball fell out of the sky, she caught it and touched it down in the corner. The second was a solo effort. She ran down the sideline in front of us, zigzagging inside and outside players like they were skiing poles, then she put the ball down in the opposite corner.

And, most impressively, even though she'd made the angle of the conversion difficult for herself, she nailed both kicks.

Conor wasn't sure she would.

'Ronan O'Gara would struggle for this kind of range,' he said.

But I'd seen her practise. I'd fetched and carried balls for her and watched her hit the post from the corner so many times.

'Well done, Aoife!' we shouted at her when the session was over. 'You were amazing!'

We wandered onto the pitch, Conor picking his

way slowly with the tips of his crutches. Peter and I were talking about Aoife's second try.

'If a man had scored it,' I said, 'we'd all be saying it was the greatest try ever scored. It would already have a million views on YouTube.'

As we got closer to Aoife, we noticed that she was talking to an older woman, who was scribbling in a notebook. It turned out that she was a reporter from one of the newspapers.

'So what do all of your friends think of you playing rugby?' she asked.

'What do you mean?' Aoife said.

'Well, they must think you're absolutely MAD, do they?'

'Why would they think I'm mad?'

'I mean, rugby! It's a boys' game, isn't it?'

'You just watched thirty girls play it. Did you think any of us wasn't up to it physically?'

'Er, I suppose not. Do you also like girly things, though?'

'Girly things?'

'Yes, like pretty dresses. Like having your make-up done. Like having nice nails.'

'Why are we talking about those things?'

'I think our readers would be interested in knowing that you're also, well, normal girls.'

'Of course we're normal girls! Why can't you write about us as serious sports people – instead of treating us like freaks?'

I felt like shouting, Well said, Aoife!

'I'm just trying to come up with an angle,' the reporter said.

'You want an angle?' Aoife replied. 'Okay, I'll give you an angle. Do you know where I got changed for training tonight?'

'Er, no,' the reporter replied.

'In my mum's car. And that's where I'll get changed back into my clothes now. We have no access to showers and toilets when we train. You see this Ireland training kit that I'm wearing? Do you know who paid for it?'

'I presume it's provided by someone.'

'If I was a boy, it would be. But we have to pay for our own. And when we play for Ireland, we have to pay for our own jerseys. That's how seriously we're taken.'

Conor, Peter and I were listening to this interview, totally spellbound.

'Are you guys hearing this?' Peter asked. 'She's amazing!'

It was true – she was amazing.

'Fair play to her,' he said.

'And there's more,' Aoife added. 'We're playing France in the Six Nations in February and we're being asked to pay for our own flights and accommodation.'

'But you're representing your country!'

'That's what it means to play rugby for Ireland when you're a girl. I'm going to have to ask my mum and dad to fork out the money to send me to Paris so that I can captain Ireland against France. A month after that, we're supposed to be playing England in London. And I'll have to ask them for the money to send me there as well, even though I know they can't afford it.'

'This is disgraceful,' the reporter agreed. 'You're treated like second-class citizens. People need to know about this.'

And the sight of my friend speaking up for herself like that helped me make up my mind what I was going to do next.

21 'Hi, I'm Gordon D'Arcy!'

I can't say that I wasn't nervous going back – that would be a lie.

But the move to UCD made things a bit easier. Because suddenly we were ALL in a new environment. It was sort of like starting a new school.

As a matter of fact, nobody even noticed me for the first ten minutes I was there. They were all too busy checking out our new, state-of-the-art training facilities. There were all sorts of machines for lifting weights. There was a sauna and a steamroom for sweating out all the toxins in your body after training. And then, most exciting of all . . .

There was a cryogenic chamber!

It looked like a giant fridge – except the door only went up to your neck. One of the staff was explaining how it worked when I arrived.

'You walk inside,' he said, 'and you'll be exposed to extremely cold air – we're talking minus 170 degrees Celsius – for between two and four minutes.'

'Minus 170?' Dan Hansen said.

I could tell he was wondering how it might affect his hair.

'That's right,' came the reply. 'Exposing your tired limbs to extreme cold helps you recover more quickly. It will reduce injuries, increase energy, improve sleep – and it will make you feel great!'

There was a real buzz of excitement about the place.

'Hey, Gordon,' a voice said. It was Leo Cullen. He was the first to notice me. 'How's the tummy?'

'It's, em, much better, thank you,' I said.

'Welcome back,' BOD said.

'Thanks,' I told him.

'You look paler than you did last time,' he said. 'Definitely less orange.'

I laughed. It was good to laugh at yourself. If I'd learned one thing in my life, it was that.

I could see Bully glowering at me across the room. He probably never expected to see me again. But here I was, back once more – and trying to take his place in the team.

I just smiled at him. It seemed to make him even madder.

Then it was time to train.

Joe was waiting for us on the pitch. He told us all to stand around him in a circle.

'Today,' he said, 'is a new start for Leinster Rugby. I want you to forget about everything that's happened up until now. This is Day One. You've seen the facilities?'

We all nodded. Everyone seemed very excited about them.

Everyone, that is, except Handsome.

'Yeah, they're fine and everything,' he said, 'but I couldn't help but notice that there are no hairdryers in there.'

'We don't need hairdryers,' Joe told him.

'You might not, Joe, but I certainly do. I've got my online image to think of.'

'Do you think the Munster players have hairdryers in their dressing-room?'

Joe had a point. I couldn't imagine they did.

'Have you seen the hair on some of them?' Handsome said. 'I rest my case!'

'As well as the new facilities,' Joe said, 'there's going to be a new way of doing things around here – a new set of values. We are going to be the best at everything – on and off the field. Excellence is a habit. It comes from constantly striving to be the best you can be, not just on the big days, but EVERY day. The things we do off the pitch are just as important as the things we do on the pitch. Timekeeping, consideration for your teammates, respect – these things are every bit as vital as three of you chasing a ball that's kicked in the air. I want you to focus all the time on what's best for the team – not what's best for you. We're also going to become what Munster are – a proper team. Sometimes when I watch you fellas play, some of you seem like total strangers to each other.'

That was true. There were a lot of players in the squad whose names I didn't even know!

'From now on,' he said, 'before every training session, I want you to shake each other's hands.'

'What?' asked Bully. 'Everyone's hand?'

'*Everyone's* hand,' Joe repeated. 'Go on – do it now! And if you don't know someone's name, I want you to introduce yourself to them.'

So we all started to 'mingle' – as they call it at parties. We were suddenly all shaking hands and saying:

'Hi, I'm Gordon D'Arcy.'

And:

'Hi, I'm Isa Nacewa.'

And:

'Hi, I'm Seán O'Brien.'

And:

'Hi, I'm Malcolm O'Kelly.'

And:

'Hi, I'm Cian Healy.'

And:

'Hi, I'm Leo Cullen.'

And:

'Hi, I'm Shane Byrne.'

And:

'Hi, I'm Johnny Sexton.'

And:

'Hi, I'm Rob Kearney.'

And:

'Hi, I'm Dan Hansen – but please refer to me only as Handsome or Damn Handsome because I need to protect my brand identity.'

And then, suddenly, I felt my hand grabbed and squeezed really, REALLY tightly. I looked up and found myself looking into the eyes of Graham Bull.

'Hi, I'm Gordon D'Arcy,' I said.

'I can't believe you came back,' he said. 'That was a BIG mistake.'

Then he loosened his grip on my hand and he walked away.

'Okay,' Joe shouted, 'let's do some work!'

We trained for two hours. It was probably the most enjoyable training session I'd ever had. It was hard work, but it was fun. The new surroundings made it feel like a real break from the past. Players who had previously kept to their own little groups were suddenly mixing with other players.

Joe was pleased because I saw him quietly smiling to himself a few times.

At the end, Malcolm suggested we play a game called Red Bum. It was essentially a game of catch and toss – but with a difference.

The rules were these:

1. You stand in a circle with a group of teammates or friends.
2. One person is nominated to start. He must throw the ball to someone. As it leaves his hands, he must shout the name of the intended receiver.
3. The receiver must then clap his hands once before he catches the ball. You can increase this to two, three or even four times as the game goes on.
4. The first time a receiver fails to clap his hands before receiving the ball – or drops

the ball – he is assigned a letter from the words 'Red Bum', starting with an R.

5. As soon as a player has all the letters to spell out 'Red Bum', he is out of the game. And he must stick out his bum for one of his teammates to throw the ball at it. Although not too hard!

6. The winner is the player who has never had a 'red bum'.

It was the kind of game that suited those with fast hands and quick reflexes. I could pretend that it was meant to sharpen up our ball-handling skills ahead of the return match against Toulouse. But that would be a lie.

It was just a lot of fun.

I was out third from last, leaving BOD and Shaggy as the last men standing. It was a tense final shoot-out between them. Both of them were on U and the clap count was up to four when Shaggy fumbled the ball and had to take his punishment.

A red bum.

Only two players, I noticed, weren't part of the fun. Felipe and Johnny Sexton. They stayed on the pitch, practising their kicking together. I watched them, totally mesmerized, as they sent ball after ball sailing through the air and between the posts.

They were both perfectionists – like Aoife. When Johnny missed a kick, I could see that it bothered him. His punishment was to force himself to retake the kick again and again and again until he'd done it perfectly – ten times in a row!

Only then would he move on.

It was fascinating to watch two masters – and now rivals for the same jersey – still working together without a sign of jealousy between them. Felipe got what it meant to be a team player before the penny dropped for the rest of us.

We all went back to the dressing-room. I noticed that everyone was staring at the cryogenic chamber. We were all fascinated by it, but a little bit afraid of it as well.

'Who's going to go first?' Leo Cullen asked.

'Not me,' said Shaggy.

'No way,' said BOD.

'Me neither,' said Handsome. 'It might dry out my hair – and I'm on a shortlist of three to do a hair gel ad.'

'I'll do it,' I said. 'I'll go first.'

All of the other players clapped and cheered and shouted:

'Go on, Darce!'

I stripped down to just my shorts. One of the staff handed me a pair of gloves, a pair of knee-high socks, a hair net and a pair of wooden clogs. I put them on. Then the metal door was pulled open and all I could see inside was white-coloured steam. Even from a distance of ten feet away, I could feel how cold it was.

I was already shivering!

'Go on, Darce!' they all shouted at me.

I couldn't back out now without looking very stupid. So I took one step forward, then another, then another, my body tensing the closer I got to the chamber.

I gulped.

Then I stepped inside and the door closed behind me.

I turned around to face the rest of the players. My chin was resting on the top of the door.

'What's it like?' everyone was asking.

And I made the mistake of saying:

'It's not as cold as I thought it was going to b—'

But then the man operating the machine said:

'I haven't turned the temperature down yet.'

And then he did.

And . . .

Oh! My! God!

I let out a scream:

'AAARRRGGGHHH!!!'

What's the coldest thing you can imagine?

Picture yourself in the North Pole. You're indoors. Outside, it's snowing. And someone challenges you, to win a bet, to take off all your clothes, walk outside and roll around in the snow.

Can you imagine how cold that would feel?

Well, this was about four hundred times COLDER than even that!

I shut my eyes tight and tried to pretend I was somewhere else.

'What's it like, Darce?' they kept asking me.

But I couldn't answer because I had to clamp my upper and lower teeth together to stop them from chattering.

After the longest two minutes of my life, the door finally opened and I jumped out.

'Never again!' I said. 'Never! Again!'

Everyone was laughing and high-fiving me and telling me that I was some man for one man. And for the first time since I joined the Leinster squad, I felt like I fit in.

And then I watched Bully take Mum's Walkman out of his bag and put the headphones on his ears. And then he started singing that he had friends in low places.

22 'Angry Ireland Captain Hits Out!'

It was Evening Study time.

I was sitting in the library with Conor and Peter and about a hundred other students. I had my Geography book open on the chapter entitled 'The Water Cycle', which we had been told to study by Mr Trent – and to make sure we knew it 'back to front'. It was all about how rain was formed. I tried my best to read it, but it was VERY boring and I couldn't even focus on the words.

So, instead, I pulled out the newspaper that I had hidden underneath the book and I started reading about the Leinster match against Toulouse this weekend. According to the report on the back page, Joe Schmidt was expected to make a number of changes to the team.

A line at the end of the report said: 'Gordon D'Arcy has recovered from the upset tummy that ruled him out of Leinster's last four matches – but Graham Bull is expected to keep his place at inside-centre.'

I wasn't surprised. I didn't think I would come back to the squad and walk straight into the team. I would just have to be patient and make sure I was ready when I was called upon.

Father Billings was supervising Evening Study.

'THIS IS WHAT I LIKE TO HEAR,' he said. 'THE SOUND OF COMPLETE AND UTTER SILENCE.'

Everyone in the library laughed. It was well known that Father Billings couldn't hear anything. He was deaf as a post, which was why he shouted all the time. And the library was anything BUT silent. There was pandemonium, as there always was when Father Billings was left in charge of us. Suddenly, the sound of a loud fart rang through the library.

PPPHHHAAAAAARRRRRRTTT!

Everyone laughed.

As well as deaf, Father Billings was also flatulent, which is why all of the boys called him Farter Billings. And because of the deafness, he had absolutely no idea that he had this problem:

PPPHHHAAAAAARRRRRRTTT!

Suddenly, I was watching his nose twitch.

'HAS SOMEONE LET OFF WIND?' he asked. 'THERE IS THE MOST AWFUL SMELL IN THIS LIBRARY!'

For some reason, his eyes fixed on Peter.

'YOU, BOY!' he said. 'WAS IT YOU?'

'Me?' Peter asked, at the same time looking deeply offended.

'YES, YOU! ARE YOU RESPONSIBLE FOR THAT VILE SMELL?'

'No, I'm not!'

'WELL, AT LEAST YOU'RE HONEST ENOUGH TO ADMIT IT!'

Everybody roared with laughter – including me and Conor. It was very funny.

'I didn't admit it!' Peter said

'SPEAK UP, BOY!' Father Billings shouted. 'I CAN'T HEAR A WORD YOU'RE SAYING!'

'I SAID IT WASN'T ME WHO FARTED!'

'YES, I KNOW IT WAS YOU WHO FARTED! WE'VE ALREADY ESTABLISHED THAT FACT! I SHALL HAVE TO HAVE A WORD WITH JANICE IN THE CAFETERIA! I THINK YOU'RE ALL EATING TOO MANY BEANS!'

'I DIDN'T DO IT!'

'WHAT'S THAT?'

'IT WAS, EM . . . SOMEBODY ELSE!'

'OPEN A WINDOW? YES, THAT'S A VERY GOOD IDEA!'

I was laughing so much now, I couldn't catch my breath.

'WHAT?' Peter shouted.

'A WINDOW!' Father Billings shouted back. 'GO AND OPEN ONE!'

Peter stood up – humiliated – and made his way

to the window. He opened it up and a gust of cold air blew into the room.

'AND IF YOU INSIST ON BREAKING WIND LIKE THAT IN THE FUTURE,' Father Billings said, 'YOU CAN SPEND YOUR EVENING STUDY PERIODS OUT IN THE FIELD WITH BESSIE THE COW! DO I MAKE MYSELF CLEAR?'

Father Billings broke wind again:

PPPHHHAAAAAARRRRRRTTT!

And even Peter, returning to his desk, began to see the funny side of it.

'Why doesn't he just switch on his hearing aid?' he asked, at the same time laughing.

'He says he doesn't want to waste the batteries,' Conor said. 'He only uses it for emergencies.'

'But every day is an emergency – he can't hear a thing!'

'Oh my God!' I suddenly blurted out.

'What's wrong?' Conor asked.

I was flicking through the rest of the newspaper and I came across an article about Aoife. It must have been written by the reporter who was at training that day. The headline read:

'Angry Ireland Captain Hits Out!'

I showed it to Conor.

'Oh, wow!' he said.

'What does it say?' Peter asked.

So I read it out loud for them:

'*Ireland captain Aoife Kehoe has criticized the Irish Schoolgirls Rugby Federation for what she says is the unfair treatment of female rugby players in this country. Kehoe, who will lead Ireland into the first ever Six Nations tournament for schoolgirls in the New Year, claims that female players are treated like second-class citizens when compared to male players. Among her list of complaints, Kehoe says that she and her teammates have NO DRESSING-ROOMS in which to change and shower; are required to BUY THEIR OWN JERSEYS; and are forced to cover the cost of their own FLIGHTS AND ACCOMMODATION when playing for Ireland abroad.*'

'Good on her!' Conor said.

'Oh, no,' I said. 'Listen to this bit. *When asked to comment, the President of the Irish Schoolgirls Rugby Federation, Jeff Smythe, said that it should be considered an honour to play for your country and that Kehoe should stop whingeing.*'

Conor shook his head.

'I know my cousin,' he said, 'and she will NOT be happy with that!'

The bell sounded. Evening Study was over. We all stood up and started to make our way out of the library.

'WAIT UNTIL THE BELL SOUNDS!' Father Billings shouted.

He hadn't heard it.

'NOT UNTIL THE BELL SOUNDS ARE YOU PERMITTED TO LEAVE!' he shouted.

Everyone ignored him.

PPPHHHAAAAAARRRRRRTTT!

'WAS THAT IT?' he asked. 'YES, I THINK I JUST HEARD IT!'

We walked outside. Conor was lagging slightly behind me and Peter, picking his way along on his crutches.

'That was really fascinating,' Peter said, 'wasn't it?'

'What was?' I asked.

'The chapter in the book about how rain is formed. The way vapour rises, cools and changes into tiny water drops, which form into clouds.'

'Er, yeah,' I said. 'It was, em, interesting alright. So what are we going to do now? Do you want to watch some TV in the common room?'

We had an hour and a half to ourselves before we had to go to bed.

'I thought I'd go back to the dorm,' Peter said, 'and read the chapter about the Water Cycle again.'

Okay, there was no real surprise there.

'What about you, Conor?' I asked.

'I, em, have to do something,' he said.

'Do something?' I asked. 'What is it?'

'It's just, em, a thing.'

He seemed a bit shifty to me.

'What thing?' I asked.

'It's a just a thing,' he said, suddenly blushing, 'with a few friends.'

'Which friends?' I asked.

Peter and I were his only friends in Clongowes – or so I thought.

'You wouldn't know them,' he said. 'They've no interest in rugby.'

Up ahead, I could see four older boys leaning against a wall. They looked a bit, well, rough to me.

'Conor!' one of them said. 'What kept you?'

'Sorry, lads,' he replied, 'I had to go to Evening Study.'

'Hurry up. We've got work to do.'

Out of the corner of his mouth, Conor said, 'I'll see you back in the dorm later,' then he went off with the boys, following them as quickly as his crutches would allow.

'Who are they?' I asked Peter, wondering why Conor had never mentioned these other friends before.

'I've no idea,' Peter answered.

'They look like they might be trouble,' I said.

Peter nodded. 'Yeah, I thought that too. I hope Conor hasn't gotten himself mixed up in something.'

23 *Dan Not the Man*

There was no sign of Dan Hansen.

We were sitting at the departure gate, waiting for the flight to Toulouse. And Handsome was missing in action.

He didn't report to the team hotel at 11.30 a.m. – as we were all told to do. One or two of the other players tried to phone him, but his mobile phone was switched off.

Joe didn't say anything. He just told us all to board the bus for the airport.

'Damn Handsome isn't here yet,' I heard Shaggy tell him.

'Who?' Joe asked.

'Damn Handsome . . . er, I mean, Dan Hansen.'

Joe just shrugged his shoulders. 'He was told that

the bus was leaving at midday. So now it's leaving without him on it.'

It was all anyone could talk about during the drive to the airport.

I was sitting beside BOD.

'Apparently,' he said, out of the corner of his mouth, 'he was filming this morning.'

'Filming?' I asked. 'What was he filming?'

'He got that hair gel ad he was talking about. He told one of the guys that he was going to make his own way to the airport.'

'Joe isn't happy.'

'I don't blame him. Handsome is really pushing it.'

An hour later, we were waiting to board the flight and Handsome still hadn't shown his face.

Bully went to the shop and arrived back with two trays containing eight takeaway coffees. He started to hand them out to various players who were sitting around me.

'Here you go,' he said, offering one to me.

'Er, thanks,' I said.

I could hear the surprise in my own voice. But when I went to take the coffee from him, he pulled it away.

'Oh, no,' he said, with a grin on his face, 'I don't have one for you. Only first-teamers, I'm afraid.'

One or two of his friends in the squad laughed along with him.

'I didn't want one anyway,' I said.

They laughed even louder then.

I noticed that Bully was still wearing the headphones from Mum's Walkman around his neck.

'I want my mum's Walkman back,' I told him.

'I already told you,' he said, 'it's not your mum's Walkman – it's mine.'

I was about to get into an argument with him about it when a hush suddenly descended over the boarding-gate area.

Handsome was strolling towards us with a big smile on his face. He had his gear bag slung over his shoulder and he was listening to music on a set of enormous headphones.

'Hey, guys,' he said, removing them, 'what's with the long faces?'

Joe stood up and walked over to him. We all braced ourselves for what was about to come.

'Where have you been?' Joe asked him.

Handsome laughed. 'Who are you,' he said, 'the cops?' and he looked around at the rest of us, expecting us to laugh along with him.

Nobody did.

'You were told to be at the team hotel for 11.30 a.m.' Joe said. 'Where were you?'

'Hey, chill out,' Handsome told him. 'I had a modelling assignment.'

'What kind of modelling assignment?'

'If you must know, I was filming an ad for Get a Grip.'

'For what?'

'It's a hair gel. *If you want a firm hold that lasts all day, you've got to Get a Grip!*'

Joe stared at him like he was speaking another language.

'What did I tell you last week in UCD?' he said. 'What did I say to you about values?'

'They wanted to do the shoot this morning,' Handsome said. 'I had no choice in the matter.'

'You had a choice between doing what was best for you and what was best for the team. And you chose what was best for you. Which was to show contempt for these guys.'

'So give me a punishment. Fifty press-ups or something. I'll do them one-handed!'

'How can I trust you to do it for me in a big match if I can't trust you to show up on time for a flight?'

'I'm on time for the flight.'

Suddenly, there was an announcement: 'Ladies and gentlemen, flight EI829 to Toulouse is now boarding.'

'See?' Handsome said, winking at Joe. 'I made it in loads of time.'

And that's when Joe said it:

'No, you didn't. Dan, you're out.'

'Out?' Handsome said, looking around at the rest of us. 'What's he talking about, guys?'

'By showing up late,' Joe said, 'you're disrespecting our values. That isn't The Leinster Way.'

Handsome laughed.

'Are you saying I'm dropped for this match?' he asked.

'No,' Joe told him, 'I'm saying you're dropped permanently.'

The smile disappeared from Handsome's face like water being poured from a bucket.

'You can't possibly mean that,' he said.

'I do mean it,' Joe told him. 'Now go home.'

Handsome pointed his finger at Joe.

'If you think you're going to beat Toulouse away without Handsome Dan Hansen,' he said, 'then you're dreaming.'

'We'll take our chances,' Joe told him.

'You'll regret this,' Handsome said, as he turned to go. 'All of you. Toulouse are going to hammer you – and then you'll come crawling back to me.'

Handsome pulled his enormous headphones over his ears and he walked off.

Then we boarded the flight to Toulouse for a match we knew we absolutely had to win.

24 *How to be a Sub*

I wasn't in the team.

We were sitting in the dressing-room and Joe read out the names of the fifteen players who would start against Toulouse. Mine wasn't one of them.

I wasn't surprised. Bully was playing well. And I'm sure the Leinster fans hadn't forgotten that my last contribution in a blue jersey was to fail to kick the ball out of play against Toulouse at home. There was nothing I wanted more than the opportunity to make up for that mistake. But I'd have to be patient.

Still, it's a strange feeling sitting in a dressing-room when you know that you're not going to be playing. It's like tagging along with your older brother when he goes on a date. Actually, that did happen to me once, when Ian arranged to go to the cinema with a girl while he was supposed to be babysitting me. He was dressed in white jeans and a paisley shirt, with the buttons opened to the naval. The film was some smoochy, romantic thing starring Colin Firth and Scarlett Johansson. I sat there beside them, embarrassed for him.

Okay, maybe sitting in a dressing-room when you know you're not going to be playing isn't *quite* as cringy as that. But it's still cringy enough. You feel like you shouldn't be there. Even listening to Joe's pep-talk, I felt like I was somehow intruding.

'You guys don't need me to tell you,' he said, 'that this is a match we absolutely have to win. Lose, and we're out of the competition. I hear a lot of people back home talking about the potential of this group of players. I'm sick of hearing about it. I want us to stop being a team with potential and become a team that actually wins things.'

We had a huge job on our hands. It was six years since a team had come to France and won a European Cup match. Not only were Toulouse the reigning European champions, they were unbeaten at home in nineteen games.

'While the result is important,' he said, 'don't spend the entire match thinking about it. Focus on every job at hand – making the next tackle, claiming the next lineout, winning the next scrum, making the next ten yards. Do the simple things well at the right time. If you do that, the result will look after itself. Remember I told you that excellence was a habit? Now is the time to show that. If you make a mistake one moment, then win the next moment. And the next moment. If you control what you do in the next eighty minutes, you will be able to look each other in the eye afterwards and know you did everything you could. If you give me that, I say it will be enough.'

An official stuck his head around the dressing-room door.

'*Êtes-vous tous prêts?*' he said.

'Well?' Leo Cullen said. 'Are we ready?'

'YES!' everyone shouted, and jumped to their feet.

The substitutes left the dressing-room first, to form a tunnel for the fifteen players who were starting. Joe said he wanted a word with me and he pulled me to one side.

'Remember what I told you in your mum and dad's kitchen,' he said. 'Just because you're not a starter doesn't mean you're not involved. The match doesn't start for you the moment you step onto the pitch. The match starts the second the whistle blows. Make sure you stay mentally up to speed with the game.'

'Okay.'

I joined the other substitutes in forming a tunnel at the entrance to the pitch. We clapped and patted the players on the back as they walked out. I wished Bully good luck, deciding to forget about everything that had happened and focus on what was best for the team.

'I don't need *you* to wish me luck,' he growled at me.

The Toulouse supporters were really passionate – and loud! There was a band playing in the middle of the crowd and they kept chanting, '*Olé!*'

It was a baking hot day.

I tried not to focus on any of these things as Felipe kicked the ball into the air to start the match. I warmed up in the deadball area and I did what Joe had told me to do. I followed the play as if I was actually on the pitch.

It was a surprisingly cagey start, especially for two teams who were known for their all-out attacking play. With so much on the line, no one wanted to make a mistake. Our full-back, Rob Kearney, and the Toulouse full-back, Clément Poitrenaud, kicked to the corners to apply pressure, but it was a tight game with no real try-scoring opportunities in the first ten minutes.

Even though I wasn't on the pitch, I tried to feel like I was involved, concentrating really hard, trying to figure out where Toulouse might have a weakness.

Leinster were having to work for everything. Felipe and Jean-Baptiste Élissalde, the Toulouse out-half, kicked three penalties each and it was 9–9 after fifteen minutes. And then, all of a sudden, Bully accidentally knocked heads with Poitrenaud and was knocked out cold.

The Leinster physio ran onto the pitch to treat him, then he spoke to Joe through his radio mic. Joe signalled frantically for me to come to the bench.

'Bully's got a concussion,' he told me. 'Are you warm?' meaning was I ready to go on.

'Absolutely,' I said.

And I was – both physically and mentally this time.

Bully was helped from the pitch. When he spotted me coming on to replace him, he got angry.

'No!' he said. 'You're not taking my place! No way!'

He didn't even shake my hand and wish me luck.

The game started again. I got the ball in my hands once or twice and tried to make something happen. If anything, I was ahead of the tempo of the game.

My passes were inches too far ahead of the receiver, or I was passing in contact, to try to force an opening.

I could hear the Leinster fans groaning.

'You are trying too hard,' Felipe told me.

He had a point. I had to stop thinking that I had to make up for what happened in Dublin. That match was in the past. This match was now.

'It is not about you,' he said. 'It is about the team. Remember what Joe said to us. Do the simple things well at the right time. Take a breath and play your game. Focus on the next pass, the next kick, the next tackle.'

As it happened, Felipe had an idea. We could see that part of Toulouse's strategy was for Vincent Clerc, their openside winger, to keep targeting BOD with hard tackles. Felipe gave us our instructions with just some moody looks and some finger-pointing. The next time he had the ball in his hands, we were lined up behind him, waiting for the pass. As Clerc made a beeline towards BOD, eyes blazing, getting ready to take him out, Felipe threw the most unbelievably long pass, over my head, over BOD's head, over everyone's head, into the hands of Shaggy out on the wing. Shaggy charged through the shocked Toulouse midfield, then threw it short to Felipe again. Felipe passed the ball, one-handed, to BOD. It happened so quickly that no one even saw it. The eyes of the Toulouse players were still fixed on Felipe when they realized that BOD had the ball and was putting it down between the two posts.

It was a brilliant piece of thinking by Felipe.

'So much for keeping it simple!' I said to him.

He just smiled.

We went in at half-time 19–9 ahead.

In the dressing-room, Joe said, 'Is there anything we can do about the last forty minutes of rugby?'

We all looked at each other, puzzled.

'No, there isn't,' he said. 'But we *can* control what's coming next. Remember what happened at the RDS – because the same thing is going to happen here. They will have a lot of the ball and they will score. How you react to that is what will determine this match.'

And he was right. Toulouse came back at us strongly in the second half. It felt like they had an extra forward and they were putting real pressure on us with their rolling maul. Malcolm O'Kelly pulled it down a couple of times to save certain tries and was lucky not to be sin-binned. Toulouse kicked their penalties and suddenly our lead was cut to four points.

Then Frédéric Michalak kicked a drop-goal and our lead was down to one point.

There was a real sense of anticipation in the crowd. They could feel that the game was swinging Toulouse's way. It seemed like only a matter of time before we folded, as Leinster teams had so often in the past.

But we didn't fold.

We had a lineout. Munch, our hooker, picked up the ball. The referee told him to hurry up and take it. Leo Cullen, one of our second-rows, told the referee that we'd take the throw when we were good and ready.

'We need to focus on this next passage of play,' Leo told us. 'Let's win this lineout, get our own maul going and pin them into their own twenty-two.'

Munch was one of the best lineout throwers in the world. He sent the ball high. Malcolm O'Kelly was lifted into the air and he beat Fabien Pelous to the ball by a couple of inches. We got our maul going and we managed to drive them backwards to the edge of their twenty-two. Chris Whitaker, our scrum-half, got the ball and kicked it over the maul and I chased after it as hard as I could, while shouting at Keith Gleeson to get our defensive line ready for the counter-attack. Michalak got to the ball before me. He was about to clear it, but Keith tack-led him hard. He tried to pass his way out of trouble, but he threw the ball straight to our blindside flanker, Cameron Jowitt, who crashed over the line for our second try of the match.

The French crowd, who'd thought the momentum of the match was swinging their team's way, was shocked into silence. We were eight points clear now, but we couldn't relax. Toulouse were one of those teams, like Munster, who never accepted defeat until it was over. They played an offloading game – they didn't like the ball to hit the ground. They didn't like forming rucks. They concentrated on passing the ball, before, during or after contact. It was really hard to defend against because there was danger everywhere.

The Toulouse flanker, Yannick Nyanga, was caus-ing us all sorts of difficulties, cutting our defence to pieces at will. At one point, he steamed right past me and Girvan Dempsey saved me from embarrass-ment by stealing the ball from him and kicking it clear.

Toulouse cut our lead back to five points with a penalty and the match started to turn into a real scrap. They were deep in our twenty-two and we were desperately trying to keep them out. There was a feeling in the stadium that if they scored a try and got themselves in front, then we wouldn't come back from it.

Before the match, Joe had told our wingers to be alert, because he felt that Toulouse were vulnerable out wide to the counter-attack. So when the ball was turned over, I looked up to see Denis Hickie waving his arms, in loads of space, on our twenty-two.

Felipe had the ball.

'Turbo!' I shouted, which was the team code word for 'Get the ball out wide!'

He spotted Denis and found him with a long, loping pass. Then Denis accelerated, moving up through the gears. He was, without doubt, the fastest man on two legs I had ever seen. He had been a champion 100m runner when he was at school. And now, I thought to myself, 'Oh my God, he's going to try and run the whole length of the pitch!'

I ran after him, very much in his slipstream, just to give him an option if he realized he couldn't make it all the way to the line.

Pelous threw himself at him. But Denis was too fast for him and Pelous found himself grasping at thin air.

As he reached the Toulouse twenty-two, Clerc, who was pretty fast himself, was coming across to

close Denis down. Denis looked inside and saw me running just behind, screaming for the ball. He threw it to me. There were two Toulouse players in front of me. But between them, I could see a clear path to the line. The only question was whether or not I had the speed to make it through the gap.

If I scored the try that won the game, it would allow me to forget forever what happened in the first match in Dublin. I could make myself a hero with the Leinster supporters!

But then I remembered what Felipe had told me.

This wasn't about me and my need to make amends. It was about the team.

I saw that Denis was in space now and had a far easier route to the line. So I threw it back to him and he found another gear before crashing over the line in the corner.

After that, there was no way back for Toulouse. And we were into the quarter-finals of the European Cup.

25 *Trouble*

'How is rain formed?'

Oh, no! I was pretty sure that Mr Trent was talking to me.

'Miiisssttteeerrrr D'Aaarrrcccyyy,' he said, 'I'm talking to *you*.'

Yeah, I thought so.

'Rain?' I asked, stalling for time.

'Yes, rain,' he answered. 'How is it formed?'

'Em, I think it sort of just falls from the sky, doesn't it?'

'But how does it get in the sky in the first place?'

'Oh, I definitely know this one,' I said, as if the answer was on the tip of my tongue.

Behind me, I could hear Peter whispering, 'Vapour rises, cools and changes into tiny water drops . . .'

And I repeated what I thought I'd heard.

'Vader rises, cruel and chained into slimy otter tots.'

'Whoever is attempting to prompt Miiissstttee errrr D'Aaarrrcccyyy, can they please desist immediately?' said Mr Trent. 'Miiisssttteeerrrr D'Aaarrr cccyyy, you were supposed to have this chapter read for today.'

'Unfortunately,' I said, 'I was away in France at the weekend. I was playing for Leinster against –'

'Frankly,' he said, 'I don't care who you were playing for at the weekend. I gave you this assignment a week ago. I want you to go to the Principal's office and explain to him why *you* – and you alone! – felt you shouldn't have to read about the Water Cycle.'

'I'll read it now, Mr Trent.'

'It's too late, Miiisssttteeerrrr D'Aaarrrcccyyy. Mr Cuffe's office – now!'

I stood up and walked out of the classroom. My heart was pounding. I knew I couldn't go to Mr Cuffe's office. He'd already told me that he would stop me playing rugby if he had any more complaints from my teachers about me not doing my work. So I decided to disappear for the rest of the period. It was lunchtime in twenty minutes anyway and I knew that Aoife would be outside, practising her kicking.

I headed for the rugby pitch.

'Hey, Aoife,' I said.

'Oh, hi, Gordon,' she replied. 'I saw the Toulouse match on TV. You were amazing.'

'Was I?'

'I'm saying the *team* were amazing.'

'Oh, right. So does that mean you're not a Munster fan any more?'

Conor and Peter had both said they were warming to Leinster.

'No, I'm still a Munster fan,' Aoife said.

'But you'll be cheering for us against Harlequins in the quarter-final,' I said, 'right?'

'Let's just say, if they played like that all the time, then I'd definitely be a fan.'

'Hey, I saw the piece in the paper. You didn't get into trouble for saying those things, did you?'

'Not at all,' she said. 'Jill Gillespie, our coach, said she was proud of me for saying what I said. She said it's a captain's role to stand up for her teammates.'

'So is anything going to be done about it?'

'I'm going to write a letter to that Jeff Smythe.'

'Is he the guy who said you should consider it an

honour to play for your country and you should stop whingeing?'

'Him, exactly. I'm going to write to him and point out that it isn't whingeing to ask that we be treated the same way as the boys.'

'You're totally right, Aoife.'

A moment later, the school started emptying out. I could hear the shouts and screams of hundreds of boys excited to be on their lunch break.

'I better go,' she said. 'I took an early lunch.'

She ran at the ball and sent it straight between the two posts.

She picked up her tee.

Just as I was about to retrieve the ball for her, I heard someone call my name.

'Gordon!'

I turned around and saw Peter racing across the pitch towards me.

At first, I presumed he was going to tell me that Mr Trent knew that I hadn't gone to Mr Cuffe's office. But it wasn't about me at all.

'It's Conor!' he shouted.

He had Aoife's attention immediately.

'Conor?' she said – because she was very close to her cousin. 'What about him?'

'I think he's involved in something very, very bad,' Peter said.

'Why do you say that?' I asked.

'Those older boys he went off with last week after Evening Study – they were waiting outside the classroom when Geography ended. He went off with them again. I was worried about him because, you know, Gordon, he's been so secretive lately. So I followed them for a little bit and I overheard one of the older boys say something about a robbery.'

'A robbery?' I said. 'What could they be robbing?'

'I was thinking maybe the tuckshop?' he said.

'Oh, no.'

'I overheard Conor say that he had the whole robbery worked out in his head and he'd explain the plan to them in the Main Assembly Hall.'

'Is that where they are now?' I asked.

Peter nodded.

'Let's go,' I said

'I'm coming with you,' Aoife said. 'We have to stop this thing before it goes too far.'

26 *Armed Robbery*

We made our way to the Main Assembly Hall.

Aoife pulled up the hood of her sweater to hide the fact that she was a girl walking around a school for boys.

'What are we going to do?' she asked.

'What do you mean?' I said.

'Well, are we going to just burst in and tell them we know what they're planning?'

'We don't really know anything yet,' Peter said. 'We have no actual proof.'

'So how are we going to get proof?' I asked.

Peter clicked his fingers.

'I've got it!' he said. 'We'll sneak in through the backstage area, then we'll climb up into the flies to spy on them from up there.'

'Into the what?' I said.

'The flies,' he said. 'It's the space above the stage, where they stand to work the curtains and the lights.'

We slipped through a door into the backstage area, then we climbed up seven flights of metal steps to a wooden walkway directly above the main stage. We suddenly had a fly's-eye view of the assembly hall – and I suddenly remembered how terrified I was of heights!

'Oh my God,' I said, 'I think I'm going to be sick.'

'Shush,' Aoife whispered. 'Listen.'

I could see Conor below me. He was leaning

against the stage with his crutches in his hands. The older boys were standing around him.

'The robbery has to be made to look real,' he said.

'Okay,' one of the older boys said. 'I don't think that's going to be a problem. Especially with this gun I'm carrying.'

I gulped. We all did. Conor had clearly got himself caught up with a bad crowd.

'So when you walk into the restaurant,' we heard him say, 'you're going to hear the words, "Welcome to McWonderburger, Wexford! What's *your* beef?" And that's when you're going to demand all the money in the cash register.'

Peter gasped. 'Oh my God,' he said, 'he's going to rob my uncle's burger bar!'

'Keep your voice down!' I said, punching him in the arm. 'You're going to get us caught.'

'Who's up there?' a voice below us shouted.

It was one of the older boys.

Aoife put her finger to her lips. 'Ssshhh!!!'

'I didn't hear anything,' Conor said. 'Let's continue with the plan. You're going to tell the idiots behind the counter to fill up this bag with money.'

Peter was rubbing his arm where I'd punched him.

'That hurt,' he said.

'I'm sorry,' I told him. 'It's just you were talking really loudly. You were going to give us away.'

Then he thumped me back.

'Ouch!' I said, holding my arm.

'Will you two give it up?' Aoife hissed.

'There *is* someone up there!' one of the boys said.

Suddenly, there was a whirring sound, like some kind of engine was kicking into life. Then the plank on which we were standing started to move.

'What's happening?' I asked.

'They're lowering us to the ground,' Aoife said. 'Nice job, lads.'

The plank on which we stood started descending towards the stage. I could see one of the older boys standing in the wing, pressing a large red button.

As we got nearer to the ground, Conor finally recognized us.

'Gordon?' he said. 'Peter? And – I don't know who that one is.'

Aoife pulled down her hood.

'Oh,' he said, 'it's my cousin, Aoife.'

'Yes,' she said, 'and we know what you're up to! You've been caught red-handed!'

'What do you mean?'

'You were planning to rob McWonderburger in Wexford,' I said, 'and we've rumbled your game.'

I must have heard that line on a TV cop show.

'Planning to rob McWonderburger?' Conor said, laughing. 'Lads, we're putting on a play!'

'A what?' Peter asked.

'A play! It's a comedy caper I've written about what happens when someone tries to pull a stick-up in McWonderburger in Wexford and how the three idiots behind the counter end up accidentally foiling the robbery.'

We were silent for about ten seconds.

'Okay,' Peter said, 'that conversation I overheard as I was leaving Geography is starting to make sense now.'

I noticed that three of the boys were wearing McWonderburger uniforms. Canary-yellow shirts, bright green trousers, plastic cow snouts and red baseball caps with horns. One of them was wearing glasses like Peter's and one of them was wearing orange fake tan.

'Wait a minute,' I said. 'The idiots behind the counter – are they supposed to be us?'

'Er, yeah,' Conor said awkwardly. 'Obviously, I've exaggerated them a bit for comic effect.'

Aoife thought the whole thing was hilarious.

'I never knew you were interested in drama,' she said, laughing.

'I wasn't,' he told her. 'But, seeing as I can't play rugby this year because of my stupid leg, I can't just stand around watching you play all the time. So I thought I needed to do something myself. Gordon's always telling me how funny I am.'

'You are,' I told him. 'You're hilarious.'

'So I wrote this play. We're hoping to put it on at the end of the school year.'

'Conor,' I said, 'this is amazing! Why didn't you tell us?'

'I thought you might think it was a bit lame or something.'

'Lame? It's anything but lame! It's exciting!'

He smiled at us.

'Did you really think I was going to carry out an armed robbery on McWonderburger?'

Peter, Aoife and I gave each other sideways glances.

'Of course not!' we all said at once.

27 *Video Nasty*

It was our last team get-together before Christmas and we were all feeling a little bit giddy, especially after the victory over Toulouse.

Everyone, that is, except Bully. Out of the corner of my eye, I could see him staring at me while I was doing my stretches. He hadn't forgiven me for replacing him in France and this time playing well.

He didn't say, 'Well done,' to me after the match. He didn't speak to me at all during the journey home from France.

Joe let us know, in no uncertain terms, that we were not going to be allowed to take it easy, just because we didn't have another match until the spring.

'I think we learned something about ourselves against Toulouse – we *can* handle pressure and it can make us a better team. But remember something – we've still won absolutely nothing. That was a brilliant performance, but it won't be good enough to beat Harlequins. Because to win trophies, as Munster have demonstrated, you need to improve with every match. Let's go to the video room.'

I looked at Leo Cullen.

'The video room?' I said. 'What are we watching? I hope it's one of the *Avengers* movies!'

Leo laughed.

'I think this video is going to be about villains more than heroes,' he said.

A few minutes later, I found out what he was talking about. It wasn't one of the *Avengers* movies. It was a video of our match against Toulouse – with all of the good bits edited out.

Joe had decided to make regular video analysis sessions part of our preparation for matches. Except he didn't see any point in rewatching all of the things we got right. As he saw it, we could do that on our own time. He wanted to show us the mistakes we'd made. Which seemed a bit harsh to me. The match was finished. We'd won. We were in the last eight of the European Cup. What was the point in reliving the mistakes we made along the way?

We all squeezed into the room where Joe had decided to show us clips of all our howlers.

'Video nasties,' Malcolm O'Kelly called them.

And the first – oh, no! – was one of mine. I recognized it straight away. I had thrown a wide pass to BOD, but I knew from the moment the ball left my hands that it was a bad one. The nose of the ball was facing downwards, which was why it ended up around BOD's bootlaces. I'd seen BOD catch bad passes many times before, but this time I hadn't given him much of a chance and he'd knocked it on. I waited for Joe to tell me that my passes needed to be better. But he didn't. He looked at BOD and he said:

'The good players catch those.'

I decided to hold my hands up.

'It *was* a terrible pass,' I said.

But Joe was letting us know that no one – not even our best player – was above criticism. In fact, the better the player, the more was expected of him.

'The pass needed to be better,' Joe agreed, 'but those passes – the bad ones – still need to be caught. So what are we going to do about it?'

'Practise it,' I said, 'in the New Year.'

'When?' Joe asked.

'Er, the New Year?' I said.

Bear in mind, it was just a week to go until Christmas and we didn't have another match for ages.

'How about now?' Joe said.

'Now?' I asked.

'I want all the backs to go outside and do the passing drill I showed you before.'

This was a drill the All Blacks used to do. We had to run the length of the field, passing the ball quickly between us, first from left to right. Then, when we reached one twenty-two-metre line, we'd switch the direction from right to left. Then, when we reached the halfway line, we'd switch the direction again. Then, when we reached the second twenty-two-metre line, we'd switch direction one last time. It was very difficult to do, because players run and pass the ball at different speeds. The idea behind the exercise was the more you practise, the more familiar the action becomes. And the rule was that you had to play thirty successful passes in a row before you could stop for the night.

'That's it,' Bully said, 'I'm going home.'

'But we haven't done it yet,' BOD argued.

'Joe won't know.'

'But *we'll* know,' I said.

This was what Joe meant when he said that a good

culture was one where the players, not the coach, enforce the standards.

'Darce is right,' said Chris Whitaker. 'We should keep doing it until we pass the ball thirty times in a row. Even if we're here till three o'clock in the morning.'

'Then you stop playing me bad passes,' Bully said.

'I think the point of this drill,' BOD said, 'is that we don't become frustrated and annoyed with each other. It's about working together to solve the problem.'

It took us two whole hours, but we finally managed to make it from one end of the pitch to the other in thirty inch-perfect passes. But Bully was furious with me for contradicting him. He thought I'd made him look small in front of the others.

When I got back to the dressing-room, he had already changed back into his clothes. I could see that he was struggling – with his ageing body, with the threat to his place, with the changes that were happening all around him. So I tried to be nice to him.

I stuck out my hand and I said, 'Merry Christmas, Bully.'

But he refused to shake my hand.

Instead, he reached into his kitbag and he took out Mum's Walkman. Then I watched in horror as he let it drop onto the tiled floor!

And then he stepped on it!

I heard the sound of plastic cracking and in that moment my heart broke. Mum's Walkman cracked under his foot.

'That's what I'm going to do to you after Christmas,' he said.

28 *My Algebra Nightmare*

'What is 2a plus 2b divided by 2c?'

Mr Rowland was being especially boring that afternoon. The last day before the school holidays always dragged by. But he was trying to teach us something called algebra and I couldn't stop myself from yawning.

'Are we keeping you awake, Miiissstttteeerrr D'Aaarrrccccyyy?' he asked.

'Er, sorry?' I said.

'I think you mean, "Sorry, *Sir*!" Perhaps *you* can answer my question, then? What is 2a plus 2b divided by 2c?'

What in the name of God was he talking about? Was he seriously asking me to add and divide letters? I looked around me, wondering did anyone else consider this the most ridiculous question they'd ever heard.

'There's no point in doing that,' Mr Rowland said. 'The answer isn't over your shoulder. I'm going to ask you one more time. What is 2a plus 2b divided by 2c?'

I decided to take a guess.

'Is it twelve?' I asked.

Twelve was my shirt number against Toulouse. But I could tell from his reaction that it wasn't the answer he was looking for.

'Twelve?' he said. 'How on Earth did you come up with that answer?'

'Er, it was a guess?'

'A guess? Haven't you been listening to a single word I've been saying this afternoon?'

The truth was, I hadn't. I was thinking about getting home for the Christmas holidays. I was also thinking about Mum's Walkman. Not only was the cover broken, but it now played Garth Brooks at such a slow speed that it sounded like whalesong:

'Iiifff tooommmooorrrooowww neeeveeerrr cooo mmmeeeesss . . .'

I hoped Mr Rowland would grow bored of asking me for the answer and move on to somebody else. But he didn't.

'Do you even know the answer to the *first* part of the equation?' he asked. 'What is 2a plus 2b?'

'What is 2a plus 2b?' I repeated.

There were titters from the other boys. I was thinking, am I the only one here who doesn't know the answer?

'Come on, figure it out,' said Mr Rowland. 'What is 2a plus 2b?'

'Em, I don't know how to add letters,' I said. 'I only know how to add numbers.'

There was loud laughter in the classroom. Mr Rowland silenced it with an angry look.

'We've been doing algebra for a week now,' he said.

This came as news to me.

Luckily, the bell went, saving me from any more embarrassment.

As we left the school, some of the other boys were patting me on the back and saying, 'That was hilarious, Darce!' and 'I don't know how to add letters – brilliant!'

I laughed along with them and pretended it had all been a big joke.

Then I went back to the dormitory with Conor and Peter and we packed our things, excited about going home for the Christmas holidays.

'What is 2a plus 2b?' I said mockingly as I stuffed some clothes into my bag. 'I put him in his place, didn't I?'

But neither Conor nor Peter seemed to find it as funny as the rest of the boys.

'When is the next bus to Wexford?' I asked.

'Ten minutes,' Conor said.

'We'll have to run if we're going to catch it.'

I noticed Peter and Conor exchange a look.

'Gordon,' Peter said, 'did you *really* not know the answer to the question?'

'Of course I didn't,' I said. 'He was asking me to add letters.'

'But that's what algebra is,' he told me.

'But what's the point of it?' I snapped back. 'I'm not going to need to know how to do that, am I? Do you honestly think that's going to come up after we leave school?'

'He's only trying to help you,' Conor said. 'You've been falling behind in *all* your classes.'

He was right. In every single class, teachers were talking about subjects we'd apparently been covering for weeks – except I had no memory of any of it. I hadn't been listening. I'd been drifting off into my own little world, thinking about . . .

What *had* I been thinking about?

Rugby, probably. The excitement of playing for a new team. Messing up against Toulouse. The business with Bully. Trying to fit in with a new group of teammates. The pressure of not wanting to disappoint the Leinster fans again. I hadn't realized how much space it had taken up in my head.

'It's just that Mr Cuffe gave you that warning,' Conor reminded me, 'that if you didn't keep up with your schoolwork, he'd stop you playing rugby altogether. And things are going so well for you with Leinster.'

'If you need any help with any of your subjects,' Peter said, 'I'd be more than happy to give you grinds.'

'I'm fine,' I told him.

I wasn't, of course. But it was typical of me that I would end up having to learn the hard way.

29 A Christmas Miracle

I arrived back in Wexford for Christmas to a big surprise.

Well, *several* big surprises, it turned out.

The framed photo on the sideboard of Dad with Peter Stringer, holding the European Cup, was gone. And so was the one of him with Paul O'Connell and Donncha O'Callaghan, where Donncha is giving him rabbit ears. The one of him in his Munster jersey with his arm around Ronan O'Gara had been replaced with a selfie of him and Joe Schmidt taken in the kitchen.

But the biggest surprise of all was that Dad was drinking his tea out of a Leinster mug.

'Where did you get that?' I asked.

'What, this old thing?' he said. 'I've had this for years.'

'No, you haven't,' I said. 'It looks brand new. You always drank your tea out of a Munster mug!'

'A Munster mug?' he said, all innocence. 'But we *live* in Leinster.'

'I'm not going to argue with you,' I told him. 'I'm just glad you've been converted.'

Mum took my clothes out of my bag to do my laundry. She found her broken Walkman.

'What happened to it?' she asked.

'I, em, dropped it,' I told her.

'Oh, Garth!' she cried as she put the headphones on and listened to the whalesong version of 'Friends in Low Places'. 'Oh, Garth, I'll never forget you!'

On Christmas Eve, I managed to find a shop in a little backstreet in Wexford Town that sold Walkmans. And I used some of the money I'd saved during my time in McWonderburger to buy one for her. She was thrilled when I presented it to her on Christmas morning.

'Garth is back!' she kept saying, listening to her favourite songs on repeat while practising her line-dancing in the kitchen. 'It's a Christmas miracle!'

I called to see Conor on St Stephen's Day. I couldn't believe what he was wearing. No, it wasn't a really embarrassing Christmas jumper with a reindeer, or a snowman, or Santa Claus, on the front.

It was a Leinster jersey.

I couldn't help but laugh.

'Conor,' I said, 'what is *that*?'

'This?' he said. 'It was a Christmas present.'

'It's a Leinster rugby jersey.'

'I know it's a Leinster rugby jersey.'

'And why are you wearing a Leinster rugby jersey?'

'Because I'm *from* Leinster, Gordon.'

'Oh my God, you're worse than my dad.'

'What do you mean?'

'You *were* a Munster fan – just like him.'

'Well, now I'm a Munster *and* a Leinster fan.'

'Since when?'

'Since you started playing for them. And since they started doing well.'

'Don't worry, Conor, there's plenty of room on the bandwagon.'

It felt good that people were finally sitting up and taking notice of what we were doing. And supporting *their* team.

While I enjoyed being home for Christmas, I couldn't wait to go back to training again in the New Year. Joe Schmidt was one of the wisest men I'd ever met and I had learned so much from him in just a few weeks.

We were two matches away from reaching the European Cup final. And, while I was trying my best not to think that far ahead, it was difficult not to get excited about what the New Year might bring.

The holidays eventually ended, and I was back at the bus station in Wexford Town, waiting to board the coach to Kildare.

Conor was getting a lift because he was still wearing his plaster cast and because Hughie had banned him from his bus for the rest of his natural life. Peter had gone away with his family for New Year's and wouldn't be arriving back to school for a few more days.

So I climbed onto the Kildare bus alone. I couldn't help but notice that Hughie had a giant sticker saying 'LEINSTER!' across the top of his windscreen.

That was certainly new.

'Where's your friend today?' he said.

'My friend?' I asked.

'That Conor Kehoe,' he said. 'The little pup!'

'Oh, his dad is dropping him to school,' I told him. 'He broke his leg a few months ago.'

'Well, just as long as he knows that he'll never get on board this bus again – him and his harmonica!'

I made my way down the aisle towards the back of

the bus. That was when I spotted Aoife being dropped off at the bus station by her mum. It seemed to me that she was acting a little shiftily. She was trying to get rid of her mum, insisting that she leave – and when she did, Aoife started looking over her shoulder to make sure that no one was watching her.

She started walking towards the Kildare bus. But when she reached the door, she didn't get on board. She kept on walking. And then she climbed onto the next bus.

It was the bus to Dublin!

I had to find out what was going on, so I picked up my bag and I got off the bus.

'Where are you going?' Hughie shouted after me. 'I'm leaving in sixty seconds – with or without you.'

I ignored him. I climbed onto the Dublin bus. It was packed with people. Aoife didn't notice me as I walked down the aisle towards her. She was reading something. I sat down beside her.

'You know you're on the wrong bus?' I said.

She looked up. I'd given her a fright.

'Oh, it's you,' she said. 'What are you doing on this bus?'

'I was going to ask you the same question,' I told her.

'I'm going to Dublin.'

'Why? You're not moving schools, are you?'

'No,' she said. 'I got this in the post before Christmas.'

She handed me a letter. The logo at the top said it was from the Irish Schoolgirls Rugby Federation.

'Can I read it?' I asked.

'Be my guest,' she said.

So I read it:

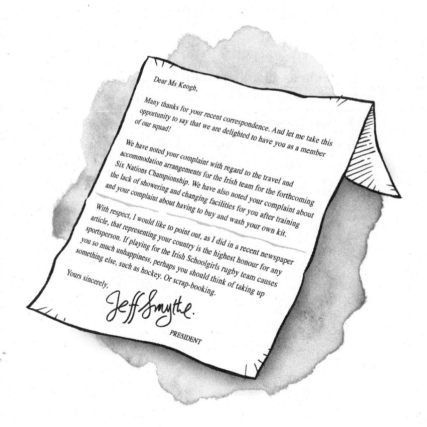

Dear Ms Keogh,

Many thanks for your recent correspondence. And let me take this opportunity to say that we are delighted to have you as a member of our squad!

We have noted your complaint with regard to the travel and accommodation arrangements for the Irish team for the forthcoming Six Nations Championship. We have also noted your complaint about the lack of showering and changing facilities for you after training and your complaint about having to buy and wash your own kit.

With respect, I would like to point out, as I did in a recent newspaper article, that representing your country is the highest honour for any sportsperson. If playing for the Irish Schoolgirls rugby team causes you so much unhappiness, perhaps you should think of taking up something else, such as hockey. Or scrap-booking.

Yours sincerely,

Jeff Smythe.

PRESIDENT

'He, er, spelt your name wrong,' I said.

'I know he spelt my name wrong,' she said, snatching the letter back from me.

'Oh my God,' I said, 'what a –'

And then – yes – it's possible that I may have used a bad word.

'Sorry for swearing,' I said.

'Oh, don't worry,' Aoife replied. 'I called him the same name, and lots of other names, when I read the letter.'

'So what are you going to do?'

'I'm going to go and *see* him.'

'What? Seriously?'

'The address is there. It's on Fitzwilliam Square. You better get off this bus or you'll –'

It was too late. I watched the Kildare bus pull out of its berth next to us with a flustered-looking Hughie at the wheel.

'It looks like I'm coming with you,' I said.

'Come if you want,' she said. 'Let's see what this Jeff Smythe person has to say for himself.'

I had to admit, I already felt sorry for the man.

30 *Jeff Smythe Meets His Match*

We eventually reached Dublin. The offices of the Irish Schoolgirls Rugby Federation were just a short walk from the bus stop.

I had to run to keep up with the length of Aoife's stride.

'Are you sure you should be doing this?' I asked her.

'What do you mean?' she said, her bag slung over her shoulder. 'You read the letter.'

'What I mean is, why are you taking this on yourself?' I asked.

'Because I'm the captain,' she said.

'But what about the other girls? How do they feel about the way they're being treated?'

'The same – presumably.'

'You mean you haven't spoken to them about it?'

'I don't need to. I can handle it myself.'

'I'm just saying, Aoife, this isn't what teamwork looks like.'

'You've won, what, one match with Leinster – and suddenly you're an expert on teamwork?'

'I'm just worried that you're maybe taking on too much. It's a lot of weight for one person to carry.'

'I'm well capable of carrying it, thank you.'

We found the building – a four-storey Georgian house on Fitzwilliam Square. Aoife didn't hesitate. She took the steps two at a time and pushed the heavy front door. I followed closely behind her.

A receptionist smiled at us from behind a desk.

'And how might I help you, young lady?' the woman said.

'I want to talk to your boss,' Aoife said, marching straight past her towards a door with the words *Jeff Smythe* on it.

'You can't go in there,' the receptionist said. 'Mr Smythe is very, very busy.'

Aoife pushed the door anyway. Mr Smythe was sitting behind a desk.

And he was fast asleep!

'Very busy?' Aoife said, looking at the receptionist with one eyebrow raised.

'Mr Smythe likes his morning nap,' the woman said, 'especially when he's eaten a big breakfast.'

Aoife slammed her bag down on his desk.

'WAKE UP!' she shouted.

The man woke with a jolt. He must have still been dreaming because he said:

'Waiter, I'll have another bottle of the Bordeaux.'

But then his eyes slowly adjusted to his surroundings and he realized he wasn't in his favourite restaurant after all. He looked at me.

'You're Gordon D'Arcy!' he said.

'Er, yeah, I am.'

'And *I'm* Aoife Kehoe!' Aoife said.

'Who?' he asked.

He really wasn't helping himself.

'AOIFE KEHOE!' she bellowed at him, then she spelled it out for him, correctly. 'K, E, H, O, E. I'm the captain of the Ireland Schoolgirls rugby team.'

Jeff looked at the receptionist.

'Susan,' he said, 'I didn't have any appointments in the diary for this morning, did I?'

'No,' Susan told him. 'They just walked straight past me.'

Aoife produced the letter.

'I wanted to talk to you about *this*!' she said.

'What is it?' he asked.

'It's a letter – you sent it to me before Christmas.'

'Ahhhhhh,' he said, the penny finally dropping, *'you're* the girl who wrote to me with a list of demands as long as my arm. You want us to build you dressing-rooms and put you up in hotels and all sorts. Well, I think I explained the Federation's position more than adequately in my letter.'

He turned to me then.

'So, Gordon,' he said, 'do you think this is going to be Leinster's year? Harlequins are going to be a tough team to beat.'

'Excuse me,' Aoife said, 'I haven't finished talking to you yet. As a matter of fact, I haven't even started. But you *are* going to listen to what I have to say.'

Jeff Smythe rolled his eyes, then he said: 'Fine, I'll hear what you have to say.'

'I play rugby for Ireland.'

'Yes, I'm well aware of that.'

'Just like Ronan O'Gara plays rugby for Ireland. Just like Brian O'Driscoll plays rugby for Ireland. Just like Gordon here plays rugby for Ireland.'

'I'm not sure it's the *same* thing – but continue.'

'When they play in the Six Nations, they're not asked to pay for the jerseys they wear. They're not expected to pay for their flights to Paris, or to London, or to Cardiff, or to Edinburgh, or to Rome. They're not handed a hotel bill and told, "Thanks for representing Ireland – the room comes to seven hundred euros." They don't have to get changed in a car and go home from training without having had a shower.'

'But you're not comparing like with like.'

'The Irish Schoolboys team are playing in their Six Nations next month. Their flights and hotels are paid for by their Federation. They don't have to pay for their own jerseys – and, by the way, they don't have to wash them themselves either. When they train, they have access to dressing-rooms and showers.'

'You can't compare the two.'

'Why not?'

'Because, well, they're –'

'What? Boys?'

'Well, yes. And you're –'

'Girls?'

'That's right.'

'We train just as hard as any man or boy. When we play a match, we put our bodies on the line just the same as any man or boy. Why should I be treated any differently?'

Jeff Smythe chuckled to himself, then he looked over Aoife's shoulder at Susan.

'Have you ever heard the likes of it?' he said.

Without warning, Aoife unzipped her bag and turned it upside-down, emptying a big pile of mucky jerseys, shorts and socks onto his clean desk.

'What are you doing?' he said.

'This is the kit we trained in before Christmas,' she said. 'I told the other girls to give it to me. I told them they'd done their own laundry for the very last time.'

Jeff Smythe held his nose. The kit had been stuffed into the bag for the best part of a month and it stank!

'Fine,' he said, 'we'll look after your kit. We'll provide you with jerseys, shorts and socks for training and for matches – and I think we could probably stretch to having them washed as well. But that's all.'

He swept the dirty laundry off his desk and onto the floor.

'That's not all,' Aoife told him. 'When we play for Ireland, I want *all* of our travel expenses to be covered.'

'Susan,' Mr Smythe said, 'can you show this girl out, please?'

But it was clear from Susan's expression that she wasn't on his side any more.

'No,' Susan told him, 'I think you should hear what she has to say.'

'But we don't have the money to meet all these *demands*,' he insisted.

'Yes, we do,' Susan told him. 'I know what's in the Federation's bank account, remember?'

Jeff Smythe breathed a deep sigh, then he said, 'I've shown myself to be more than reasonable.'

'Unless you agree to this,' Aoife said, 'the next thing I drop on your desk will be a petition. I'm going to stand outside the stadium the next time the Ireland men's team are playing and I'm going to ask

EVERYONE to support equal rights for women rugby players. Gordon, you'd sign it, wouldn't you?'

'I'd be honoured to sign it,' I said. 'And I'll pass it around the Leinster dressing-room. I could even ask Joe Schmidt to sign it.'

Jeff Smythe breathed another deep sigh.

'Okay,' he said, 'we'll cover the cost of your flights to Paris and London. But just your flights.'

'No,' Aoife told him, 'you'll also cover our hotel accommodation.'

'Well, just try to keep the bills down, will you?' he said. 'No room service. Or nuts from the minibar. We're not made of money. Now, I think I've done enough compromising for one day.'

'No,' Aoife said, 'you haven't. We still have no dressing-rooms or showers.'

'We're not going to build you dressing-rooms with showers!' he said.

'I'm not asking you to,' she told him. 'In future, I want us to train and play all of our home matches . . . in Donnybrook Stadium.'

'What?' he said.

'Donnybrook Stadium!' Aoife repeated.

'But the Ireland Schoolgirls team couldn't fill a corner of that stadium.'

'We could if you told people that we're playing. You never publicize our matches.'

'Donnybrook Stadium! I can't possibly agree to that!'

'Gordon, do you really think Joe Schmidt would sign my petition?'

Jeff Smythe raised his hands in a gesture of surrender.

'Fine, fine, fine!' he said. 'We'll fly you to away matches, put you up in hotels, pay for your kit to be laundered, publicize your results and your upcoming fixtures and move all of your matches to Donnybrook Stadium. Is that everything?'

'No,' said Susan, 'I would like a pay rise.'

'Give her a pay rise,' Aoife said.

'Otherwise,' Susan said, 'I quit.'

'Okay, okay, okay,' he told her, 'you can have your pay rise. You can have whatever you want. Just, please, leave my office – and let me go back to sleep.'

Susan smiled at Aoife.

'You know,' she said, 'those girls are lucky to have a captain like you.'

And she was right. It's one thing to put yourself on the line on the pitch, but to do it out there in the real world takes character and courage.

I was so proud to be Aoife's friend.

31 *A Bully Beaten*

'I hope you all had a good Christmas,' Joe Schmidt said, 'and that you're looking forward to getting back to work.'

We were sitting around in the kitchen area next to the dressing-room, having a cup of coffee, trying to warm ourselves up before we started training. The thought of the quarter-final against Harlequins had us all buzzing with excitement.

'I want to introduce you to someone,' Joe said – and suddenly I noticed a man standing behind him. It would have been difficult not to notice him. He was the tallest man any of us had ever seen.

'Guys,' Joe said, 'I want you to meet Rocky Elsom.'

'How are you going, boys?' Rocky asked.

It was clear from his accent that he was from Australia.

'I mentioned to you that I was going to be bringing in a few new faces,' Joe said. 'Rocky is a blindside flanker. I think he could offer us something a little extra against Harlequins.'

Before Joe had a chance to explain what that might be, Rocky walked over to the stove, picked up the coffee pot, which was full of boiling hot coffee, and drank the entire thing down in one go.

Do NOT try that at home, by the way – you will burn your throat very badly.

But I suspected that the 'something extra' that Rocky was bringing was that he was as hard as nails.

We all shook hands with him and welcomed him to the squad.

A short time later, we went outside to train.

It was a freezing cold January night – one of those nights when you could see your breath appear as fog in front of your face. The thing I loved about that kind of weather was that you had to keep moving to stop your joints from freezing.

Bully made a big point of ignoring me and as usual he didn't shake my hand at the start of the session. I didn't make an issue out of it.

Joe wanted us to work on match preparation. And, with that in mind, he had come up with a variation on the game of Sevens that he wanted us to play. It was called Never Ending Defence. He split us into two teams of five. Then there were two players who were called Floaters – they played for whichever team happened to be defending. The attacking team kept the ball until they either scored or made a mistake, then the possession would swap over to the other team, and so would the two Floaters. It meant there were always five players trying to get past seven defenders. It was Joe's way of preparing us for a really tight match against a team who would defend like their lives depended on it.

The only problem with Never Ending Defence is that it's exhausting. You're either attacking in a five-against-seven situation, or you're giving everything you've got to try to stop the other team scoring a try. There is never a moment when you can rest.

And Joe made sure of that.

After an hour, some of the players were complaining they were tired.

'It's okay to be tired,' Joe said. 'I expect you to be tired if you're working hard. But never let the opposition see that you're tired. Never show weakness. If you're tired, stand up tall with your shoulders back and fake it until you get your breath back. You'll keep playing until I blow this whistle.'

Rocky was putting us all to shame. He was one of

the two Floaters. And it was clear from the effort he was still putting in that he was a man who hated losing more than he enjoyed winning.

Joe realized that we needed more people like that.

My legs were beginning to feel really heavy. We'd been playing for an hour – twenty minutes longer than the length of each half in a match situation. And this was far more intense because there were no breaks in play.

I was on the attacking team when Shaggy threw the ball blindly over his shoulder, somehow knowing that I was going to be there. I caught it, wrong-footed BOD and headed for the line with the ball tucked under my arm. Bully was on the opposition. I tried to sell him a dummy, but he didn't buy it. He tackled me low and front-on – perfectly legally, but he hit me so hard, I felt my back teeth vibrate in their sockets!

My back hit the hard ground and I was winded for about thirty seconds.

I didn't mind the tackle so much. Once I got my breath back, I was fine to carry on. What I didn't like was that Bully didn't help me up. It was one of Joe's rules that if you tackled one of your teammates in training, you were supposed to offer him a hand-up afterwards.

'Maaate?' Rocky said to him. 'You're supposed to pick him up. He's your teammate.'

But Bully just ignored him.

I was mad as hell. And then I remembered Aoife fighting her corner in Fitzwilliam Square that afternoon. And she inspired me to do what I did next.

The next time Bully had the ball in his hands, I ran straight at him. He saw me coming, but I covered the ground between us quicker than he expected and before he knew what was happening . . .

BANG!

I threw my arms around his waist, stopping him dead in his tracks, then I lifted him clean off the ground and started running backwards with him. He held onto the ball, but I carried him about twenty yards before depositing him on the flat of his back.

'Great tackle!' Rocky shouted. 'What a hit!'

But Bully wasn't happy at being shown up like that. He jumped to his feet and he roared:

'That was a foul!'

'It was a fair tackle,' Joe told him. 'It was no foul, Bully.'

Bully stared at me and I stared back at him, just to let him know that I wasn't frightened of him.

Joe instructed us to shake hands.

'Make up, fellas,' he said. 'It how we do things, remember? It's The Leinster Way.'

I stuck out my hand.

'I'm not shaking his hand,' Bully insisted.

'Bully,' Joe said, 'I told you how things were going to be from now on. We settle our disputes and we move on together as a team.'

'I'm not shaking his hand,' Bully repeated.

'Bully, you're making this decision for yourself,' Joe told him. 'I've asked everyone to make sacrifices for the team. One of them is that we respect each other. If you can't shake Darce's hand, or anyone else's for that matter, whatever your difference, then you can't be a part of this team.'

'What, you'll drop me just for not shaking his hand?' Bully said.

'In case the message hasn't reached you yet,' Joe said, 'no one is bigger than the team.'

But Bully's pride wouldn't allow him to back down in front of the squad.

'Right,' he said. 'Goodbye and good riddance.'

Bully turned and walked back in the direction of the dressing-room. And I knew, to my great relief, that it would be the last time I ever saw him.

32 *Trust Issues*

I'd been back at school for a couple of weeks. I was in the cafeteria one morning, standing in the breakfast queue, trying to remember what class I had first that morning.

I thought it might have been Maths – or maybe even Science.

And that was when I heard my name called. The version of my name that told me instantly that I was in trouble.

'MIIISSSTTTEEERRR D'AAARRRCCCY YY!!!'

I turned around. Oh, no, I thought. It was Mr Cuffe.

'Come with me,' he said.

I followed him out of the cafeteria to his office,

knowing that I was in some kind of trouble. He sat down in his chair with his elbows on the desk, making a steeple out of his index fingers.

'Mr Trent told you to come and see me before Christmas,' he said, 'and you didn't.'

'Errr,' I stuttered, trying to come up with an excuse quickly.

'There's no use trying to deny it, Miiissstteeerrr D'Aaarrrccccyyy. I know everything. I have in front of me the results of your Christmas tests.'

I noticed a small stack of A4 pages on the desk in front of him. He went through them one by one, telling me my marks for each subject.

'History,' he said. 'Five!'

'Five?' I said. 'That's not too bad.'

'That's out of one hundred, Miiissstteeerrr D'Arrrccccyyy.'

'Okay, that *is* bad.'

'Geography. Two!'

'Is that out of –'

'Yes, it's out of one hundred. They're *all* out of one hundred.'

'Fair enough.'

'Maths. Three. Science. Seven. English. Six. Irish. Two. French. Four.'

He put down the pages.

'Need I go on?' he asked, looking at me over the top of his glasses.

'No, Mr Cuffe,' I said.

'Your schoolwork is not of a standard that I consider acceptable. Do you understand me?'

'Yes, Mr Cuffe.'

'Your teachers inform me that you continue to be non-attentive in class.'

'Non what?'

'It means you don't listen, Miiisssttteeerrrr D'Aaarrrcccyyy. You daydream your way through the day – no doubt thinking about rugby.'

'That's not true.'

It *was* true. It was completely true.

'You'll remember our conversation before Christmas,' he said, 'when I told you in no uncertain terms that unless I saw a marked improvement in your attitude towards your schoolwork, there would be no rugby for you?'

'Mr Cuffe, please,' I begged, 'I'm doing really well for Leinster. We're two matches away from playing in the European Cup final.'

'I'm sorry, Miiisssttteeerrr D'Aaarrrcccyyy, you *were* warned. I'm going to speak to your parents and apprise them of the situation. I told you that this school is very proud of all your achievements on the rugby field – but you are here, first and foremost, to learn.'

'I will learn,' I promised.

'It's too late.'

'Please,' I said, suddenly bursting into tears. 'Don't take away my rugby. It's the most important thing in the world to me.'

'You have left me with no choice,' he said.

'Just give me one more chance,' I begged him. 'I'll knuckle down and I'll do my schoolwork.'

At that moment, there was a knock on the door. Mr Murray stuck his head around it.

'I'm sorry, Mr Cuffe,' he said, 'I just got your message.'

Mr Cuffe stood up.

'What we feared has come to pass,' he said, pacing the floor. 'Young Miiissstteeeerrr D'Aaarrrcccyyy's schoolwork has deteriorated to such a degree that he might as well not be here at all.'

Mr Murray looked at me.

'Is this true, Gordon?' he asked.

I couldn't lie.

'Yes, Mr Murray,' I said, unable to even look at him.

I felt like I'd let him down badly.

'Gordon,' he said, 'you were warned about this.

It's not fair that all of the other boys have to work hard at their schoolwork and you don't.'

'I will,' I told him. 'I promise this time.'

'You promised last time as well,' said Mr Cuffe, picking up the phone. 'I've heard just about all I want to hear from you on the subject. I'm phoning your parents and then I'm phoning this Joe Schmidt person.'

'Wait,' Mr Murray said.

'Wait?' Mr Cuffe asked. 'What am I waiting for?'

'Just put down the receiver for a second, Mr Cuffe. Gordon, will you make me a promise that you'll knuckle down this time?'

'I will,' I told him, bawling my eyes out. 'I'll stay up all night studying if I have to.'

'No one is asking you to do that,' he said. 'We're just asking you to take your schoolwork seriously.'

'I will. I promise.'

'Promise is just a word, Gordon,' said Mr Murray. 'I'm sure you don't promise Joe Schmidt that you'll do things and then fail to deliver, do you?'

'No,' I said.

'Because he'd drop you from the team, wouldn't he?'

'I suppose he would.'

'From what I've read in the newspapers, Joe is a

big believer in values. He believes that if you don't work hard and show discipline, you're showing disrespect to your teammates. And he trusts the players to take it upon themselves to do the right thing.'

'Yes, Mr Murray.'

'So why don't we do something similar here?' he said, turning to Mr Cuffe.

'What are you talking about?' Mr Cuffe asked.

'Well, I think Gordon understands now that to ignore his schoolwork is to show disrespect to his classmates and his teachers. But what if we tell him that we trust him to put it right?'

'Personally,' Mr Cuffe said, 'I'm against giving the boy any more chances. But I like to think of myself as a fair man. So this is the deal I'm going to offer you, Miiissstttteeerrr D'Aaarrrcccyyy. The Easter exams are exactly ten weeks away. If you don't pass them, then you will not be permitted to play rugby for Leinster, or anyone else for that matter, ever again.'

'Your very last warning,' said Mr Murray. 'We're putting our trust in you.'

'Thank you,' I said. 'I won't let you down.'

I left Mr Cuffe's office in a daze. I didn't know what I was going to do. The exams were due to take place at Easter – just after the semi-final of the European Cup. The results would be coming out three days before the final. If Leinster made it that far, I wouldn't be allowed to play in it unless I passed my exams.

And, to be totally honest, there was very little chance of that happening. I couldn't possibly learn enough about each of my subjects – not in ten weeks anyway.

I walked to the Maths room. It was empty. Then I realized it must be Science this morning after all. Which shows you how interested I was in what was going on in school.

I walked into the Science lab. The class had already started. All of the other boys were wearing white lab coats. I apologized to the teacher, Mr Kavanagh, for being late, then I pulled on my own lab coat and sat down next to Peter.

He could see that I had been crying.

'Hey,' he whispered, 'what's wrong?'

And then I said what I would soon discover were the three most important words in the English language. Three words no one should EVER be too proud to say. Three words that, when strung together in this particular order, can act like a magic spell that will change your entire world. And the words I said were these:

'I need help.'

33 *Ten Weeks to Save Myself*

Peter sat me down at my study desk. There was a stack of books to my right and it was about two feet high.

'So,' he said, 'where do you want to start?'

'What do you mean?' I asked.

'Which subject do you want to start with? Maths? English? History? Geography? Irish? Science?'

'I don't know,' I told him. 'There's just so much that I have to learn. Look at all these books! How am I going to get all that information into my head?'

'By taking it one step at a time,' he said. 'Now, which subject do you *hate* the most?'

'Geography,' I said, without any hesitation. 'I really, really, really HATE Geography.'

'Okay,' he said, pulling a book from the top of the stack, 'let's start with Geography, then.'

That *wasn't* what I wanted to happen.

He opened the book and he put it down in front of me.

'Chapter One,' he said. 'The Water Cycle. How rain is formed. Let's start here.'

'Okay,' I said, wondering what was going to happen next. 'What do you want me to do?'

'Read it,' he said.

'Read it?'

'How are you going to learn it if you don't read it?'

'You don't understand, Peter. My problem is that

when I read something, it just refuses to go into my head.'

'Read it again, then.'

'What, twice?'

Conor laughed. He was lying on the bottom bunk, reading the script for his play, clearly amused by Peter's efforts to tutor me.

'How many times do you think I have to read my lines before I know them?' he asked.

'I don't know,' I said.

'Well, it's definitely not once, Gordon. Look, if Joe Schmidt told you that you had to improve on a particular skill – say, for example, passing off your left hand – how many times would you practise it?'

'I don't know,' I told him. 'As many times as I needed to.'

'You wouldn't just do it once and then say, "Hey, it didn't work. I'm not perfect at it – so I'm not going to bother"?'

'No, I'd keep on practising it until I got it right.'

'So why do you think studying is any different?'

I looked at Peter. He was nodding his head. I'd never thought about it in that way before.

'But I don't understand,' I said. 'Peter, you only have to read something once and you remember it forever. It goes into your head. With me, it doesn't. Lads, I'm stupid.'

'You're not stupid,' Peter said. 'Look, we all learn different things at different rates. It's like Conor said, there might be a particular rugby skill that you have to practise fifty times before you get it right. But it could take me five hundred times to perfect. Or it could take Conor five thousand times.'

'Unlikely,' Conor said. 'I'd definitely pick it up quicker than you, Peter.'

'The point I'm trying to make,' Peter said, 'is that the end result is the same – we are all capable of learning the skill. It's just that some of us will have to work on it harder and longer than others.'

I was looking at Peter, aghast.

'You're not telling me,' I said, 'that I might have to read this chapter five thousand times, are you?'

He laughed.

'Why don't you start by reading it once,' he said, 'and we'll see where it goes from there?'

And so that's what I did. I read the chapter entitled 'The Water Cycle'. And when I finished reading the twenty pages, I went back to the start and I read them again. And when I finished reading the twenty pages for a second time, I went back to the start and I read them again. It was far from riveting. But I read it all the same. And by the end of it, I knew . . .

Absolutely nothing!

Seriously, I couldn't remember a single thing I'd learned from the hour I'd spent reading the chapter. I tried to explain this to Peter.

'Good work,' was all he said. 'Now, let's move on to Maths – because I know you hate that almost as much as Geography. Okay, algebra. Are you ready to find out the answer to the question: what is 2a plus 2b divided by 2c?'

I nodded. But, at the same time, I looked at the stack of books – and I thought about how little time I had. And I knew, deep down, that passing my exams was going to be virtually impossible.

34 *A Plan*

Without Bully around, the atmosphere at training changed completely. It felt like a weight had been lifted from my shoulders. And everybody else seemed to feel the same way. Nobody missed the dark shadow he cast over us all with his constant bad humour. The proof of that was that I never heard his name mentioned again.

At the same time, I didn't dare to think that the number twelve jersey was now mine. With Joe Schmidt, you couldn't take anything for granted.

It was a Thursday evening, three days before we played Harlequins in the quarter-final of the European Cup. We were sitting around the dressing-room in UCD, waiting to go outside to train. It was a freezing cold night and the rain was pouring down.

'I wonder does he have a plan?' I said.

'Who?' BOD asked.

'Joe,' I said. 'I wonder has he figured out how we can beat Harlequins.'

BOD laughed.

'This is Joe Schmidt we're talking about,' he said. 'He has a plan to beat any team in the world. The question is, can we, the players, execute that plan?'

'Where's Rocky?' Shaggy asked.

That was a good question. He wasn't in the dressing-room. As a matter of fact, I hadn't seen him since I'd arrived forty minutes ago.

'The last time *I* saw him,' Malcolm said, 'was about an hour ago when he said he was going into the cryogenic chamber to wake himself up.'

'Wake himself up?' Shaggy said.

'Yeah, like taking a cold shower in the morning.'

'But he couldn't have been in there for an hour,' I said.

I'd spent two minutes in there and I thought my body would never be warm again.

We all looked at each other with our mouths wide open. Then we ran in the direction of the cryogenic chamber.

The door of the chamber was closed. The room was full of freezing cold steam, which meant we couldn't see anything.

'Is he in there?' Shaggy asked.

'I can't see him,' I said.

Malcolm called his name: 'ROCKY? ROCKY? ROCKY?'

There was no response.

I asked the question that was on everyone's lips:

'You don't think he's –'

'No,' BOD said. 'No way.'

'It's minus 170 degrees Celsius in there,' I reminded him. 'There's no way anyone could survive for an hour in there.'

Suddenly, we heard the door open. And, through the freezing fog, a giant figure emerged. It was Rocky. He was whistling 'Waltzing Matilda' and acting like he'd just got out of the shower – a *hot* shower.

'How are you going, boys?' he said when he saw us all standing there with shocked looks on our faces. 'I'll tell you what, maaate – an hour in that thing would really wake you up before training!'

We all fell around laughing.

Joe called us outside.

The rain was still coming down in sheets and there was a cold wind blowing across the pitch that made you feel like the world was a cryogenic chamber.

'Tonight,' Joe said, 'I'm going to show you how we're going to beat Harlequins.'

'Please not another game of Never Ending Defence,' I heard Malcolm whisper.

'We're going to play another game of Never Ending Defence,' Joe said, 'but with a twist.'

'Is the twist going to be that it's a lot shorter?' Munch asked.

Joe laughed.

'The twist,' he said, 'is that the attacking team aren't going to run with the ball. They're going to kick it – and they're going to contest in the air.'

'No running at all?' I asked.

Running with the ball and passing were my strengths as a player.

'It's not going to be that kind of game against Harlequins,' he said. 'The team that wins on Saturday will be the team that's best at the kick, the chase and the follow-up hit.'

So he divided us into teams. The Floaters were Felipe and Rocky. They played with whichever team was attacking, so that it was always five players trying to stop seven players from scoring. Felipe would kick the ball long, usually into the corners. The attacking team would chase the ball and then contest it.

'And remember,' Joe said, 'the game isn't over until I've blown this whistle.'

270

Felipe kicked the ball deep into the opposition half. I hared after it, along with Rocky and Jamie Heaslip. Rob Kearney rose like a salmon leaping to catch it perfectly. And, just as his feet hit the ground again, I tackled him around the waist, then Rocky and Jamie arrived to help me drive him back.

'That's it, guys!' Joe said. '*That* is how we're going to beat Harlequins!'

35 *In Our Own Hands*

We were sitting on the big, blue Leinster team bus on our way to Dublin Airport. It felt strange. It wasn't like being on the Ireland bus, when people stopped, and clapped, and waved, and gave us a thumbs-up. No one really paid the slightest bit of attention to us as we drove past.

Plus, I couldn't help but notice that there were a lot of people walking around the streets in red jerseys. Munster had beaten Perpignan in the first quarter-final the night before. It seemed that the Lunster fans were out in force.

I was sitting next to Leo Cullen.

'There can't be *that* many Munster supporters living in Dublin,' I said. 'Where are all the Leinster jerseys? We're playing in a European Cup quarter-final in ten hours and I haven't seen one.'

'We haven't earned it yet,' he said.

'Earned what?' I asked.

'The people's love,' he said. 'The people's respect. All they know about us is that we win a lot of big matches, then we collapse once the pressure comes on. Honestly, I'm not sure if I'd be a Leinster fan if I didn't play for them.'

'But we're a different team now,' I tried to remind him.

'Are we?' he asked. 'We haven't proven that yet. So we beat Toulouse. That's all. We still haven't won anything.'

'So what do we have to do for the people to respect us?' I said. 'Beat Munster?'

Leo looked over his shoulder, then he said, 'Don't let Joe catch you talking about Munster.'

'Why not?' I asked.

'Because he'll say that's typical of us,' he said, 'getting ahead of ourselves. Thinking about the semi-final when we're not even in it. And he'd be right. If you have one eye on the semi-final, then your head isn't in *this* game. That's one of the reasons we've lost so many of these tight matches – not focusing on the job in hand.'

It was impossible not to be inspired by Leo's passion.

'We have a massive battle on our hands tomorrow,' he said. 'We have to beat Harlequins in their own ground – in front of their own fans.'

'It's going to be a tough match,' I agreed.

'It's not going to be a tough match,' Leo said, staring out the window. 'It's going to be a war.'

I felt my stomach muscles tighten. That usually happens at some point before every big match. It's the moment you realize the size of the task you're facing and what's at stake. Sometimes it happens when you're in the dressing-room beforehand. Sometimes it happens when you walk out onto the field. Sometimes it doesn't happen at all – and those are usually the days when you underperform.

With Harlequins, it happened on the morning of the day of the match, while we were still on the M1 in Dublin.

We finally reached the airport. We pulled up outside and Johnny O'Hagan, our kitman, started pulling all of our training equipment from the belly of the bus. I watched Rocky walk over and start helping him. Seeing this, I decided that I should probably help as well. And so did BOD. And so did Munch. And so did Shaggy. And so did Malcolm.

As I was carrying a tackle bag into the terminal building, I noticed Joe standing off to one side, smiling to himself. This, I realized, was what he wanted all along. Players taking on responsibilities and others following their lead without needing to be told. Every single player carried a tackle bag, a sack of rugby balls or some other piece of training equipment into the airport.

It was a small thing, but it felt huge.

We checked in our bags, then we made our way up the escalator to the security screening area. As I was walking through the metal detector, I heard a little boy say to his father:

'Daddy, what team is that?'

And his father replied, 'I've no idea. I don't think they're anyone important.'

That really stung me.

BOD walked through the metal detector behind me.

'Did you hear that?' I asked him.

'He's not wrong,' Brian said. 'Until we actually win something, there's no reason for anyone to know who we are.'

As we were making our way towards the gate, I bumped into Dad and Ian. I was delighted. I had no idea they were travelling to England for the match.

'We were going to surprise you,' Dad said.

'You have,' I said. 'I can't believe you're coming to London.'

'Well,' Ian said, 'the surprises don't end there. Wait till you see this.'

He pulled open Dad's coat. And I could see that he was wearing a Leinster jersey.

I laughed.

'If only Donncha O'Callaghan and the rest of your Munster heroes could see you now,' Ian said.

'I've always had a soft spot for Leinster,' Dad said. 'And my youngest son is playing for them now. Sure, I'd have to wear a bit of blue, wouldn't I?'

'I'm glad to see you've been won over,' I said.

'Are you playing?' Dad asked me.

'I don't know,' I told him. 'Joe hasn't announced the team yet.'

'But I read that Graham Bull has gone from the squad. A disciplinary issue, according to the papers.'

'There are other players who are equally capable of filling in at twelve,' I said.

'Oh, well – fingers crossed, eh?'

A voice came over the P.A. system saying that the nine o'clock flight to Heathrow was now boarding and would all passengers please make their way to the gate.

'That's me,' I said.

'We're on the eleven o'clock,' Dad said. 'We might see you on the other side. Good luck tomorrow, son.'

'Yeah,' Ian added, 'don't get our hopes up and then let us down again!'

I said we'd do our best.

I boarded the flight along with the other players. I looked at my ticket. My seat was 22B. It was an aisle seat on the right-hand side of the plane. As I walked down the plane, I counted the seats ahead of me and I saw I would be sitting next to . . .

Felipe Contepomi.

Felipe wasn't one for deep, meaningful conversations.

Oh, well, I figured, at least I'd get some time to read. I took out the novel that we were supposed to be studying for English. It was called *Animal Farm* by George Orwell.

Felipe was lost in his thoughts, no doubt playing out various match scenarios in his head. As I sat into the seat next to him, he smiled at me and I nodded back at him.

Joe Schmidt was sitting behind us. We had been in the air for about fifteen minutes when the captain announced that we could all remove our seatbelts. Joe stood up and stuck his head over the back of my seat.

'Hey, Darce,' he said, 'how are you doing?'

'Er, good,' I said, laying my book face-down on the table in front of me.

'Ah, *Animal Farm*!' he said. 'What do you think of it?'

'I've, em, just started it,' I told him. 'It's all about animals on a farm who can talk.'

He chuckled to himself.

'The thing is,' he said, 'it's an allegory.'

'It's a what?' I asked.

'An allegory is a story with a hidden meaning. Yes, he's writing about a bunch of animals who take over a farm. But really he's writing about the Soviet

Union under Joseph Stalin. You know who Joseph Stalin was, don't you?'

'He was the leader of the Soviet Union,' I said, 'between 1922 and 1953,' and at the same I thought to myself, Okay, how did I know that?

Joe smiled.

'Very good,' he said. 'I like that you're keeping up with your schoolwork, Darce.'

Joe was a schoolteacher before he became a rugby coach.

'Anyway,' he said, 'I just wanted to let you know that you're going to be starting at number twelve tomorrow.'

'What?' I said. 'Really?'

'You seem surprised,' he said.

'It's just, well, I didn't want to take anything for granted.'

'The reason I'm telling you now and not later is because I want you to start preparing yourself mentally for it. It's your first time starting a match for Leinster. And, like I said on Thursday night, it's going to be a very different match from the Toulouse game. There's not going to be the same opportunity for you to show off your skills – do you get me?'

'Yeah.'

'Remember the drills we've been doing. That's what all those games of Never Ending Defence were about. Tomorrow is going to be just like that. You're going to find yourself running into a brick wall of a defence. I've spoken to Felipe. It's really important that you two work together. I want you to chase every single ball that Felipe kicks into the opposition half and try to be the first tackler when the defender catches it. Good luck, mate!'

Joe sat down again and I took a deep breath. Felipe smiled at me. And I felt my stomach muscles clench even tighter.

It wasn't long before the pilot announced that we would soon begin our descent into London-Heathrow Airport.

I thought to myself, in forty-eight hours, we would all be on a plane flying in the opposite direction. We would either be winners, looking forward to a European Cup semi-final against the mighty Munster. Or we'd be losers, with nothing to look forward to except more knowing smiles and more people saying, 'Typical Leinster!'

But the good news was that it was all in our own hands.

36 *A Proud Leinsterman*

The noise was ear-splitting. There were only fifteen thousand fans at the Twickenham Stoop, but it sounded like every single one of them was screaming outside the door of our dressing-room.

Joe was forced to raise his voice to make himself heard above it.

'Can you all hear me?' he asked.

'Yes!' we told him.

'Okay,' he said, 'this is it. This is where things start to get serious. This is the quarter-final of the European Cup – and this is where most people are expecting our journey to end. And do you want to know why? Because they think we don't have the bottle for a match like this one. A year ago, two years ago, three years ago, this is a match I would have put money on Leinster to lose. As a matter of fact, I would have bet my house on it. Because I would have known the kind of effort it takes to beat a team like Harlequins in front of their own supporters – and I would have known that Leinster weren't capable of it. But you're a different team now. Right?'

'Yes,' we all shouted.

'Well, we need to show them that – show them the work we've been doing since before Christmas. Harlequins are the kind of team who squeeze you until you crack. Today is the day we don't crack. Because we're tougher now than we were last season – not just physically, but mentally. We don't do it for ourselves any more. We do it for each other. Those are our values. Remember them today, because they're important. Discipline. Respect. Teamwork. The Leinster Way.'

We all looked at each other and nodded.

'If we win this afternoon,' Joe said, 'it won't be remembered as a classic match. But it will be remembered as the day that something changed for Leinster. Today is the day that people realize that we are finally a serious team. We know how to win playing the pretty stuff. But we know how to win ugly too. We know how to win those matches where you have to fight for every inch of ground. Never

Ending Defence – remember? You'll find out today why I let those games go on until you were beyond the point of exhaustion. Anything worth fighting for has to be earned. And if we win today, we will have earned it – believe me. And, who knows, you might even enjoy yourselves out there!'

The dressing-room was a poky little room that was barely big enough to hold the fifteen players and the eight substitutes. But Joe and about seven members of the backroom team were also squeezed in there. There was a table in the middle, full of bandages and drinks and cups of tea and sandwiches. It was so tight in the room that I started to feel claustrophobic. And, as the kick-off time approached, the noise outside grew more and more deafening.

Joe named the starting fifteen. One by one, we were handed our jerseys. I looked at the crest. For the first time, I could say that I felt proud to play for Leinster in the same way that I felt proud to play for Ireland. I pulled the jersey over my head and I stood up and found about three inches of space to perform some stretches.

Leo gave us his captain's talk, which was an extension of what he'd said to me on the bus back in Dublin.

'We are stepping into a war zone,' he said. 'These guys are a big, strong, physical team. Whatever you've faced in the past, forget about it. You won't have experienced anything like the intensity that these guys bring to the game. Look at this dressing-room. There isn't room to move in here. That's what it's going to be like out on the pitch. But we focus, we fight for everything and we don't take a backward step.'

The referee knocked on the door and told us that it was time.

We walked out of the dressing-room and we lined up in the tunnel. A few seconds later, the Harlequins players lined up beside us. Leo was right. They were enormous. I found myself standing next to Will Greenwood, the Harlequins number twelve. He was one of my favourite players. He'd won the World Cup with England and played for the Lions. But he didn't look like an inside-centre. He looked more like a second-row – or a high-jumper! He was a giant! I nearly pulled a muscle in my neck looking up to see his face.

He smiled at me.

'Good luck,' he told me.

'Yeah, you too,' I said.

As tall as he was, I was really looking forward to

playing against him and finding out how good I could be.

We walked out onto the pitch. The noise level rose still further.

I looked around for the Leinster supporters. There were a few hundred of them, huddled together in a corner behind one of the goals. I hoped that Dad and Ian had a good view.

Leo gave us our final instructions.

'Remember,' he said, 'work and work and work. And never, ever, ever stop concentrating.'

And a few seconds after that, the ball was in the air and the match was under way.

Joe's prediction was absolutely right. From the first minute, it was obvious that there would be no room for us to play our pretty passing game. Whenever one of us received the ball, there wasn't room to take a single step forward – there was always a Harlequins player, or sometimes two, standing immediately in front of us, barring our way. They seemed to have an extra man everywhere.

The tackling was ferocious, just as Leo had warned us it would be. He said they would probably try to soften us up a bit early on – just to see if we had the appetite for the battle.

But we stood up to them. And we tackled them back just as hard as they tackled us.

After about ten minutes, Chris Robshaw, the Harlequins number eight, emerged from a ruck with the ball in his hands. He advanced about three steps and I suddenly found myself standing directly in front of him.

My survival instinct was telling me to get out of the way. But I couldn't, because I knew this was my tackle to make.

Still, I felt like I was standing on a railway track, attempting to stop an express train using just my body.

I fixed my eyes on his waist and I launched myself at him. Every nerve ending in my body braced itself for the impact.

BBBOOOOOOMMMM!!!

It hurt.

I mean, it REALLY hurt.

But when my head cleared, I was relieved to discover that my arms were wrapped around his waist. Well, part of the way round – he really was huge! And, to my surprise, I'd managed to wrestle him to the ground. He spilled the ball and it was kicked out of touch for a lineout.

'Great tackle!' I heard Shaggy shout.

'Well done, Darce!' said BOD.

It was my first big test of the match and I'd passed it. I put my hand out and helped Chris up off the ground.

'For a little lad,' he said, 'you tackle like an elephant.'

Which I decided to take as a compliment.

For the people watching, it was a poor match. And we could hear the sighing and the tutting from the crowd, who wanted to see tries – or even a few fancy passing movements.

But this wasn't going to be that kind of match.

Most of it was played between the two twenty-twos. Only rarely did either team make it further. We'd gain ground, then we'd lose ground, then we'd lose some more ground, then we'd gain it back. And the ball passed back and forth between us. We'd have it, then Harlequins would take it from us, then we'd win it back from them, then they'd win it back from us.

During a break in play, Felipe caught my eye and told me that it was time to start putting our kicking plan into action. He did this without speaking any words to me. He just rolled his eyes from right to left and whistled, which was his way of telling me that the next time he got the ball he was sending it high into the opposition twenty-two.

A minute or so later, Chris Whitaker pulled the ball out of a ruck and passed it back to Felipe, who immediately put his boot to it and sent it fifty yards down the field. I hared after it. And so did Rob Kearney. He got there first and managed to catch the ball with a spectacular high catch that he must have learned playing Gaelic football.

Whenever Harlequins looked like they might be about to mount a try-scoring move, Rocky Elsom always appeared to snuff it out. Everyone kept looking around to make sure there was only one Rocky Elsom on the pitch – he seemed to be everywhere at the same time.

At half-time, it was still 0–0!

What Joe had said was true. I couldn't imagine anyone wanting to watch a recording of the game in ten years' time. But Joe was delighted with us.

'It might not feel like it,' he said, 'but that first forty minutes was the best forty minutes of rugby you've ever played.'

We knew that was the highest kind of praise.

I looked around the dressing-room. Most of our players were hurt in some way or other. I noticed Isa Nacewa and Luke Fitzgerald, Cian Healy and Malcolm O'Kelly, Shane Jennings and Jamie Heaslip, all comparing war wounds.

'I know it's a lot to ask,' Joe said, 'but give me another forty minutes of that. And I promise you, something will give. Trust me, guys, this is going to be a one-score game. All it's going to take is one tiny bit of magic at the right moment to win it.'

We walked back out onto the pitch and the war resumed.

We got our kicking game going again. Every time, it was a race between me and Rob Kearney to see who could get to the ball first. Sometimes it was me, sometimes it was Rob. Usually, it was Harlequins full-back Mike Brown, then one of us would have to launch ourselves at him and try to tackle him to the ground.

Then the match would go back to the same pattern as before. Gain a few metres, then lose a few metres, while we all ran around putting out fires.

And then, about fifteen minutes into the second half, I noticed that Mike Brown had this habit of straying out of position. He always seemed to be about five metres further forward than he should have been.

I mentioned this observation to Felipe during a break in the play.

'Felipe,' I said, 'can I talk to you about something?'

'Darce,' he said, 'do not disturb. You can see I am thinking. I am always thinking.'

'Mike Brown keeps moving out of position,' I told him. 'I think he's vulnerable if you kick the ball over his head.'

Felipe thought about this for a moment. He moved his lips silently while he performed some kind of calculation in his head. But he didn't say anything back to me.

There were about ten minutes left. The match

was still scoreless and I had forgotten all about my advice to him. I had the ball in my hands right on the halfway line. There was no space for me to move forward, so I ran sideways with the ball, along the line, then I spotted Felipe in a little bit of space just behind me.

I threw the ball to him. He caught it and then, without the slightest hesitation, launched it high into the air, over Mike Brown's head. I raced after it. Rob raced after it. Brown was caught flat-footed and he spun around to see where the ball had landed. But it bounced unexpectedly to the left – and suddenly, Felipe appeared out of nowhere, to get to the ball first!

In a single movement, he bent down and scooped up the ball, before running fifteen metres to the line and depositing the ball underneath the posts.

Our little corner of the stadium erupted.

Felipe kept pointing at me.

'Your idea,' he said, tapping the side of his head with his index finger. 'Clever idea by Darce.'

He added the conversion and we were 7–0 ahead with less than ten minutes to go.

Those ten minutes were the toughest I ever faced on a rugby pitch. Most of the other Leinster players said the same thing. We were exhausted. We were out on our feet. But still Harlequins kept attacking us in wave after wave after wave.

I thought I would never hear the final whistle. But, eventually, mercifully, it came.

All of us – Leinster and Harlequins players – fell on the pitch, empty from eighty minutes of pure effort. I was sure I could have slept there and then on the spot where I collapsed.

Then our supporters started to invade the pitch. They began pulling us up, one by one, and telling us how proud they were of us.

Chris Robshaw helped pick me up.

Suddenly, I heard my name roared from behind: 'GORDON!'

I spun around. It was Ian. He'd run onto the pitch with Dad and they were sprinting towards me. Ian threw his arms around me. Then Dad did too. When they let go, I could see that they both had tears in their eyes.

'You'll get at least one more wear out of the jersey this year, won't you?' I said.

'No one will ever again say that Leinster are soft after that!' Ian said. 'No one!'

'It'd make you proud to be a Leinsterman,' Dad said.

I'd never heard anyone say that before.

'So you're not a Munster supporter any more?' Ian asked.

'I'll tell you this for nothing,' Dad said. 'I'll never watch another Munster match again.'

'You'll have to,' I reminded him. 'We're playing them next.'

37 'Is Prince William In?'

Joe was so pleased with our performance that he gave us the following day off. The video analysis could wait another twenty-four hours, he decided. Our flight back to Dublin wasn't until the late afternoon, so we decided to do a tour of London.

From the top of a tour bus, we saw all the famous sights.

We saw Big Ben and the Houses of Parliament.

We saw St Paul's Cathedral, one of the biggest and most famous churches in the whole world. It was destroyed during the Great Fire of London in 1666 and had to be totally rebuilt.

We saw the Tower of London, where the Crown Jewels are kept. They were the property of the Queen of England and, according to the tour guide, they were the most valuable and heavily guarded collection of precious stones in the world.

For a minute, I allowed myself to fantasize about stealing them.

'How would you do it?' BOD asked.

'Well,' I said, 'I was thinking that Rocky and Cullen and Malcolm could tackle the guards.'

'They're called Beefeaters,' said Shaggy.

'Okay, they can tackle the Beefeaters. Then someone fast –'

'Me,' said Luke Fitzgerald, putting up his hand.

'Okay,' I said, 'Lukey could run in and open all the doors, while I followed with a sack.'

'With the word SWAG written on the side?' asked Malcolm.

'Good idea,' I said. 'I'm taking you on as my main details man.'

'And what would you do with them afterwards?' BOD asked. 'How would you get them through customs?'

'I wouldn't keep them,' I said. 'I'd post them back to the Queen. Although I might keep one or two – to pay for the postage.'

They all thought that was hilarious.

We saw Trafalgar Square, which was named to commemorate Lord Horatio Nelson's victory over

the French and Spanish at Trafalgar in 1805. It was one of the fiercest battles ever fought, according to the tour guide.

'You didn't see Leinster against Harlequins yesterday, did you?' asked Isa Nacewa.

We all laughed.

'Er, no,' the tour guide said. He clearly wasn't a rugby fan.

'I can guarantee you,' Isa said, 'that that was a hundred times harder.'

We still had the aches and pains to prove it.

Eventually, we stopped outside Buckingham Palace.

'Here we are, BOD!' the players started shouting. 'This is your stop!'

BOD was apparently pals with the Queen's grandson Prince William, who would one day become the King of England. He was even invited to his wedding at Westminster Abbey.

'Hey,' said Malcolm, 'let's see can we get into the house by dropping Brian's name with the guards.'

We all stood up.

'Guys,' BOD said, 'please don't embarrass me!'

But nobody listened. We all clambered down the stairs and off the bus, then we ran up to the gates, with BOD running behind us, shouting:

'Guys, please don't do this!'

The guide had told us that the guards who stood outside Buckingham Palace, protecting it from intruders, were called the Queen's Guard. They wore red jackets and tall, black, fluffy hats that were called Busbys.

Malcolm walked up to one of them and said, 'Is, em, Prince William in?' like you would say if you called to one of your friends' houses and his or her dad answered the door.

'Do you have an appointment?' the Queen's Guard asked.

'No,' Malcolm told him, 'but that guy there is one

of his best mates. BOD, what did you buy him for a wedding present? An electric blanket, wasn't it?'

Poor BOD was mortified.

We laughed and laughed and laughed. And something struck me then. We weren't a collection of little cliques, all enjoying our own private jokes in our own quiet corners of the dressing-room. Bully was gone. Damn Handsome was gone. We'd seen off Harlequins by playing the kind of rugby that nobody believed we were capable of. And we had to face the mighty Munster next.

But for the first time, it really felt like Leinster were a team – and a team that I was proud to play for.

38 *Wide of the Post*

'You played great!' Conor said.

'Did I?' I said, trying my best to sound modest.

'Not *you*,' he said. 'Don't start getting a big head again – like you did when you played for Ireland! I'm talking about Leinster. I watched the match with my dad. He kept saying, "They're going to buckle – any minute now," but you didn't!'

Peter nodded. 'I never saw Leinster play like that before,' he said.

I bit into my apple. It was lunchtime and we were sitting in the cafeteria.

'It sounds to me like you two have got a bit of a dilemma,' I told them.

'A dilemma?' Peter asked.

'Yeah,' I said, 'we're playing against Munster next. Who are you going to be cheering for?'

Conor and Peter exchanged an embarrassed look. 'What?' I said. 'Seriously?'

Conor shrugged. 'You don't expect us to stop supporting Munster,' he said, 'just because you're playing for the other team, do you?'

'Well, yes, I do,' I said. 'I'm your best friend. I can't believe you'll be watching the match, wanting me to lose.'

I looked at Peter.

'You as well?' I asked.

'I told you,' he said, 'we're *all* Munster fans in our house.'

I looked away. And then I heard a snigger. I looked back at Conor and then at Peter. They both burst out laughing.

'Of course we're going to be supporting Leinster!' Peter said.

'As a matter of fact,' Conor added, 'we've already booked our tickets!'

I laughed. They really had me fooled.

The excitement was already building ahead of the match. Lansdowne Road, the stadium where the biggest rugby matches were played, was being rebuilt, so a decision had been made to move the game to Croke Park, the home of the GAA and the biggest stadium in the whole of Ireland. They were expecting a crowd of more than 80,000 people to be there.

There was a lot of work to be done between now and then, however – on the rugby pitch *and* in school.

'So,' said Peter, changing the subject, 'how are you getting on with *Animal Farm*?'

'I finished it on the flight back from London,' I told him. 'It turns out it's not just a book about talking animals. It's an allegory.'

I watched Peter's face brighten.

'That's very good,' he said. 'And what's an allegory?'

'It's a story with a hidden meaning,' I told him. 'In this case, the author, George . . . er, something or other –'

'Orwell.'

'That's it. He's writing about the Soviet Union. And Napoleon, the pig, is really Joseph Stalin, who we're also learning about in History. He took over the Soviet from, er, Valerie Lennon.'

'Vladimir Lenin,' Peter corrected me.

'That's right,' I said. 'Valerie Lennon is a woman from Ballyvalloo who my mum knows from line-dancing.'

'See, that's a really good way of remembering important names,' Peter said. 'Just think of someone you know who has a similar name. So when you're trying to remember the name of the man who led the Russian Revolution and started Communism in the Soviet Union, just picture your mum's friend from line-dancing.'

'What, Valerie Lennon?'

'Yes. Picture her standing on a raised platform, addressing a big crowd of angry workers in Moscow.'

'But Valerie Lennon's never been to Moscow. The only time Valerie Lennon left Wexford was to go to the Phoenix Park in Dublin to see the Pope in 1979.'

Conor laughed.

'But the funny picture in your head,' Peter said, 'of your mum's friend in her line-dancing gear addressing angry workers in Moscow will trigger you to remember the leader's *real* name. Vladimir Lenin. I do that kind of thing all the time.'

'Really?'

'Of course. Use anything that helps you to remember.'

I sighed. 'But that's *all* I can remember,' I said. 'I know what an allegory is and I know that the leader of the Russian Revolution sounds like a friend of my mum's who doesn't like leaving Ballyvalloo, but I still can't remember how rain is formed. I still don't know what 2a plus 2b divided by 2c is.'

'Keep working at it,' Peter said. 'You'll be surprised at how much you've actually learned.'

We'd all finished eating. Conor pushed his seat back, then pressed down hard on the table to get himself upright. Then he picked up his crutches.

'Let's go outside and see Aoife,' he said. 'She's practising her kicking.'

There were just four days to go until Ireland's opening match in the Schoolgirls' Six Nations Championship.

Peter and I stood up and we all headed outside. Conor could move on his crutches as fast as we could walk now.

'So how much longer?' I asked him as we headed for the rugby pitch. 'Before you get the cast removed, I mean.'

'A few more weeks,' he said. 'And do you know what I can't wait to do?'

'Throw a rugby ball around with me and Peter?' I asked.

'No – have a good scratch! My leg is itching like mad under the plaster! I have to keep putting things down there to scratch it – a pool cue, a wire coathanger, Mr Rowland's pointing stick!'

Up ahead, we spotted Aoife. She was standing on the pitch at the point where the touchline met the tryline, a sack of rugby balls spilled open on the ground beside her.

'She's practising unbelievably hard,' Conor said. 'She was here this morning at half-seven. I saw her out the window. And she was here last night as well.'

'You know your cousin,' I said. 'She's a total perfectionist. And she wants to play well against France.'

'Yeah,' Conor said, 'but she was practising exactly the same kick all the time – trying to hit the post from the corner.'

We watched her perform her routine. Four steps backwards, then three to the right. Then she ran at the ball and sent it sailing into the air . . .

. . . and twenty feet wide of the post.

'Whoa!' Conor said. 'That was terrible.'

Then we watched as Aoife looked up at the sky and let out a loud, animal roar:

'Aaaaaggggggghhhhhh!!!!!!'

Then she kicked the tee in frustration.

'Let's go and see if she's okay,' Conor said.

We made our way over to her.

'Aoife?' Conor said.

She seemed lost in her own world. He had to say her name a second time before she heard him.

'Aoife?' he said. 'Is everything okay?'

'No,' she snapped. 'I can't get this kick right.'

'It's just, well, you were here until late last night. And early this morning.'

'Don't tell me how long I've been practising it,' she roared at him. 'That'll only make it worse.'

Peter tried to keep things jollying along. That was his way.

'You must be looking forward to Paris,' he said.

'It's not a holiday,' she snapped.

'Hopefully you'll get a chance to see the sights,' I said. 'The Eiffel Tower is amazing. I saw it when I played for Ireland.'

'I don't have time to think about things like that,' she said. 'I'm captaining Ireland in the Six Nations Championship.'

From where I was standing, she didn't look well. Her face was pale and her nose was red and runny.

'Aoife,' I said, 'maybe you should be in bed.'

'I'm not going to bed,' she said. 'We're leaving for Paris in three days' time. And if I can't nail kicks like this, then Emma Ormsby is going to have to take over my kicking duties. And I am NOT going to let that happen.'

'Is there anything we can do to help?' Peter asked.

'Yes,' she said. 'You can leave me ALONE!'

39 *Dingo*

Things started to change after we beat Harlequins. You could see it happening slowly. Dad put a Leinster poster in the window of the bank and customers would ask him if his son could get Rocky Elsom and Brian O'Driscoll's autographs for them. According to Mum, there were people walking around Wexford Town wearing Leinster jerseys as fashion items.

We heard that similar things were happening elsewhere. We'd proven that Munster weren't the only team in Ireland worth supporting. People from Kildare, Kilkenny, Longford, Meath, Offaly, Wicklow and Westmeath, who'd previously cheered for Munster, were suddenly switching sides.

Ian said that, among his friends, being called a Lunster was just about the worst insult you could throw at someone, especially now that the two teams were about to play each other. Supporting Munster when you came from Leinster was now the act of a traitor!

There was no doubt that we had created a stir.

With the match still weeks away, it was already being described in the newspapers as rugby's All Ireland final.

Meanwhile, Aoife's Ireland team were creating a buzz of their own. They beat France in Paris by 25–3. Aoife landed the Woman of the Match award for her performance, which included two of her team's three tries. Ever the perfectionist, though, she kept focusing on the three kicks she missed and not the four she nailed. Conor reckoned this was down to the cold she was suffering from during the week of the match. But she'd promised to take it easy in the days leading up to Ireland's second match against Wales in Donnybrook that Friday night.

There was lots to be excited about, even though Joe Schmidt was keen to remind us that we'd still won absolutely nothing. It had been ten days since we'd beaten Harlequins and he decided it was time to bring us back down to Earth.

'Look, I'm proud of what you did in London,' he said. 'It was a battle and it wasn't easy. You fought tooth and nail for each other. The defence was incredible. You trusted each other. And you've changed people's perceptions of you. In future when people use the phrase "Typical Leinster", they'll be talking about qualities that no one knew we possessed – like resilience, like strength of character, like mental toughness.

'But the time for congratulating ourselves is over. You don't need me to tell you how tough Munster are going to be – especially now that they've seen how we played against Harlequins. The secret is out. They know now that we're not the Leinster of old. They know they're going to have to be at the top of their game to beat us. Which they will be. And that's why we have to be at the top of ours.

'Remember what I said to you when we talked about values – we are what we do every day. We have to be better against Munster. The moment we stop improving is the moment we'll start losing. So the job of beating Munster starts today. There's a few things I want us to try. But we need to practise them and practise them and practise them if they're going to work. So let's get started.'

Joe was convinced that the way to beat Munster was to use our passing game and our pace. This was music to my ears. It was my kind of rugby. But, he said, their defence was so good that we couldn't beat them playing an obvious kind of rugby. Instead, he had a number of specific moves in mind, which he said would surprise them, and which he wanted us to rehearse over and over again, as if they were dance steps, in the weeks leading up to the match.

There was one particular move that was really ambitious, but also very difficult to pull off. Joe called it Dingo, which is the name of a wild dog found in Australia. The plan was that, at some point in the match, Felipe would say the magic word, 'Dingo', and we would slip into position. I would move behind Felipe to his left and Shaggy would move behind him to his right. Nine times out of ten, Munster would expect him to offload the ball to me. But Felipe would switch the direction of the play and Shaggy would make a run like he was expecting to receive it. But it was a decoy run. Rocky would come storming through, intercept the pass and run straight through the Munster defence.

We practised it over and over again against five of our defenders. But we just couldn't get it right. Either Felipe threw the pass too long, or the ball was intercepted by the opposition instead, or Rocky arrived too late, or he arrived too early and knocked the ball on, or he ran straight into a defender with the ball. It was a move with so many working parts, all of which had to work in sync with each other. And the timing had to be exactly right because we realized, through practising it, that Rocky would only have a split-second of time to get through the gap in the Munster defence.

We must have practised it for an hour and a half without managing to pull it off once. We were so disappointed. That's how committed to the cause we all were. If you failed something, you took it personally.

'Leave it for tonight,' Joe said. 'We'll try it again the next day. Let's try a different one.'

Suddenly, rain started thundering down on us.

'Whoa, where did that come from?' Rob Kearney said.

And, from out of nowhere, I found myself thinking, 'Heat from the sun turns water into vapour, which rises into the sky, where it turns into droplets of water, which merge with other droplets of water, forming clouds. When the droplets of water become too heavy, they fall as rain.'

And my next thought was:

'Whoa, where did *that* come from?'

When I got back to school that night, I couldn't wait to wake Peter to tell him that I knew how rain was formed. But when I got to the dormitory, I discovered that my two friends were awake. They were sitting on the edge of their beds with worried looks on their faces.

'What's wrong?' I asked.

'It's Aoife,' Conor said. 'She collapsed tonight – while she was practising her kicking.'

'Oh my God!' I said. 'Is she okay?'

'I don't know!' he said. 'They've taken her to hospital.'

40 *Exhaustion*

Aoife was sitting up in the bed when we arrived at the hospital. She looked awful. She also looked about as unhappy as I'd ever seen her look.

'I've got laryngitis,' she said.

I'd never heard of it before.

'What's that?' I asked.

'It's a sore throat,' she answered. 'It's not a big deal.'

'It's slightly more serious than a sore throat,' Conor said. 'Your mum told my mum that you were suffering from exhaustion.'

'I thought you looked a bit under the weather lately,' I said. 'You've run yourself into the ground, Aoife.'

A nurse arrived then. She asked Aoife to sit forward and she plumped up her pillows.

'This is ridiculous!' Aoife told her. 'I'd like to discharge myself – right now!'

The nurse laughed.

'You are NOT discharging yourself!' she told her. 'What you need is rest.'

'I'll rest next week,' she promised. 'I have to play a match against Wales on Friday. Can you please bring me the relevant paperwork so that I can sign myself out?'

'You're not going anywhere, Aoife – we've been through this. Stay where you are. Your mum and dad are on the way in to see you.'

As soon as the nurse left, Aoife shot me a serious look.

'Gordon,' she said, 'hand me my tracksuit.'

It was folded neatly on a chair beside the bed.

'The nurse told you to stay in bed,' I said.

She turned to Conor.

'Conor!' she said brightly. 'My favourite cousin in all the world! Hand me my tracksuit, will you?'

'What are you going to do?' he asked. 'How are you going to get out of the hospital?'

'I'm going to climb out the window,' she said – like it was the most reasonable thing in the world.

'We're four storeys up,' I said.

'That doesn't frighten me.'

314

'But what will you do then,' Peter asked, 'once you're free of the hospital?'

'I'll go back to school,' she said, 'and practise my kicking. I missed three against France. I can't afford another performance like that.'

'Aoife,' Conor said, 'I really think you should listen to what the nurse said. If you picked this thing up because you were trying to do too much, then it stands to reason that what you need to do now is slow down.'

'They want me to rest for four weeks. That means I'll miss not only the Wales match, but the England match and the Italy match as well.'

Aoife made one last-gasp appeal to me – rugby player to rugby player.

'Gordon,' she said, 'you've played for Ireland. You're the only one who can understand what I'm going through right now. I *can't* miss this match. The girls need me.'

'Aoife,' I tried to reason with her, 'you're sick and you're exhausted.'

'Yes, I've been overdoing it recently – campaigning to try to get us equal treatment, then my responsibilities as captain of the team, then trying to stay on top of my kicking. But I'm definitely going to rest after we beat Wales.'

'Aoife, this isn't a good idea,' I said. 'Trying to play while you're feeling below par isn't good for your teammates. They need you to be at one hundred percent.'

'Please! I don't have long here. Once my mum and dad arrive, that's it – I'll never get out of here. And if I don't play against Wales, then Emma Ormsby will take over the kicking duties. And if she does really well, there's no way that I'll get the job back from her. So you see, Gordon? I actually HAVE to go!'

It really hurt me to see her so distressed. But thankfully, at that exact moment, her parents arrived.

'Aoife Kehoe!' her mum shouted at her across the ward. 'What's this the nurse is telling me about you trying to discharge yourself?'

'Hello, boys,' her dad said. 'Thank you for looking after our little princess.'

From Aoife's expression, I could tell how much she liked being referred to as their little princess.

In other words, not one bit!

'Mum,' Aoife said, 'hand me my tracksuit. I have work to do before we play Wales.'

'No, you don't,' her mum said, 'you silly thing!

You're staying here, where we can look after you and get you better!'

Aoife looked at me over her mum's shoulder. And she said:

'Thanks a lot, Gordon!'

41 *A Big Shock*

The next few weeks dragged by. The entire country was talking about our upcoming match against Munster at Croke Park. But the time passed so slowly that I thought the day would never come.

My life was consumed by two things. Rugby and schoolwork. When I wasn't obsessing about the first, I was trying my hardest to focus on the second.

Rugby came naturally to me. Studying was something I had to force myself to do. It often involved reading pages and pages of a book and then realizing that I didn't understand a word of what I'd just read. Then I'd have to reread it – sometimes five or six times before I could close the book – and then I would test my knowledge by trying to explain it to Peter.

The following day, whatever I'd learned was usually gone from my head. But at strange moments – like when I was lifting weights with BOD and Johnny Sexton – random facts would pop into my head.

Like, for instance:

The Irish Civil War (1922–1923) was fought between two sides who took opposing views on the Treaty with Britain that followed the War of Independence.

And then, one evening, in the middle of one of Joe Schmidt's team talks, where he was telling us that we would have to stop Ronan O'Gara dictating the match:

Pythagoras's Theorem says that, with a right-angled triangle, the square of the length of the hypotenuse equals the sum of the squares of the lengths of the other two sides.

And don't worry – I had no idea what any of it meant either! But something was clearly happening. It was like when we practised a particular passing move in training – we'd perform it so many times that suddenly you didn't have to think about what you were doing any more. It came to you as naturally as breathing.

'I've suddenly got all this random stuff in my

head,' I complained to Peter in the dormitory one night.

He howled with laughter.

'Gordon,' he said, 'that's called LEARNING!'

The only problem was that I kept forgetting. And I knew that I couldn't afford to do that. If we beat Munster, and then I failed my exams a few days later, I wouldn't be allowed to play in the European Cup final. I simply HAD to pass them. But it was going to be very difficult.

With Leinster, I was still learning too. Joe taught us lots of new passing moves that he hoped would catch Munster by surprise. But we never did manage to pull off the Dingo move and we decided to give up on it.

I was aware of the sudden buzz around the Leinster team from the growing interest of the rest of the school. The other boys would stop me in the corridor, or sit next to me in the cafeteria, or tap me on the shoulder during Evening Study, then ask me questions, like:

'Is Rocky Elsom really as big as he looks on TV?'
And:

'Who's the best kicker – Felipe Contepomi or this new Johnny Sexton guy?'

But it wasn't until a week before we played

Munster, when we returned home for a weekend break, that I started to see how many ordinary people were suddenly taking an interest in this Leinster team.

I was used to seeing the streets of Wexford decorated with purple-and-yellow bunting. Purple and yellow were the county colours. And when the hurling team was playing in the Championship, those colours were everywhere.

But when I returned home that weekend, the bunting was blue and white!

And nobody was talking about Munster any more. They were all talking about Leinster like they'd been supporting them all their lives! I was being stopped all the time by people who wanted to shake my hand and tell me that we'd made them feel really proud to be from Leinster!

I'd heard people say they were proud to be from Wexford before. And I'd even heard people say they were proud to come from particular parts of Wexford – like Enniscorthy, or Gorey, or Curracloe. But I'd never heard anyone say that they were proud to come from Leinster.

While we were home for the weekend, Conor, Peter and I decided to go visit Aoife. She'd been off school for three weeks now, but her mum had told Conor's mum that she was on the mend.

Ireland had beaten Wales 12–6 in Donnybrook thanks to Emma Ormsby's four successful penalties from four attempts. Then they went to London and beat England by 26–24. And all without Aoife. I couldn't even imagine how difficult it must have been for her having to sit out most of her first Six Nations.

I wondered whether she was still angry with me for not handing over her tracksuit so that she could climb out of the window of the hospital.

Conor knocked on the door and Aoife's dad answered.

'Hello, fellas,' he said.

'Hello, Uncle Eddie,' Conor said. 'Is Aoife in?'

'Yes,' he said, opening the door for us, 'she's in the living room. She'll be absolutely thrilled to see you.'

Aoife *was* thrilled to see us. And she seemed to have forgiven me for not helping her to escape. She gave us all a hug, then we sat down and caught up on what had been happening over the past few weeks.

Conor told her that the rehearsals for his play were going really well, and that he was having the plaster cast removed from his leg in two weeks. Peter said that he'd been to a lecture in the

Trinity College School of Medicine and he'd decided that he definitely wanted to be a doctor when he grew up.

And I told her what had been happening with Leinster and how the whole country seemed to be talking about the match against Munster the next week.

'I saw your dad driving to work the other day,' she said, 'and he was wearing a Leinster hat and scarf!'

I laughed.

'I know,' I said, 'ever since the Harlequins match, he's been describing himself as "a Leinsterman – born and bred".'

They all thought that was hilarious.

'Doesn't your dad have a *Munster Forever* sticker on the back of his car?' asked Peter.

'Not any more,' I said. 'He peeled it off the other day. Now he denies that he ever supported them! "Munster?" he says. "No, I think you must be confusing me with someone else. Yeah, I think you're confusing me with Eddie Kehoe – Aoife Kehoe's dad!"'

They all laughed.

Since we were talking about rugby, I asked Aoife when she was planning to return to training.

'I'm not,' she said.

I looked at Conor. Conor looked at Peter. Peter looked at me.

'What are you talking about?' Conor asked.

Aoife just shrugged her shoulders.

'I've decided that I don't want to play rugby any more,' she said.

'You mean EVER?' I asked. 'Even when you're fully better?'

'There are more important things in life than rugby,' she said.

I knew she didn't mean that. I wondered was she on some kind of medication.

'So have you, like, officially retired?' Conor asked.

Aoife nodded.

'I phoned Jill Gillespie,' she said, 'and I told her I was giving up rugby.'

'You can't give up now,' I said. 'You're two matches away from winning the Six Nations.'

'Yeah,' said Conor. 'If you beat Italy and Scotland, you'll have done the Grand Slam.'

'That wouldn't have happened without you,' I reminded her. 'You can't just give up.'

'They don't need me any more,' she said in a flat voice. 'They have Emma Ormsby.'

'Emma is a great player,' I told her. 'You're a great

player. And Ireland are a much better team when both of you are playing.'

'Yeah, maybe you just took on too much,' Peter suggested. 'You were the captain. You were the out-half. You were the kicker –'

'You were the one knocking on doors,' I reminded her, 'demanding equal treatment for the girls. And you got it, Aoife. That's why you can't walk away – not with the Grand Slam to come.'

But she just shook her head.

'I'm not sure I even like rugby any more,' she said.

42 *The Fear of God*

The drive to Croke Park on the afternoon of the match is something I will never forget. The bus struggled to make its way down the narrow streets, which were teeming with people, all dressed in blue or red.

That was when my heart started to beat VERY hard in my chest.

As we drove past them, the Munster supporters cupped their hands around their mouths and booed us – but in a good-natured way. They were famous for their passion. But our supporters were showing that they could make just as much noise.

They were chanting: 'LEIN-STER! LEIN-STER! LEIN-STER! LEIN-STER!'

Everyone seemed to be having a great time. I noticed that there were groups of friends walking to the stadium together, some wearing the blue of Leinster and some the red of Munster. There were husbands and wives, even families, divided by their support for the two teams.

'My dad is actually from Kerry,' I heard Johnny Sexton say.

'Yeah,' BOD told him, 'my grandmother is from Limerick.'

There was a feeling in the air that Leinster might at last have produced a team to put it up to the mighty Munster. The question was, could we finally deliver on our promise – or were we going to flop, like we had so often on the big days?

I spotted Mr Murray, making his way to the stadium. I waved at him and he smiled and waved back at me.

Seeing so many Leinster fans making their way to the stadium made us all feel a new sense of responsibility. We had a lot of first-time supporters now. We didn't want to let them down.

It took what seemed forever for the bus to thread its way through the throngs of people and reach the safety of the car park. And all the time I could feel the tension building in my chest.

This felt even bigger than the Grand Slam decider against Wales – even though there was no trophy for the winner. It just seemed to matter more to so many people.

The bus pulled up outside the stadium and we all climbed off. I looked up. In front of me, on top of a very high plinth, was a statue of a man with an enormous beard. Leo Cullen told me that it was Michael Cusack, an Irish teacher from County Clare, who had founded the GAA. We all followed the tradition of touching the base of the statue for luck, then we made our way to our dressing-room.

Joe named the team. There were no surprises. Most of the players who played so well against Harlequins would have been very disappointed not to make the starting fifteen.

I was sitting directly opposite Johnny Sexton. I could tell from the look on his face that he really wanted to play, but you could understand why Joe had to go with Felipe. Johnny was one for the future. Everyone was certain of that.

Through the wall of the dressing-room, we could hear shouting. Next door to us, Paul O'Connell, the Munster captain, was roaring at his teammates:

'WE MUST PUT THE FEAR OF GOD INTO THEM!'

Some of us had played with Paul for Ireland and were familiar with his pre-match pep-talks. But hearing it through the wall, knowing that I was part of the 'them' this time, sent a cold ripple of fear down my spine.

I think everyone else felt the same way. Joe must have picked up on it because he said, 'You can all hear Paulie next-door, I presume?'

'I'd say they can hear him down in Thomond Park,' I said.

'Don't worry,' BOD said, with a grin on his face, 'we'll quieten him down when we go out there.'

'That's what Munster are famous for,' Joe told us. 'That kind of passion you can hear from Paulie. Pride in the jersey. They know what it means to play for Munster. It's an honour. It's a privilege. But I think you guys are beginning to understand that playing for Leinster is a pretty special thing as well. Maybe we don't have the history that those guys have. But maybe our history is all ahead of us. We have a chance today to write the first page of it. What will it be? That's up to you to decide.'

Then he handed each of us our jerseys. I pulled mine over my head.

Leo Cullen stood up then to give us his captain's speech.

'You heard what the coach said,' he told us. 'Let's do something today that people will talk

about in ten years' time. Let's produce a performance that ends forever the idea that we're a bunch
of chokers.'

The noise outside in the stadium suddenly
swelled. The Munster fans had found their seats.
And their voices. Fifty thousand of them were singing 'The Fields of Athenry' – but it sounded like
twice that number.

'We're going to go out there and hit them with
everything we've got,' Leo said. 'We're going to go
at them like . . . like blue thunder!'

Like blue thunder! I loved that phrase. I could see

that everyone else did too because the dressing-room was suddenly full of smiling faces.

'BLUE THUNDER!' Felipe shouted.

'BLUE THUNDER!' BOD shouted.

'BLUE THUNDER!' I shouted.

Then Nigel Owens, the referee, stuck his head around the door of the dressing-room.

'Well?' he said. 'Do you boys want to play this match or not?'

What a stupid question, I thought.

We walked out of the dressing-room. The Munster players were already standing in a line, waiting to go out. We went and lined up beside them.

The tension between us was unbelievable. They knew they were in for a match.

I was standing next to ROG.

Out of the corner of his mouth, he said, 'Your knees must be knocking, Darce, are they?' He had a wry smile on his face.

'I think I'll be alright,' I told him. 'You just worry about yourself, ROG.'

The crowd was chanting:

'MUN-STER! MUN-STER! MUN-STER! MUN-STER!'

ROG turned around and looked at BOD, who was standing behind me.

'Are there *any* of your fans in the stadium?' he asked. 'Or is there a sale on in Brown Thomas or something?'

BOD knew that ROG liked to wind people up. He just stared straight ahead and said nothing.

'Okay,' Nigel Owens shouted, 'let's go, boys!' and he led us out of the tunnel.

The noise was so loud that the ground seemed to shake. The stands were a sea of red and blue – but mostly red.

We all warmed up, then Nigel told us it was time. We won the toss and Leo said that we would kick off. Then we took our positions on the pitch and we waited for the whistle.

'This is it, Gordon,' I thought. 'This is going to be the biggest test of your life.'

Nigel blew his whistle and Felipe launched the ball high into the Munster half.

43 *Blue Thunder*

The noise was so loud that the players struggled to hear the lineout calls. I had to really shout to make my voice heard – even when I was talking to a player standing next to me. And whenever someone made a big tackle, the noise went up another few levels again.

There were only three minutes gone when we were awarded a penalty just inside the Munster half. It was an opportunity to score the first points of the match and settle ourselves down. It wasn't a particularly difficult kick. I'd watched Felipe put balls between the posts from this position ten times in a row. In normal circumstances, he could have kicked it over in his slippers.

But these were not normal circumstances.

He went through his usual, no-fuss, pre-kick

routine. He counted three steps backwards, took a sharp turn, then counted two more to the side. He looked up at the posts once, then down again. Then he ran at the ball and sent it flying towards the goal. I could tell from the moment his boot connected with it that it wasn't a good kick. It left the tee, wobbled a bit in the air, then drifted right and wide of the post.

The Munster fans cheered.

It was one of those matches where you knew you wouldn't get a second to relax. A lot of the Leinster and Munster players were friends with each other away from rugby. But you wouldn't have known that down on the pitch. In the first five minutes, three of our players needed medical attention, and there was a lot of pushing and shoving going on off the ball.

Nigel called Leo and Paulie together and he told them to tell us to cool it.

Felipe was starting to feel his way into the game. He received a ball from the ruck, sold David Wallace and Alan Quinlan a dummy and put a drop-goal between the posts, to make up for his missed penalty.

We led for only three minutes before the game started to turn in Munster's favour. First, Cian Healy got sent to the sin-bin for running across the

Munster winger Ian Dowling, meaning we were down to fourteen men for the next ten minutes. Then, ROG kicked Munster level. And then – the worst news – Felipe got injured.

We were attacking the Munster line. He had the ball in his hands and he tried to change direction. But, as he did, he slipped and twisted his knee. It was obvious from his face that he'd hurt himself very badly. Felipe was a player who would happily play through all sorts of pain. But he couldn't continue this time. He was heartbroken. As he hobbled off the pitch, he had tears streaming from his eyes. His season was over.

Johnny Sexton was going to get his chance after all. As he walked past him, Johnny tapped Felipe on the cheek to tell him he was sorry for him.

Felipe looked at him and said, 'Forget it – go and smash it!'

Johnny's first touch of the ball was going to be a kick at goal. That was pressure. His first big match for Leinster. He was coming on to replace one of our most important players. And his first job was to kick a penalty.

Silence fell over the stadium.

Johnny picked up the ball and put it in the tee. He took four steps backwards. He looked up at the goal, then down at the ball, then he ran at the ball and sent it straight between the posts.

It was clear that here was a young man with nerves of steel!

We were 6–3 ahead and it felt like the game was swinging back our way. Johnny started to dictate the play like he'd been doing it for years. Rocky was putting in some great carries and BOD kept producing little pieces of magic that made you think it was only a matter of time before we scored a try.

Then something amazing happened.

Johnny shouted, 'Dingo!'

We all looked at each other, wondering did he really just say what we thought he said?

'Dingo?' I asked him.

'Dingo,' he repeated.

We had practised the move hundreds and hundreds of times and it had NEVER come off – not even once! And Johnny had never practised it. He'd only ever watched us do it with Felipe. And now here he was, ready to try it in a high-pressure match. It was either very, very brave, or very, very foolish.

'Dingo?' Shaggy said. 'Definitely Dingo?'

I noticed that Rocky was smiling. He was excited about it.

We all got into our positions. I was behind Johnny

to his left. Shaggy was behind him to his right. Johnny received the ball from the ruck. Shaggy made his decoy run. Johnny made the pass. And Rocky came charging through and intercepted it. In the same motion, he slipped through a tiny gap between two defenders. The Munster players were thrown by the move, which gave him a two-second headstart in the race for the line. Rocky was a giant of a man, but he could really move. He ate up the ground, then he crashed over the line to ground the ball.

Dingo! Joe was right! It did work!

The stadium announcer said:

'The first try of the day is to Leinster's number six . . . Rooocccckkkyyy Elllsssooommm!!!!'

Our supporters roared with delight.

Johnny kicked the points to put us 13–3 ahead.

We knew that Munster would come back at us – and they did. They started to put together phase after phase, slowly turning the screw. But Rocky kept tackling the ball carrier like he was on a one-man mission to stop Munster scoring a try.

All they could manage in reply was another penalty by ROG. Then Nigel Owens blew the whistle and it was suddenly half-time. We were 13–6 ahead. We knew it wouldn't be enough, but it was a good start.

In the dressing-room, Joe told us that the job was only half done. Munster's pride had been hurt and history showed that they were at their most dangerous when the odds were stacked against them. It was going to take a mammoth forty minutes from us to win the match.

We were still buzzing about managing to pull off the Dingo move, but Joe reminded us that it would be quickly forgotten if we lost the match.

'No one goes home from a rugby match talking about a try scored by the losing team,' he said. 'People go home talking about winners. We put in a great first half – and we're in charge of what happens in the next forty minutes. How we tackle, how we react to mistakes – and whether we let Munster back into this match. I want you to attack them the way I know you can. Let's win this match.'

We understood. And we couldn't wait to get back out on the pitch again.

'BLUE THUNDER!' I shouted as we left the dressing-room.

'BLUE THUNDER!' my teammates shouted as one.

We didn't wait around for Munster to make their response. We attacked them from the kick-off. ROG kicked the ball deep into our half, then we started to string passes together and make our way down the pitch.

Ten minutes into the second half, we had a line-out somewhere around the halfway line. Malcolm O'Kelly jumped high and pawed the ball down to Chris Whitaker. He threw a long pass to Johnny, who passed to BOD, who passed to Isa Nacewa. It happened so quickly that Munster didn't have time to react. Isa burst in between two men in red and made about ten yards. I saw my opportunity. I was running to his left and I was screaming for the ball:

'I'M HERE, ISA! I'M HERE, ISA!'

I could see a clear path to the line, twenty yards in front of me. Isa played the pass to where he expected me to be. But the nose of the ball was dipping and I was going to have to catch it at shoelace level. In that moment, I remembered Joe's words after the Toulouse match:

'The good players take those.'

I had to break stride to bend down and get my whole hand under the ball – to make sure I didn't knock it on. I managed to grab hold of it, then I tucked it into my left armpit. I knew that I had three Munster players right on my heels. I kept running as fast as I could, anticipating the tackle at any moment. When it came, it was Keith Earls who tried to take

me down. But all those hours I'd spent as a kid acting as a human tackle bag for my brother, Ian, meant I knew what to do next. I switched the ball to my other armpit and, as he prepared to tackle, I used my hand to push him away – anything to buy myself an extra metre.

It wasn't a clean tackle and he only succeeded in knocking me off balance. I was still ten yards from the line. I stumbled forward a couple of steps before I fell face forward onto the ground like an airplane hitting the runway – except I was about three yards short of where I wanted to be! But then something magical happened. A combination of my momentum and the wet pitch sent me sliding forward over the Munster line, where I grounded the ball.

The stadium erupted. And, for the first time, it sounded like there were more of our fans than theirs in Croke Park.

Munster were rattled.

My teammates congratulated me. Somehow, I'd managed to pick up a dead leg in the course of scoring. I limped back to the middle of the pitch while the stadium announcer said:

'The second try of the day is to Leinster's number twelve . . . Gordon D'Aaarrrcccyyyy!'

There was another loud roar. One of the team physios ran onto the pitch and asked me if my leg was okay. I told him it felt a bit dead, but I was sure I could run it off.

I noticed that Paulie had gathered all of the Munster players around him in the in-goal area and he was giving them a serious talking-to. It was clear to him that this wasn't the Leinster team of a year ago.

Johnny narrowly missed the conversion – but then I hadn't made the angle easy for him by scoring in the corner!

We were winning 18–6.

But we knew enough about Munster to know they were far from beaten. Second-half comebacks were their speciality. They'd done it time and time again. We knew we needed to score another try.

Munster were stung into action. They attacked us and it took a Herculean effort by all of us to keep them out. We were bracing ourselves for half an hour of relentless Munster pressure when something very unexpected happened.

We were defending right on our twenty-two-metre line. Munster were starting to put some nice passing moves together and it seemed like only a matter of time before they would find a gap in our defence. Then ROG threw a long pass to Paulie. Anticipating what he was going to do, BOD stepped forward . . .

And he intercepted the ball before it could reach Paulie!

Then he set off on a seventy-metre run to the Munster line, sprinting all the way, with ROG haring after him. I'd raced both of them when we played for Ireland and they were equally fast. But BOD had the advantage of a three-metre head-start.

'GO ON, BOD!' we all roared as we watched him disappear into the distance.

Then he slid under the posts and grounded the ball.

The Leinster fans celebrated wildly in the stands while the Munster fans went unusually quiet. They knew, just as we knew, that there was no way back for their team now.

But still the end came as a huge relief. We had done it. We had finally beaten the mighty Munster!

Ryle Nugent, the TV commentator, made his way onto the pitch while we were celebrating. He asked if he could do an interview with me and BOD.

BOD was still out of breath from running almost the entire length of the pitch to score his try!

'What a performance!' Ryle said. 'This team has really answered the critics who say that Leinster always choke on the big occasions and –'

BOD cut him off.

'We've proved nothing yet,' he reminded him. 'We still haven't won anything – and for this group of players, that isn't good enough. We want to put that right, but there's no trophy for beating Munster today. So we're not going to be patting our-selves on the back just yet. We still have a European Cup final to win.'

And that's when I was suddenly brought back down to Earth again. Because I remembered Mr Cuffe's warning – that if I didn't pass my exams next week, I wouldn't be allowed to play for Leinster again.

My own battle to get to the European Cup final wasn't over yet. The exams were starting soon. And if I didn't pass them, I knew that this was the end of the road for me.

44 Cast Away!

Aoife laughed.

'Now that's a sight I thought I'd never see!' she said.

She was talking about me reading my Maths book.

I suppose she had a point!

We were back at the hospital, sitting in the waiting room, waiting for Conor's name to be called. Today was the day he was finally having his cast removed.

'You didn't have to come,' he told me. 'You should be back at school, studying.'

'I didn't want to miss this moment,' I said. 'Anyway, I can study here, can't I?'

'Have you got your head around algebra yet?' Peter asked.

'I think so,' I said.

'Just follow the rules as I explained them to you and you'll be okay.'

'I have to be,' I reminded him. 'If I don't pass these exams, there'll be no European Cup final for me.'

Northampton had won the other semi-final and we would be meeting them in Cardiff in just under two weeks to decide who would be the Champions of Europe.

'There's no way Mr Cuffe would stop you from playing in the final,' Aoife said, 'even if you failed your exams.'

'He would,' I told her. 'The only reason he let me play was because Mr Murray persuaded him to give me another chance. But I've used up all my lives now.'

'What,' she said, 'even though you were one of Leinster's best players against Munster, he would tell Joe Schmidt that you couldn't play against Northampton?'

'Absolutely,' I said. 'You didn't see how angry he was with me after Christmas.'

Aoife hadn't changed her mind about giving up rugby. Ireland had beaten Italy 52–9 to set up a Grand Slam decider against Scotland in Donnybrook. Emma

Ormsby was the Woman of the Match, scoring three tries and landing all of her kicks. I still thought that Ireland were better with both of them in the team, but Aoife changed the subject every time I brought it up.

A doctor appeared then.

'Conor Kehoe?' he said.

Conor manoeuvred himself into a standing position. Then his dad handed him his crutches.

'This is hopefully the last time you'll be needing these!' he said.

'Is it okay if we come with him?' Peter asked the doctor.

He laughed.

'What are you,' he said, 'his fan club? Of course – come this way.'

Conor picked his way into a small examination room. It was a tight squeeze, but we all managed to fit in there – me, Conor, Peter, Conor's dad, Aoife and the doctor, who introduced himself to us as Dr Kennedy.

Conor lay down on the bed. Dr Kennedy produced a hand-held, circular saw.

'Er, please be careful with that thing,' Conor said. 'Even if I never get to play rugby again, I've kind of gotten used to having *two* legs, okay?'

Dr Kennedy laughed.

'You are a hoot,' he said. 'But please don't make me laugh while I'm cutting through the plaster – otherwise you might end up losing the entire limb!'

Suddenly, there was a loud, grinding sound as the saw's teeth ate into the plaster and our nostrils were filled with the smell of burning. As the plaster cast opened, things started to fall out of it onto the floor. Like, for instance:

A pencil!

Two pens!

A screwdriver!

A stick of rock with *Greetings from Wexford* written through it!

Nobody bent down to pick it up. I doubted if anyone would be prepared to eat it now.

'I take it you were trying to scratch your leg with these things?' Dr Kennedy said.

'Er, yeah,' Conor replied. 'It was seriously itchy in there.'

And then, unbelievably, a TV remote control fell out onto the floor.

'I was wondering where that got to!' Conor's dad said. 'That's been missing for months!'

We all laughed.

Finally, the cast was off.

'Now stand up very slowly,' Dr Kennedy said. 'You haven't used that leg for months. It's going to be very weak until you build up the muscles again.'

Conor moved himself into a sitting position on the side of the bed.

'Give me a hand, Darce, will you?' he said.

I stood on one side of him and his dad stood on the other. He put his arms around our shoulders and he lifted himself off the bed and onto the floor.

'You're right,' he said, 'it feels very weak.'

'That's only natural,' the doctor said.

'Do you think I'll ever be able to play rugby again?' Conor asked.

'It's far too early to tell,' he said. 'But why don't you learn to walk before you try to run?'

'That sounds like good advice,' Aoife said.

'Hey,' Conor said, 'at least I'll be able to appear in the school play next week!'

'Are you actually in it?' I asked.

'Yeah,' he said, 'I wrote a part for me – just in case I got the plaster cast off in time!'

Dr Kennedy demonstrated some exercises that Conor should do four times a day to strengthen his muscles again.

Then we left.

Conor used his dad and me as makeshift crutches as he hobbled towards the door. But by the time we reached the car park he was able to limp without any support from us.

We got into his dad's car. I was keen to get back to school. I had a long evening of studying ahead of me.

We eventually reached Kildare. Conor's dad said he'd drop Aoife off at St Bridget's before he drove us back to Clongowes.

He drove through the gates, then up the long driveway to the school. Aoife was getting out of the car and saying goodbye to us when we heard some-one call her name:

'Aoife!'

It was another girl – around Aoife's age. She approached the car.

'Emma?' Aoife said. It was Emma Ormsby. 'What are you doing here?'

'I got a lift out here,' Emma said, 'because I wanted to talk to you. I asked were you in school and they said you were away for the afternoon.'

'Er, yeah,' Aoife said. 'My cousin was in hospital having his plaster cast removed.'

'Jill said you've given up rugby,' Emma said.

'Yeah, I have,' Aoife said.

'Please don't do it.'

'What?'

'Please don't give up. We need you.'

'You don't need me, Emma. I read about what you did against Italy. You're amazing.'

'Aoife, we wouldn't be where we are today without you.'

'That's not true.'

'It is true. We owe you everything, Aoife – including an apology.'

'An apology?'

'We let you do everything. When we were being told that we had to pay for our own jerseys and our own flights and hotels, you were the one who stepped forward and said it wasn't good enough. You were the one who wrote to the Federation. And then, when they wouldn't listen, you were the one who banged on their door and told them that things had to change. And, at the same time as doing all of that, you were trying to be our captain, our kicker, our best player on the pitch. You had all of that pressure on your shoulders and we should have done more to help.'

Aoife shrugged. 'It's fine,' she said. 'I'm glad things worked out.'

'Aoife,' Emma said, 'I didn't come here alone today.'

Emma looked over her shoulder and shouted:

'GIRLS?'

And suddenly, from the back of a white minibus, about twenty girls emerged. They started walking towards the car. I noticed that Jill Gillespie was with them. She smiled at Aoife.

'This was *their* idea,' she told her. 'I just agreed to drive the bus.'

'We don't want to face Scotland without you,' said one of the girls. 'You're not only our captain – you're our inspiration. Aoife, please come back.'

Aoife just burst into tears. But they were tears of happiness.

'Please come back!' the others said. 'We need you.'

'Say YES!' Conor shouted.

Aoife dried her eyes with the back of her hand. Then she said . . .

Well, what do *you* think she said?

45 *Chip Up, Champ!*

'Darce,' Malcolm said, 'come outside for a second, will you?'

'Er, what for?' I asked, instantly suspicious.

'We've got a surpise for you.'

Okay, now I was actually worried!

'What kind of surprise is it?' I asked.

'Just come on,' he said. 'It wouldn't be a surprise if I told you what it was, would it?'

I followed him out of the dressing-room. UCD was quiet this evening. And I was about to find out why. All of my teammates were gathered around the goal at one end of the training pitch.

'What's going on?' I asked.

'Well,' said Malcolm, 'you know the way you're the joint-holder of the Leinster chin-ups record, along with Bully?'

'Er, yeah.'

'Well, tonight, we've decided that you're going to have a crack at owning the record outright.'

'*You've* decided?'

'*We've* decided,' said BOD, stepping forward with a stopwatch in his hand. 'The record stands at fifty-eight. Leo, do you want to lift Darce up to the crossbar bar there?'

'Hang on,' I said. 'I'm faster when I'm listening to my Workout Playlist.'

'What's on your Workout Playlist?' Johnny Sexton asked. 'I've got my iPod here.'

'Er, do you have anything by Garth Brooks?' I asked.

There was suddenly silence.

'Garth Brooks?' Shaggy said. 'What, the country and western singer?'

'Yeah,' I said.

'The fella that all the oul ones listen to when they're doing their line-dancing?'

'My mum wouldn't be happy hearing herself described as an oul one, but yes.'

'I've got some Garth Brooks on *my* iPod,' said Cian Healy.

Cian was a part-time DJ with *the* coolest taste in music – so this came as a bit of a surprise to everyone.

He raced over to his jeep, jumped in and reversed it over to the side of the pitch. He wound down the window. Seconds later, I could hear Garth warbling the opening lines to 'Friends in Low Places'.

I nodded at Leo to tell him I was ready, and he lifted me up so that I could reach the bar.

'Sixty seconds,' BOD announced, 'starting from . . . NOW!'

The other players counted the chin-ups off as I completed them:

'Forty-five . . . forty-six . . . forty-seven . . .'

And I could hear the excitement in their voices as Malcolm said, 'Ten seconds left!'

I was exhausted. My muscles were aching, but I dug deep and kept going.

'Fifty-eight . . . FIFTY-NINE . . . SIXTY . . .'

'TIME'S UP!' BOD shouted.

There was a huge cheer as I dropped down off the bar.

Malcolm raised my hand like a boxer who's just knocked out his opponent.

'The new Leinster chin-ups champion!' he said. 'Gooorrrddddoooonnn D'Aaarrrcccyyy!!!'

I noticed Joe standing there, clapping and cheering along with everyone else.

'Well done, Darce!' he shouted.

'Thanks,' I said.

I suddenly realized how much I loved being part of this group of players. They weren't just my teammates – they had become my friends.

And my heart sank a little bit, because I still didn't know for sure if I'd be going to Cardiff with them. The exams were due to begin the following morning. If I didn't pass every single one of them, I knew that this might be the last time we were all together like this.

Joe decided it was time to train.

'Okay,' he said, 'as Darce is going to no doubt find out as the Leinster chin-ups champion, when you're at the top, everyone wants to knock you off your pedestal. It's the same with us. The secret's out. We're the team to beat now. I don't know if I need to remind you of this, but all you've done is win a semi-final. And you don't get anything for winning semi-finals. Beating Munster was such a big deal, you might start thinking that the hardest part of the job is done. But it's not. Northampton are a great team. But *they're* not the team I'm worried about. The team I'm worried about is us.'

We all looked at each other. This was difficult to hear, especially coming off the high of what we had done at Croke Park.

'Finals are different,' he said. 'You've never been in one before, but you're about to find that out. The pressure of the occasion will affect you in all sorts of ways. That's why I want us to focus on our mental preparation for this match. Like what happens if we have to chase the match? We haven't been behind in a game all season. What if it happens against Northampton and we have to come from behind to win? How would we do it?'

'By thinking calmly,' Johnny said. 'By forgetting about the score and focusing on the next play.'

'But are we capable of that?' Joe asked. 'Between now and the final, I want you to think about that a lot – about that scenario. What happens if the occasion gets to us? What happens if we freeze in the first half and we find ourselves behind? Do we have it in us to reset and then come back? Because that's what we might have to do if we're going to win the European Cup next week. Okay, let's go out there and train like a team that really wants to be remembered.'

We all made our way to the middle of the pitch.

'Darce,' Joe said, 'can I have a word?'

'Er, yeah,' I said.

'What's up? You look like there's something on your mind.'

I sighed.

'I might not be able to play next week,' I told him.

'What?' he said.

I couldn't even look at him.

'I've got exams,' I told him, 'starting tomorrow. Mr Cuffe said that if I don't pass them, I won't be allowed to play rugby any more.'

Joe looked shocked.

'Darce, you're one of our best players,' he said. 'We need you.'

'I know,' I told him. 'But that was the deal I made with him. No exams, no rugby.'

Now, it was Joe's turn to sigh.

'So what are your chances of passing these exams?' he asked.

I shrugged. The truth was I had no idea.

'I've been working really hard,' I told him.

'Ah,' he said, 'that's why you were reading *Animal Farm* on the flight home from London.'

'I sort of let my schoolwork slide,' I said. 'Mr Cuffe was going to stop me playing rugby after Christmas. He said he'd give me one last chance – provided I passed everything.'

'I hope you do,' Joe said, 'I'm counting on you to pass. As a matter of fact, we all are.'

I resolved that I would give it one last push. As

soon as I returned to school from training, I would sit down and study some more. The following day's exams were Maths and Geography. I would read the books from cover to cover and make sure I knew everything there was to know inside-out.

And I would do it even if it meant staying up all night.

46 *The Toughest Test*

I woke up the following morning with a sudden start.

Where was I?

I knew I wasn't in bed. I lifted my head. I couldn't believe it. I was still sitting at my study desk. I must have fallen asleep while I was revising.

Conor woke up.

'Have you not been to bed yet?' he asked.

'Er, no,' I said, 'I was just about to go.'

Conor laughed.

'Gordon, it's eight o'clock in the morning,' he said. 'It's time to get up.'

Peter's alarm sounded then.

'Gordon?' he said, appearing confused. 'You're dressed already!'

'He hasn't been to bed yet,' Conor told him.

'What, you stayed awake all night?' Peter asked.

I suddenly felt a panic rising in my chest.

'No, I was reading my Maths and Geography books,' I said, 'and I must have . . . NOOOOOO!!!!!!'

'What?'

'I fell asleep! I didn't actually finish reading what I was supposed to read!'

'It's too late now,' Conor said. 'The exams are starting in an hour.'

'An hour?' I said.

I was now more nervous than I was before we played Harlequins or Munster. My heart was beating fast and my mouth was dry.

'Gordon,' Peter said, 'you need to calm down.'

'Peter,' I said, 'I can't remember anything.'

'Of course you can.'

'I can't.'

I was telling the truth. I could recall absolutely NOTHING of what I'd learned over the past few weeks.

'I don't understand it,' I said. 'It was in there last night and now it's not in there any more.'

'Don't panic,' Peter told me. 'You know this stuff.'

'I don't know anything, Peter. My head is literally empty.'

'Gordon, it's like rugby. All the things you've learned

and think you've forgotten will come back to you when you need them. You just have to relax, okay?'

'Let's get some breakfast,' Conor said.

They both got out of bed and got dressed.

'I don't have time for breakfast,' I told them. 'I'm going to try and read that chapter that I didn't finish last night.'

But Peter closed over my Maths book.

'Trust me,' he said. 'Let's go and eat something.'

We went to the cafeteria and queued up with the other boys. Conor told Janis, the dinner lady, that I'd have sausages and beans. I carried them over to the table, but I was too nervous to eat anything.

I was probably the only one feeling like this. These were only mid-term exams. They didn't really count for anything – except for me. The European Cup was on the line. Maybe even my entire rugby career.

Maths was first. And I couldn't remember a thing.

'The right angle of the hypotenuse,' I muttered, 'is something, something, something . . .'

'Gordon,' Peter said, 'just relax, okay?'

I wanted to relax. But this was something completely new to me. I'd never really cared about schoolwork before. Now, it was suddenly everything.

The bell sounded.

I stood up.

'This is it,' I said.

I followed the traffic of boys from the cafeteria to the exam hall. In the hallway outside, I ran into Mr Murray.

'Gordon,' he said, 'I just wanted to wish you good luck with your exams. I know how much is riding on it for you.'

'I can't remember anything,' I told him.

'What?'

'I'm serious, Mr Murray. I've been studying for the past few weeks. Every spare second I had. When I wasn't playing rugby, I was reading my school-books. But now I can't remember a single fact I learned in all that time.'

'Gordon, relax.'

'I wish people would stop telling me to relax.'

'What happens if you go out on the rugby pitch and you don't control your nerves?'

'You make mistakes.'

'Exactly. This is no different, Gordon. Pretend you're about to play a rugby match – okay? Lots of deep breaths. Eight seconds in, six seconds out. Relax and focus.'

I did what he told me to do. I walked into the exam hall and found my desk. I closed my eyes and

I focused on my breathing. I managed to calm myself down.

'Wake up!' said Mr Rowland.

I opened my eyes. In front of me on the desk was an examination paper, turned face-down, and a booklet in which to write my answers.

'This is no time to be sleeping,' he said.

Then he walked back up to the top of the room and he said:

'Your examination starts in five seconds, four, three, two – you may turn over your exam papers now.'

I turned mine over and I stared at it.

'Mock Exams' it said at the top of the page.

Underneath, it said: 'Mathematics.'

And then underneath that, it said: 'PASS: 40%.'

That was one piece of Maths I didn't need explained to me.

I looked at Question 1.

'Oh, no!' I thought.

It said:

'What is $2a + 2b \div 2c$?'

I looked up at the ceiling of the examination hall. And I took a deep breath. And then something truly amazing happened.

I realized that I knew the answer.

47 A Night of Drama

'Well?' I asked.

'Well what?' Aoife said.

'You know what I'm talking about! Are you back training with Ireland?'

'Yes,' she said, 'I am.'

I was thrilled to hear it.

'I knew you couldn't give up rugby!' I said. 'You love it too much.'

'I do,' she said. 'But I've also learned a valuable lesson. Girls are awesome.'

'Er, yeah,' I said, smiling, 'I suppose they are. But then you always thought that, didn't you?'

'If I thought they were so awesome, then why did I try to do everything by myself? I should have involved Emma and all the rest of them. No matter how strong we think we are as individuals, we're even stronger when we work together.'

'I suppose I learned a similar lesson,' I said. 'We should never be too proud to ask for help. If it wasn't for this guy sitting beside me' – and I flicked my thumb at Peter – 'I don't know what I'd have done.'

Peter shrugged modestly. But it was true.

'So how did the exams go?' Aoife asked.

'I don't know,' I said.

And that was the truth. Maths and Science were okay, I thought. But the French and Irish papers were really hard. And I didn't have a clue how I'd done in English and Geography.

'When are you getting your results?' she asked.

'Tomorrow morning,' I told her.

Meaning the day before we were due to leave for Cardiff.

'Oh, God, Gordon,' Aoife said, 'I really hope you get them. It would be so unfair if you weren't allowed to play in the final.'

Peter shushed us. Conor's play was about to start.

'Ladies and gentlemen,' Mrs Crummy announced from the stage, 'we now come to the final play in our Theatre Evening. It's written by Conor Kehoe and it's called *Welcome to McWonderburger, Wexford.*'

The curtain went up. On the stage, there was a counter that was almost identical to the one in the shop where we worked in Wexford. And behind the counter were two McWonderburger employees – who were supposed to be me and Peter.

A man walked up to the counter.

'Welcome to McWonderburger, Wexford!' Peter's character said. 'What's *your* beef?'

My character was wearing headphones while flipping the burgers on the grill and he was singing along to his Walkman. The song was 'Friends in Low Places'.

The audience laughed.

He was also wearing LOADS of fake tan.

The man produced a gun.

'Give me everything in the till,' he said.

Except Peter's character couldn't hear him because my character was singing so loudly. And he couldn't see the gun because his glasses were fogged up from all the steam from the kitchen.

'What did you say?' Peter's character asked. 'What are our meal deals?'

The audience fell about the place laughing.

'NO!' the robber shouted, 'I TOLD YOU TO GIVE ME ALL THE MONEY YOU'VE GOT IN THE TILL!'

My character was still singing along to my Walkman at the top of his voice – but then he added in some line-dancing moves.

The audience howled with laughter.

'Yes, I'd be happy to explain them to you,' Peter's character said. 'There's the McWonderburger – a quarter-pound beef patty, with onions, lettuce, tomato and mayonnaise, on a bun.'

I turned around to Peter and I said, 'Is that what we're really like?'

Peter shrugged.

'Yes!' Aoife said, then she laughed.

'There's the McWonder Wonderburger,' Peter's

character said, 'which is three quarter-pound beef patties and four slices of cheese, with gherkins (eugh!), onions, lettuce, tomato and mayonnaise, on a bun. There's the McWonder Wonder Wonderburger – six quarter-pound beef patties, eight slices of cheese, twelve slices of bacon, with gherkins (yuck!), guaca-mole, salsa, onions, lettuce, tomato and mayonnaise, on a bun.'

'I HAVEN'T GOT TIME FOR THIS!' the robber yelled.

'There's the McWonder Wonder Wonder Wonder-burger – twelve quarter-pound beef patties, sixteen slices of cheese, twenty-four slices of bacon, black and white pudding, peanut butter, two fried eggs, a deep fried banana, a slice of pizza and two hot dogs, with gherkins (it's just WRONG!), guacamole, salsa, onions, lettuce, tomato and mayonnaise, not on a bun, but sandwiched between two custard-filled doughnuts.'

Peter and I started to laugh along with everyone else.

It was hilarious!

'Don't forget about the hidden menu item,' I heard Conor's voice say. Then he stepped onto the stage – dressed in the Benji the Dinosaur costume.

The robber swung around, pointing the gun at Benji.

'The McWonder Wonder Wonder Wonder Wonderburger,' Conor told him, unable to see the gun because some kids had stuffed napkins in the eyeholes. 'That's rumoured to be a whole cow in a bun. Although we'd have to check the kitchen to find out if we even have any whole cows.'

'Put your hands above your head,' the man ordered him.

'I'm afraid that's not possible,' Conor said. 'I only have these little dinosaur arms that barely even reach my mouth.'

'I mean it, Barney.'

'Oh, I'm not Barney. I am legally required to point out that I am, in actual fact, Benji, another purple dinosaur with no connection whatsoever to the popular anthropomorphic Tyrannosaurus Rex of the same colour.'

At that point, people in the audience were almost choking, they were laughing so much.

It was absolutely brilliant.

The play ended with the robber giving himself in to the police out of frustration, while Peter's character chased after him, holding a giant, inflatable cow between two buns, shouting, 'YOU FORGOT

YOUR MCWONDER WONDER WONDER WONDER WONDERBURGER!'

At the end, the audience gave the show a standing ovation.

Conor and the actors took three curtain calls.

'BRAVO!' Aoife shouted. 'BRAVO!'

I turned around to the man behind me and I said proudly, 'The characters on the stage were actually based on us!'

And the man laughed and said, 'You must be complete idiots, then, are you?'

'Yes,' I said, laughing. 'I suppose we are!'

Conor smiled and waved in our direction. And in that moment, I was as proud of my friend as I knew he was of me.

48 *The Moment of Truth*

I woke early the following morning with a heavy feeling in my stomach. I felt like I'd swallowed a grapefruit whole.

'Is anyone else awake?' I asked.

Peter wasn't because I could hear him snoring:

HOOOCCCKKK...ZZZUUUUUU!!!!!

HOOOCCCKKK...ZZZUUUUUU!!!!!

'Conor?' I asked. 'Are you awake?'

He didn't answer me. I climbed down the ladder as quietly as I could and put on my clothes. I walked out of the dormitory. The entire school was still sleeping. I checked the time. It was 6.30 a.m. I pushed the bar on one of the emergency doors and I went outside.

It was a cold, crisp morning and I set off on a walk. The birds were singing in the trees, excited to be facing into a new day. I felt exactly the opposite. All I felt was dread. The exam results would be out that morning. And if I failed, I wouldn't get to play in the biggest match of my life.

It was no wonder my mind was all over the place. I walked and walked and walked, thinking about how unfair it would be to miss the European Cup final, especially given how hard I had worked to try to pass my exams.

After a while I realized that I'd walked about three miles, so I turned around and walked back again.

By the time I returned to the school, it was a hive of activity. All of the other boys were getting dressed and heading to the cafeteria for breakfast. No one seemed to be talking about the exam results. I could think of nothing else.

I walked into the dormitory. Peter and Conor were talking about the play last night.

'There was a woman sitting two rows in front of us,' Peter was explaining, 'she was laughing so hard, I thought she was going to need oxygen.'

'It was one of the funniest things I've ever seen,' I agreed.

They turned their heads and saw me for the first time.

'Gordon,' Conor said, 'where have you been?'

'I was just out walking,' I said. 'Thinking about, well, you know.'

'Your exam results,' Peter said.

I nodded.

'Let's go and see Mr Cuffe,' Peter suggested.

'What, now?' I asked. 'It's only eight o'clock.'

'He should be in his office by now.'

'Wait,' I said, 'maybe I don't want to know.'

Conor laughed.

'What do you mean, you don't want to know?' he asked.

'What if the results are bad?' I said.

'You're going to find out sooner or later – might as well be now.'

'Come on,' Peter said, 'let's go and see him.'

So we walked to Mr Cuffe's office. We knocked on his door, but there was no answer. Then we heard a voice behind us say:

'Yes, what is it?'

We all turned around. It was him.

'Em, I was wondering,' I said, 'do you know when the exam results are going to be released?'

He chuckled to himself.

'Miiissstteeerrr D'Aaarrrcccyyy,' he said, 'for a boy who never showed the vaguest interest in his academic career, you certainly are keen to find out how you did in these exams. It's quite the conversion you've undergone, isn't it?'

'Yes, Mr Cuffe,' I said.

'Well, run along to your first class of the day,' he told me. 'The results will be given out later in the morning.'

'Please, I can't wait that long,' I told him.

He could see that I desperately needed to know now.

'Very well,' he said, putting the key into the door of his office. 'Come with me, Miiisssttteeerrr D'Aaarrrcccyyy.'

'We'll wait here,' Peter told me.

'Good luck,' Conor said.

I followed Mr Cuffe into his office. He put his briefcase on his desk, removed his hat and hung it on a peg, then took off his coat and hung it on the peg next to it.

Every action seemed to take forever.

'Mr Cuffe,' I said, 'my results?'

'Yes,' he said, 'I'll get to them in time.'

He sat down at his desk and he opened the catches on his briefcase. He removed a large sheaf of paper – the exam results of every boy in the school.

'D'Aaarrrcccyyy,' he said to himself as he sorted

through the pages. 'D . . . D . . . D . . . Damcott . . . Daniels . . . D'ARCY! Here we are!'

He gave the page a quick once-over, then he looked up at me with a serious expression on his face.

'Well?' I said. 'How did I do?'

'Miisssttteeerrr D'Aaarrrcccyyy,' he said, 'as you will remember, you and I made a pact a number of weeks ago in this very office, with Mr Murray present. And you understood that unless you passed your exams, you would not be permitted to play rugby any more.'

I'd failed. That was why he was making this big speech.

'You probably still think it's a very harsh punishment for lack of academic success,' he said. 'But we do these things because you need to understand that schoolwork is more important than rugby.'

I stood up. I didn't need to hear him tell me that I'd failed. I started making my way to the door.

'You passed,' he said. 'Everything.'

I spun around.

'What?' I said.

'With flying colours,' he added.

He smiled. I think it was the first time I ever saw Mr Cuffe properly smile.

He handed me my results. I didn't even look at them. I didn't need to. All I needed to know was that I'd passed and was allowed to play.

I threw open the door of his office. Peter and Conor took one look at me and they knew that the news was good.

'I passed!' I said. 'I'm going to Cardiff!'

'We're coming too!' Peter said.

'What?' I said. 'Really?'

'Our dads are bringing us over.' Conor said. 'We didn't want to tell you until you knew you'd passed.'

'I thought both of your dads were Munster fans?' I said.

'Not any more,' said Peter. 'And neither are we.'

49 *Lein! Ster!*

This was it.

This was the moment.

The Millennium Stadium was full to capacity. Forty thousand of our supporters had travelled to Cardiff. We had made them believe that we were capable of achieving something special – of winning the European Cup.

Now, it was up to us to deliver.

We lined up next to the Northampton players in the tunnel.

'BLUE THUNDER!' a voice behind me shouted.

It was Luke Fitzgerald.

Suddenly, we were all shouting it:

'BLUE THUNDER!'

I'm not sure the Northampton players knew what to make of it.

I suddenly realized that my heart was beating at what felt like twice its normal rate. But I tried to remember what Joe had told us in the dressing-room:

'Play the match – not the occasion.'

Meaning, forget that it's a final. Remember that it's just another match you have to win. But that was easier said than done. Especially because we all had to file past the trophy as we walked out of the tunnel and onto the pitch. It was standing on a high table in front of us. Joe told us not to look at it, but I couldn't help myself. It was a big, silver trophy, with green ribbons tied to its handles. And I allowed myself to think how great it would be if I got to lift it in two hours' time.

As we emerged from the tunnel, the place went wild. The roof of the stadium was closed, which made it really warm. I was already sweating and I hadn't even warmed up.

I was looking up in the stands at this enormous sea of blue. Conor and Peter were in there some-where – not to mention Mum and Dad, my brother, Ian, and my sisters, Shona and Megan.

Our supporters sang:

'LEIN! STER! LEIN! STER! LEIN! STER! LEIN! STER!'

Northampton kicked off the match.

Joe was absolutely right when he said that finals were different. The occasion got to us. There were only five minutes gone when Northampton won a penalty in front of our posts. We presumed they'd kick it and take the three points. We switched off mentally – and that cost us. Northampton decided to play the advantage. Before we even knew what was happening, their number eight, Phil Dowson, had bundled his way over the line with the ball and we were behind.

We all started acting out of character, making

mistakes we wouldn't normally make. Not one or two of us, but all of us. Our forwards were giving away penalties in the scrum. I missed a tackle. BOD missed a tackle. Johnny failed to find touch with a kick. Even Isa Nacewa, who hardly ever made a mistake, ran a wrong line. Everyone was trying a bit too hard and we were losing heart when things we tried didn't come off.

It got worse shortly afterwards when their fullback, Ben Foden, waltzed through our defence to score a second try in the same corner.

We were in shock. Northampton had cut through us with ease. And we were all over the place. We couldn't string more than five passes together without losing the ball.

Then, just before half-time, Dylan Hartley, the Northampton hooker, scored Northampton's third try. This one was all about brute force. He powered his way over the line – and, beneath a huge pile of bodies, managed to ground the ball for what everyone thought was the knockout blow.

He grinned.

'This is easy,' he said. 'I thought you lads would at least give us a game!'

Our fans were stunned into silence. And I knew what they were thinking:

'Typical Leinster.'

I didn't know what was wrong. We had forgotten everything that Joe had taught us and gone back to being the team that blew it on the big occasions.

When the referee sounded the whistle for half-time, we were losing 22–6 and you would have found it hard to find a single Leinster fan who thought we could still win. No team had ever come back after finding themselves so far behind in a European Cup final. And we were playing terribly.

I wished I hadn't looked at that trophy.

I expected Joe to be furious with us when we got back to the dressing-room. But he wasn't. He was calm and measured. And he said:

'We have them just where we want them!'

I was sitting on the bench with my head down. I looked up when I heard that. I thought he was joking.

'Come on,' he said. 'We prepared for this. What if we have to come from behind to win? How would we do it? By forgetting about the score and by focusing on the next play. Their three tries didn't come from good play by them. They came from bad play by us. As a matter of fact, we played so badly, they'll be disappointed to have only scored twenty-two points. The only thing that matters now is what we do next. I really do believe that whoever scores the first try of the second half will go on to win the game. Remember, this is your match and you are in a position to control the result. Everything you do in the next forty minutes is going to define you, your teammates and your team. Just ask yourselves, how much do you want it?'

But it wasn't enough that Joe believed we could still turn the match around. We needed to believe it, too. One of us had to say it – that the match wasn't lost. And then Johnny Sexton spoke up:

'Northampton scored three tries in the first half,' he said. 'Why can't we score three tries in the second half?'

We all looked at each other.

'I'm serious,' he said. 'You think scoring three tries is beyond us? If we get one early enough, it could change the whole match. You see comebacks like this all the time in sport. If Munster can do it, why can't we?'

'You need to dig deep,' Joe said. 'You need to dig deeper than you've ever dug before.'

Suddenly, we were all looking at each other differently. I could feel a sense of resolve growing in that dressing-room.

We weren't going to take this lying down.

We were going to fight back.

We stood up.

'If you pull this off,' Joe said, 'you will be remembered forever.'

And those were the last words he said to us before we returned to the pitch.

Johnny stood, waiting to kick off the second half. He held the ball up to his face and he put three fingers up behind it, his code to let us know that he was planning to kick the ball deep and really go after Northampton. We won the restart after Shaggy tackled Dowson to the ground and Rocky drove two Northampton defenders off the ruck.

Northampton knew immediately that something had changed. We were a different team. It was in the way we went at them. Johnny said that if we scored a try early enough in the second half, it would change everything. And he started like he was determined to score it himself – just to show us that it was true.

After eleven exhausting phases of play, our scrum-half, Eoin Reddan, pulled the ball from a ruck. I was standing right behind him, waiting for the pass, to see could I move us a few feet further forward. But Eoin threw it long to Johnny, who had eyes only for the line. He charged through two Northampton defenders and grounded the ball.

Suddenly, we could hear our supporters making noise again — even if they didn't believe that we could still win the match. But I could see the self-doubt creeping into the faces of some of the Northampton players.

A few minutes later, we were back in their territory again — five metres from their line. Johnny played a beautiful wraparound pass with Jamie Heaslip, then made a motion like he was about to off-load the ball to BOD. But he had no intention of giving it to him. He was going for his second try. Four Northampton players got their hands on him — but none of them could stop him scoring again.

'YES!' we all screamed.

We had looked dead and buried. Now, with Johnny converting both of his tries, as well as adding two penalties, we were just two points behind.

Joe often talked about momentum swings in matches — about how a tide that went out also came back in again. Now the momentum was with us. But time was against us. I glanced up at the clock just before the two packs set for a scrum. We were losing 22–20 and there were only five minutes to go.

I remembered Joe's words, 'Focus on the next play,' and I snapped back to the match.

Northampton had dominated us in the scrum, but now our forwards were pushing their forwards around. Cian, Malcolm and Leo started to really throw their weight about. Cian won a penalty off the scrum, deep in our own half, which was a huge moment, because it showed that the pressure was finally getting to their forwards.

Johnny stepped up to kick for the corner. I noticed he was slowing his breathing and taking his time. I wished he would just hurry up because that clock was ticking. But he knew what he was doing. He was setting up for a spiral kick, which is so much harder to execute, but he knew we were going to need every inch we could get.

As soon as his foot struck the ball, the crowd cheered. They knew it was a good kick and, as the seconds ticked away, they knew it would give us one last chance at victory.

Leo walked to the front of the lineout and shouted, 'Tempo,' which was a code. Cian knew exactly what to do: when Leo jumped, he caught and lifted him perfectly. Leo won the ball. Our pack were driving into the Northampton forwards, trying to push them towards their tryline, but this was a final, and Northampton were doing everything in their power to keep us out.

Rocky split out of the maul and the ref called, 'Use it!'

Rocky was trying to hand off Roger Wilson, but he spilled the ball in the tackle. Amazingly, it didn't go forward, and the ref shouted, 'Play on.'

I scooped it up and started a zigzag run across the pitch, looking around for options. This was going to be our last play, so it had to count. I made a move like I was about to kick the ball over the top for Isa to collect. He made a run and he fooled both defenders, creating a tiny gap for me. I didn't hesitate. I dummied a pass, ducked down low and made a drive for the line. I slammed the ball down with one hand. I made it with millimetres to spare. That extra

ground that Johnny had gained with his kick really mattered. But the good news was that I was over the line! It was our third try of the game. For the first time in the match, we were in front – and the clock was about to turn red.

The eighty minutes were up. We won the ball from the restart and Eoin kicked it out of play. The roar from the Leinster fans was deafening.

We all hugged each other. The feeling was amazing. We had done it. We had won the European Cup!

We applauded our supporters. Some of them had been following the team for years. Some of them had joined us when this particular journey started. We all stood and tried to pick out the faces of people we knew in the crowd. It was like looking at one of those *Where's Wally?* puzzles and after a while it hurt my eyes. But then I heard someone calling my name:

'Gordon! Gordon!'

I looked across at the touchline. It was my family. Mum and Dad, Ian, Shona and Megan had made their way down to the front of the stand and were being held back by a line of stewards in fluorescent orange coats.

I pushed past the stewards and I threw my arms around Mum and Dad.

Dad had tears streaming down his face.

'I never doubted Leinster,' he said. 'I never doubted them for a minute.'

Ian laughed.

'He actually spent half-time reminiscing about all the great Munster comebacks of the past,' he said. 'Did you think it was gone yourself?'

I shook my head.

'No,' I said. 'I actually didn't. There's something different about this bunch of players. Joe has taught us to never stop believing in each other.'

I hugged Ian, Shona and Megan, and then I heard someone else calling my name. With all the noise, it was difficult to tell where it was coming from. And then I saw them, over to my left, high up in the stand, waving their arms like they were directing a plane to land.

It was Conor and Peter.

I gave them a smile and I shook my fist at them as if to say, 'We did it!'

They held up their Leinster scarves with enormous smiles on their faces. Two more former Munster fans who'd been converted.

'You'd better go,' Dad said. 'You don't want them lifting the cup without you.'

I turned around. Dad was right. The presentation

was about to be made. I raced over to the stage, which had been placed in the middle of the pitch.

I took my place at the back. But then Leo called me to the front.

'They've travelled from all over Leinster to see us do this,' he said. 'We need some more counties represented at the front here. I'm representing Wicklow. Gordon, you can represent Wexford. Where's Shane Horgan? Shane, you can represent Meath. Let's lift it together.'

I stood on one side of him and Shane Horgan stood on the other. We each grabbed a handle.

'Ready?' Leo asked.

'Yes,' we both said.

Then the three of us lifted the trophy. And suddenly fireworks exploded all around us and the crowd went absolutely crazy.

Winning the Six Nations and the Grand Slam had been great. But I was sure that this was the best day of my life.

50 *What Makes a Hero*

The two teams were lining up for the national anthems as we made our way to our seats.

I was delighted to see that the ground was packed full of people. This Ireland team had really captured the country's imagination and now it seemed that everyone wanted to be there to see if they could land the Six Nations and the Grand Slam.

We stood for 'Amhrán na bhFiann'.

Aoife stared straight ahead while everyone sang the words. She didn't look a bit nervous. She was focused on the job she had to do.

The anthem ended and we sat down.

'COME ON, IRELAND!' Conor shouted.

And that was the cue for everyone else to do the same.

'COME ON, IRELAND!' went the roar.

The first few minutes were a bit cagey, which was understandable given everything that was at stake. The Scotland team were really good. From a scrum, they forced a penalty, which their number ten put over the bar.

A few minutes later, Ireland won a penalty of their own.

Emma had clearly agreed to give up the kicking duties, because Aoife picked up the ball and put it into the tee. It wasn't a particularly difficult kick. It was from about thirty metres out, a little to the left of the posts. I'd seen her put the ball over the bar from the same distance and angle a hundred times in training.

She performed her usual pre-kick routine. But she didn't connect with the ball properly. It took off, wobbled a bit in the air, hit the post and bounced back into play again.

I turned and looked at Conor.

'It's just nerves,' I told him. 'Even Johnny Sexton misses the odd one from that distance.'

'Absolutely,' he said. 'She'll nail the next one – you'll see.'

Ireland were enjoying most of the possession. And Aoife was playing brilliantly. Every time she had the ball in her hands, a buzz of anticipation went through the crowd like an electrical charge.

If any player was likely to make something happen, it was her. Which explained why the Irish players kept passing the ball to her at every opportunity.

She'd receive it and then do something really exciting with it. A flick of her hips and she left an opponent standing still and looking stupid. A burst of acceleration and she left two more running, panting, in her wake. All around me, I could hear people saying what a phenomenal player the Ireland number ten was.

But, worryingly, Scotland were winning a lot of penalties. And their number ten was putting them between the posts from all sorts of angles. By the half-hour mark, Scotland were leading by 12–0 – totally against the run of play.

I could see Aoife's teammates looking at her, wondering could she do something. Then she played a reverse pass with Emma Ormsby and went on a mazy run, beating five Scotland players before diving over the line and touching the ball down in the corner.

'YEEEEEESSSSSS!!!!!!' we all roared.

We danced around and celebrated.

But our joy didn't last long. The try was disallowed because the touch judge said that Aoife's right foot was off the pitch.

'NO WAY!' we shouted, then we booed the decision, even though we had no idea whether it was right or not.

Aoife did everything in that first half – except score.

But with the last play of the half, she had an opportunity to put something on the board with a very kickable penalty right in front of the Scotland posts.

She stepped up to take it. If she put it over, the half-time score would be 12–3. It would be possible to come back from there. I watched Aoife shape up to take the kick. But something was wrong with her body language. I'd watched her kick so many penalties that I knew instantly when something was up. She ran at the ball. Again, her connection was poor and she sliced it. It skewed to the right of the posts.

The crowd groaned as one.

Ireland were losing 12–0. And Scotland looked like they were gaining in confidence.

'This is going to take a comeback on the same par as Leinster's,' Peter said.

'They're relying on her too much,' I said. 'It's too much pressure. She needs help down there.'

'Or,' Conor said, 'she needs to stop trying to do everything herself again. Maybe she needs to encourage other players to step up.'

The second half started.

It was hard to believe that Ireland were losing. But within five minutes of the restart, Scotland had slotted over another penalty and suddenly it was 15–0.

The crowd fell silent. Scotland were disappearing over the horizon.

But then, with the Ireland scrum-half down injured and receiving attention, Aoife pulled the ball out of a ruck herself. She dummied a pass, wrong-footing the Scotland defence, then tucked the ball under her arm and headed for the line. She dived under the posts to score a try.

'YEEEEEESSSSSS!!!!!!' we roared.

There was still hope.

Aoife kicked the conversion and we breathed a sigh of relief.

It was 15–7.

I asked Conor how long was left. He said fifteen minutes. It would hopefully be enough time. But the minutes flew by. And when I asked him again, there were only five remaining. And Ireland were still losing by eight points.

Then I saw Aoife with her hand up to her face. She was whispering something to Elaine Barrett, the Ireland outside-centre. I wondered did she have a plan.

A minute later, I got my answer.

Aoife had the ball right on Scotland's twenty-two. She passed it short to Elaine, then I watched her run around the back of her. It was a wraparound pass – a carbon copy of the move that Johnny Sexton pulled off against Northampton. But this was even cleverer. Because, while every set of eyes in the stadium was fixed on Aoife, watching to see if she could get over the line, one thing was missed by everyone – including the entire Scotland team . . .

Aoife didn't have the ball!

Elaine had thrown a dummy pass. And so, while everyone was expecting Aoife to finish the move, it was Elaine who was rushing towards the line with the ball under her arm. She scored under the posts.

'WHOA!' Conor shouted. 'DID YOU SEE THAT?'

'She made them think that she was going to do it herself,' Peter said. 'Then she suckered them.'

'Joe Schmidt would have been proud of that move,' I said.

The Ireland players didn't celebrate. Aoife kicked the conversion from right in front of the posts. But Ireland were still a point behind and this was no time to be patting themselves on the back.

I realized that I was holding my breath with the excitement of it all.

Scotland kicked off. Ireland won the restart.

'COME ON, IRELAND!' we roared.

You could see the players around Aoife growing in belief. They really thought they could win now. But the clock was against them. Soon, the eighty minutes had passed. And, though Ireland had the ball, the game would be over the second it went dead.

Aoife had the ball close to the touchline, near where we were sitting. I watched her cut inside. There was a clear channel of space in front of her. But then one of the Scotland players, in desperation, put out her arm and clotheslined her.

Aoife hit the ground holding her throat.

'REFEREE!' we shouted.

And the referee blew her whistle for a penalty.

Silence fell on Donnybrook Stadium as Aoife climbed to her feet. She was alright. But what was she going to do with the penalty? Was she going to kick it into touch and push for a try? That was risky – especially if they lost the lineout. Then it would be game over. Or was she going to take a kick at goal? This was just as risky because it was a far from easy kick. And if she missed, the match would be over.

But what happened next surprised everyone.

I saw Aoife and Emma deep in conversation. Aoife had the ball in her hands. She was shaking her head, saying, 'No.'

I wondered what was going on.

Then, suddenly, Aoife handed the ball to Emma.

Emma smiled at her and accepted the ball. She placed it in the tee.

'Oh my God,' Conor said, 'she's letting Emma take the conversion!'

'Whoa!' I said. 'That takes MASSIVE courage!'

Everything about the kick was difficult. The angle. The distance. The stadium, so loud all afternoon, was suddenly so quiet that you could hear your own breathing.

I crossed my fingers.

'Please kick it over,' Conor whispered over and over again. 'Please kick it over. Please kick it over.'

Emma ran at the ball. She got her foot underneath it and it took off like an airplane.

We watched it in what seemed like slow motion as it traced an arc through the air in the direction of the posts.

'It's on target,' Peter said, 'but I don't know if it has the distance.'

It was falling out of the sky rapidly. The only

question was – did she put enough power into the kick to clear the crossbar?

People were looking away – unable to stand the tension.

'It's not going to make it,' Conor said.

'It is,' I told him.

'It's not.'

I watched, with my heart in my mouth, as the ball hit the crossbar and bounced up into the air.

There was a collective: 'WOOOOOOOOOOO OOO!!!!!!!' from the crowd.

But which side would it land on?

It seemed to stay in the air forever.

And then it fell . . .

And when it did, it fell . . .

. . . *behind* the Scotland goal!

The referee blew her whistle to signal that the conversion was good, then blew it a second time to say that the match was over.

They'd done it! Ireland had won the Six Nations Championship and the Grand Slam!

Emma fell to her knees with her arms in the air. All of the girls ran to her. Aoife was the first to get there. She hugged her, then she and the other girls lifted Emma onto their shoulders and carried her around the pitch.

I started to think about Felipe. I thought about how he took Johnny Sexton under his wing, instead of treating him as a rival. And when it was time to hand over the kicking role to someone else, Johnny had the confidence to become our match-winner. Felipe understood what it meant to be part of a team. Aoife had learned the same lesson. Sometimes you had to let someone else be the hero.

As a matter of fact, that was one of the most heroic things you could do.

51 'I'm Looking for Gordon D'Arcy'

We were back working for McWonderburger Wexford.

And we had a new member of staff.

'Welcome to McWonderburger Wexford! What's *your* beef?'

That was Aoife talking.

Her mum and dad felt that she would learn to appreciate the true value of money if she earned her own.

Aoife wasn't happy about it. Especially on her second day, when we were told that a children's party was about to arrive.

'Aoife,' I said, 'it's your turn to wear the dinosaur costume!'

'No! Way!' she said. 'I am not playing Barney for a bunch of screaming kids!'

'No,' I said, 'you're playing Benji, another purple dinosaur with no connection whatsoever to the popular anthropomorphic Tyrannosaurus Rex of the same colour.'

'Please!' she begged. 'Don't make me do it! I'm only a girl!'

We all laughed.

'Aoife,' Conor reminded her, 'this is what equality means! You don't get to play the "I'm only a girl!" card. Especially as you're being talked about as a future captain of the senior Ireland women's team!'

'Well, that's a good point,' she said. 'These kids can be really rough. What if I pick up an injury that affects my rugby career?'

'Gordon,' Conor said, 'go and get Aoife the Benji suit!'

She was laughing now.

'No,' she said. 'Peter, I'll give you my entire day's wages for today if you play Benji!'

'I'm sorry,' he said, 'I wouldn't do it for a whole week's wages!'

I went into the back of the restaurant to retrieve the suit. And that was when the phone rang.

'Hello, McWonderburger Wexford,' I said, 'what's *your* beef?'

'What's my beef?' a voice on the other end of the line said. It was a man with a posh voice. He sounded like he might even be English.

'What's my beef?' he said. 'I haven't got a beef. Not with you.'

This happened occasionally. The phrase, 'What's your beef?' meant the same thing as 'What's your problem?' and sometimes people thought it was the opening line in an argument.

'I'm sorry,' I said, 'all McWonderburger Wexford employees are required to ask that question. How may I help you, Sir?'

'I'm looking for Gordon D'Arcy,' he said.

'This is Gordon D'Arcy,' I told him.

'Oh, good,' he said. 'Your mum told me I'd find you there. Gordon, this is Clive Woodward speaking.'

'Clive Woodward?' I said. 'Er, the only Clive Woodward I know is the one who's coaching the Lions this summer.'

'Yes, that's me,' he said.

I was lost for words.

'Well, er, well . . . em . . . why would you be ring-ing me?' I asked.

'Because,' he said, 'we're about to go to Australia. I watched you play for Leinster this year and you really impressed me.'

'Did I?' I asked.

'Absolutely,' he said. 'Gordon, how would you like to play for the Lions?'

GORDON D'ARCY

Gordon D'Arcy was first called up to play for Ireland while he was still at school. He won his first cap in 1999 and his final cap in 2015, making him Ireland's longest-serving international player. Shortly after making his first appearance for his country, he fell out of favour with management because of his 'attitude problems'. But he returned three years later, a better and more mature player. In 2004, he was named the Six Nations Player of the Tournament. He played a total of eighty-two times for his country, scoring seven tries. Partnering Brian O'Driscoll in the centre, he was a vital part of two Six Nations Championship-winning teams, including the Grand Slam team of 2009, and starred in four World Cups. He was also a member of two British and Irish Lions squads. With Leinster, he won three European Cups, a Challenge Cup and four league titles.

I hope you enjoyed *Blue Thunder*. The first book in this series, *Gordon's Game*, was a huge success and lots of you got in touch to tell me you loved it – thank you! Some of you also asked me some head-scratching questions. Here is a selection of those questions, answered as best I can.

Q. I am a really big fan. I really enjoyed reading *Gordon's Game*, which I got as a present for Christmas. I loved your book because it was really funny and about sport. I love sport! My favourite part of the book was when you got to play for Ireland and won the Grand Slam. My question is: if you could relive one rugby game you played, which one would it be?

Patrick, age 11, County Kildare

A. What a great question, Patrick! My first match for Ireland was incredible. I was on the bench, number sixteen (the sub numbers were weird back then), in the 1999 World Cup against Romania. I came on to replace Conor O'Shea. The match flew by so quickly, I barely had time to catch my breath. I picked up a loose ball just outside my twenty-two, broke a couple of tackles and then chipped the full-back. The ball bounced wickedly and I wasn't able to gather it – would have been a cool try! I wanted to keep my very first Ireland jersey because it's such a special thing for any player. Back then, you only got one jersey, so after the match Conor O'Shea gave me his jersey to swap with the opposition, so I could keep my first jersey. It's one of the reasons I loved that match so much – because rugby is always about your team and teammates.

Q. How do you manage to get over a major injury (like your arm) and come back so strong?

Dylan, age 14, Cavan RFC

A. Luckily for me, I had the best doctors, and I always followed their advice. I had three operations on my arm (bit of bone taken from my hip and elbow to fill the gaps – I had broken my arm in eight places!) and had plenty of time away from the game. A good friend of mine, Enda McNulty, is a sports psychologist, and we talked about the mental and physical side of the game. My body would recover, he told me, but I had to be mentally ready to play again. If I spent all my time feeling sad about my injury and all the things I couldn't do, I wouldn't be ready to play. So I focused on all the things I could do, like running, swimming and passing with my left hand. He also challenged me to take up a hobby that was in no way related to rugby, something I wouldn't have the time to do when I got back playing. I did a photography course and I loved it.

Q. I enjoyed your book. It is my eighth birthday today. For my birthday I got tickets to the Leinster v Munster game and a tackle bag. I saw you in Center Parcs. Who was your first Wexford Wanderers game against?

Paddy, age 8, Westmanstown RFC

A. My first game was against a touring side from Wales called Pontypridd. I was actually mistaken for my brother, Ian, who was older than me. It was a great game. I got Player of the Match, a big black eye and a bag of fish and chips. I had forgotten to tell my parents I was going to play this match and they weren't delighted that I disappeared for eight hours – and arrived home with a black eye!

Q. Really loved reading your book. I am six years old and play for Belfast Harlequins. I love scoring tries and would love to play for Ireland in the future. My questions are as follows: Who is your favourite current rugby player? What was your favourite ground to play in? Have you ever played *Fortnite*?

Quinn, age 6, Belfast Harlequins RFC

A. Three great questions!

I think James Ryan is amazing, he is so skilful and such a smart rugby player, even though he is still so young. I'd love to have played with him.

I always loved playing in Paris. It was such a fun place. The rugby was always amazing, with lots of tries. The fans were so funny, with all the hats, garlic and chickens on the side of the pitch and even a brass band in the crowd. I only won there once with Ireland and that was in 2015 when we won the Six Nations. Dave Kearney made a wonder tackle to win the match.

I don't really play video games. I'm more of an outdoors person. I cycle a lot and do Pilates. The last video game I played was called *Tekken*.

Q. *Salut*, Gordon! My name is Liam and I live in Geneva, Switzerland. I have just finished reading your book with my dad. I have the following questions for you: What has become of Aoife? What university did Peter attend?

Liam, age 8, Geneva, Switzerland

A. Aoife is still playing rugby and she is making sure that women's rugby gets as much support as the men's game. It is a tough battle, but she is doing an amazing job.

Peter is still a little young for college just yet. I think once there is a rugby team, he'd be happy to study anywhere.

Q. Hi, my name is Ben and I am nine years old. I just read your book. It's my all-time favourite. I would like to ask you a question. Who were the five players you loved when you were young and why did you like them?

Ben, age 9, Firhouse, Dublin

A.

1. David Campese. He was, without doubt, the best winger in the world when I was growing up. He was

always so confident. He used to take the touch-kicks and he'd use his left or right foot, depending on which side of the field he was on. He had this 'goose step' which everyone tried to copy, it looked like a dance move and always sent you the wrong way. He was playing for Australia at the time and they were super fun to watch.

2. Keith Wood. He *was* Irish rugby at the time. A hooker who played like he was made for every position – even out-half. He would just knock over drop-kicks. He played with a smile as well.

3. Zinzan Brooke. He hit a drop-goal in the World Cup semi-final against England in 1995 from nearly the halfway – and he was a number eight! He had amazing skills for a big man. I also loved the All Blacks jersey.

4. Francois Pienaar. When he lifted the World Cup in 1995, I thought he was a mountain of a man. He was a really impressive player, strong both as a player and as a leader. He made sure his players never took a backward step and he led by his actions.

5. Jonah Lomu. He had his own video game – kinda says it all! He was so hard to tackle. He was fast as well, wasn't selfish and made sure others scored lots of tries too.

Q. Dear Gordon, my name is Niall. I am six years old. I have just finished *Gordon's Game*. I play mini rugby for Terenure U6. Which team do you like the best? My mum would like me to play number nine so I don't have to go into the scrum.

Niall, age 6, Terenure College RFC

A. Niall, I have a couple of favourite teams. Wexford Wanderers because that is where I started and my first coach, Jimmy O'Connor, is the nicest man on the planet (if not the universe). I played with Leinster and Ireland all my career as well. However, when I was young, I always loved watching France play. They were so cool, lightning fast and played some of the most beautiful rugby in the world. It didn't matter how the game was going or what the score was, they could just flick a pass or an offload and run 80m. They were sooooo exciting to watch!

Q. Who was the tallest player you ever played with?

A. Easy. My Leinster and Ireland teammate, Devin Toner. He is 6'10" – which is an entire foot taller than me. He also has enormous feet. Size 15, apparently! I also hear he gets a grant from the government for his clothes and shoes, because he is technically a giant!

Q. **What songs are on your Gordon D'Arcy Workout Playlist?**

A. Okay, your parents will probably remember some of these. And some might seem cheesier than a McWonderburger. But feel free to put this playlist together yourselves to help with your sit-ups, push-ups and chin-ups.

1. *Take On Me* – a-ha; **2.** *Smooth Criminal* – Michael Jackson; **3.** *I Wanna Dance With Somebody* – Whitney Houston; **4.** *Sweet Dreams* – The Eurythmics; **5.** *Sweet Child O' Mine* – Guns N' Roses; **6.** *Another One Bites the Dust* – Queen; **7.** *Eye of the Tiger* – Survivor; **8.** *Never Gonna Give You Up* – Rick Astley; **9.** *Smells Like Teen Spirit* – Nirvana; **10.** *Livin' La Vida Loca* – Ricky Martin; **11.** *Wonderwall* – Oasis; **12.** *Enter Sandman* – Metallica; **13.** *Baby One More Time* – Britney Spears; and number **14.** What else could it be? *Friends in Low Places* – Garth Brooks.

If you'd like to put a question to Gordon, please send it to gordonsgamebook@gmail.com. You never know, your question might end up featuring in Book 3 of *Gordon's Game*!

ACKNOWLEDGEMENTS

Gordon D'Arcy's acknowledgements:

Writing the second book in the *Gordon's Game* series has been such an enjoyable experience, and one of the key reasons for that has been the people involved. Paul Howard and Rachel Pierce – thank you both for your infectious positivity and belief in this series. Paul, I'm especially grateful for your guiding hand in bringing what is in my head to paper, whilst adding your own unique pieces, which make these books so special. Rachel, your ability to mould a story is fantastic to watch and we are lucky to have you. Alan Nolan has done another fantastic job with the illustrations, a pleasure to work with you again.

Faith O'Grady, I'd include you in that infectious positivity and thank you again for believing in this book. To Patricia Deevy, Michael McLoughlin and everyone at Sandycore, we could not ask for a stronger team. The passion you have for books is inspiring, and the way you have supported *Gordon's Game* has been incredible – especially Louise Farrell, to whom we owe a big thank you!

Soleil & Lennon, seeing you reading and the joy it gives you brings a smile to my face; I can't wait to read these books with you in years to come.

And finally to my wife, Aoife, I couldn't do any of this without your support, love and inspiration – thank you.

Paul Howard's acknowledgements:

A huge thank you to Gordon D'Arcy for agreeing to share his stories, to entertain young readers and maybe even inspire the rugby legends of tomorrow. Thank you, Gordon, for all your hard work in making the book happen. Enormous thanks to Rachel Pierce, my editor for almost twenty years, for her wise counsel and the buckets of ideas she brought to this book, and every book we've worked on together. Thanks to Alan Nolan for your fantastic illustrations that have really helped bring the story to life. Thanks to our agent, Faith O'Grady, for getting behind the project right from the start. Thanks to Michael McLoughlin and Patricia Deevy of Sandycove for believing in it. Thanks to Louise Farrell of Sandycove for running such a great and fun publicity campaign for *Gordon's Game* and helping us bring the story directly to hundreds of kids, even if it meant that I had to dress up as a chicken. Huge thanks to Cliona Lewis, Brian Walker, Carrie Anderson and everyone at Sandycove for being the Dream Team. And a special word of thanks, as always, to Mary, my very wonderful wife.

a serioüsfun camp

*Childhood stops for seriously ill children, at
Barretstown we press play on childhood*

www.barretstown.org

Missed the first book in the series?

GORDON'S GAME

is available in paperback now!

A rugby-mad boy. A huge game. And a chance for an epic win . . . or an epic fail!

Gordon D'Arcy is an ordinary boy, but he's not so ordinary once he gets a rugby ball in his hands. He's the star player for Wexford Wanderers and dreams of one day wearing the Ireland jersey. A dream like that means hard work, raw talent and never losing sight of your goals.

But Gordon has a wild streak that often lands him in trouble. Mum and Dad think that if he can just channel his energy, all will be well.

Then something utterly mad happens and he gets a chance to live his biggest dream. Can he stay on his game and do everyone proud?

Or will trouble follow him . . . like it usually does?

WWW.PENGUIN.CO.UK